DEATH OF THE OFFICIAL

A TALE OF MEDIEVAL MURDER, MYSTERY AND SKULDUGGERY. BOOK ONE OF THE DRAYCHESTER CHRONICLES.

M J WESTERBONE

AN INTRODUCTION TO THE SERIES FROM OTHER READERS

"Plunges the reader head on into an immersive tale of humour, murder and intrigue set in a gritty depiction of medieval England that's not for the fainthearted..."

"Medieval life is cheap, nasty and short, at least for some, for others, well, its all just a game to them..."

"The grizzled old mercenary Sir Roger Mudstone, you'll love to hate him, if that makes any sense?"

"A perfect medieval villain with a troubling talent for violence. He's the kind of man who'd sell not only his own grandmother but yours too..."

"Will, Bernard and Osbert, its like Cadfael has shuffled off this mortal coil and left three much stupider understudies, enjoy the ride..."

FREE BOOK OFFER

Get your free copy of
Death Of The Messenger
The Prequel to the
Draychester Chronicles

Visit www.westerbone.com to get exclusive discounts, news on upcoming releases **and a free copy of *Death of the Messenger*,** the prequel to the Draychester Chronicles series.

OTHER BOOKS IN THE SERIES

Available Now

Book 2 of the Draychester Chronicles

Death Of The Vintner

Available Now

Book 3 of the Draychester Chronicles

Death Of The Anchorite

1
WILL IS CAPTURED

From close behind came angry shouts and the sound of running feet. The alley ended at a pair of ramshackle doors tied together with twine. Crashing through the flimsy wood, Will realised he was inside one of the city tanneries. The stench was so strong it made his eyes water. Pressing on he stumbled around in the gloom of the large shed. The tanning pits were a dangerous and stinking obstacle slowing his progress. Piles of hides blocked the way and a greasy mixture of mud, fat, hair and rotted animal flesh lay underfoot.

His two pursuers came barging through the open doorway. Will hopped onto the slippery walkway between the pits and began to run towards the front of the building. He slithered and skidded along the smooth stonework, the chasing men jumping up after him.

Reaching the far side of the shed he crashed into the wall and gasped for breath in the fetid air. Behind him there was a cry as one man lost his footing and slid cursing into a mixture of lime and two-day-old piss. The other man kept coming. Will scrambled alongside the front wall until he found an opening covered by a hanging leather hide. He hauled it aside and entered a rough wooden porch tacked onto the front of the building. Before him there was a door with a heavy wooden bar across it. He heaved the bar out of the way, shouldered the door open and stumbled out. Pausing only to drag in great lungfuls of fresh air, he set off again at a stagger up the muddy street.

He'd gone only a few yards when the two sheriff's men came crashing out of the door behind him. There was no more flight left in him and he turned to face them. Swiftly drawing his arm back, one man drove his fist into Will's nose. There was an audible crunch. Will stumbled. His feet slid on the wet cobbles and he fell to his knees. His hands rose to cover his nose, eyes squeezed shut. Head coming forwards, nose throbbing, he glared up at the man though blooded fingers. "You turd. I think it's broken. There was no need for that."

The man grinned. "Every need lad. Run again and I swear I'll break your legs. Now get up."

Will dropped his hands from his nose and struggled to his feet. He cast his eyes down in what they might confuse as a gesture of surrender. The man took a leather belt from around his own waist and said, "Come closer, hold out your wrists while I bind them."

Will moved just out of arm's reach. The man stretched out to grab him. Will raised his eyes. The man hesitated as he met his gaze. Will attacked, kicking the man hard in the right shin. He jumped backwards howling in pain.

The other man advanced, he held a heavy wooden cudgel in one hand. He hissed, "I'm going to break every single bone in your worthless body."

Will started to back away up the street. The man suddenly rushed him, the cudgel swinging at Will's head. He ducked, but the club struck him a glancing blow. It sent him spinning round and then down onto the cobbles into dark oblivion.

2

SIR ROGER RETURNS

From the very start, Sir Roger had some doubts as to the ship's sea worthiness. It wasn't a vessel you'd ever want to make a long voyage in. There didn't seem to be space for more than a handful of passengers and the shelter on deck was virtually non existent. She was clinker-built and short in both length and beam. The master had seemed competent enough in that he'd only been half drunk and swore the crossing would take at most three hours. After squinting at the sky through bloodshot eyes, the master had given his verdict on the weather. "Calm as a mill pond all the way across."

As he went aboard Sir Roger was reassured it was an authentic working ship by the smell of dead fish, old piss and someone's regurgitated breakfast. The sun had been shining as they left the French coast behind. That's when the trouble began.

As they got further out to sea, the swell increased. Sir Roger was soon hanging over the side, bringing up his own breakfast. One of the crew sniggered and slapped him on the back. "Got a delicate stomach have you matey?"

Sir Roger looked up at him with a green tinged face. The seaman grinned back revealing blackened stumps of teeth. Sir Roger croaked, "What did you say to me?"

Before the man could reply, Sir Roger reached up and grabbed him by his dirty ginger beard. With a mighty tug he dragged him to the deck and began to throttle him with one hand whilst banging his head on the deck with his other.

The last thing Sir Roger remembered was being hit on the back of the head and dragged semi-comatose to the mast. His arms and legs were lashed tight to it with thick lengths of rope. At which point he lost consciousness.

Sir Roger woke with a thumping headache to find it was dark and a howling storm appeared to be raging. His most immediate concern was the sound of the ship being violently pulled to pieces beneath him. He struggled briefly, but he was still tied fast to the mast. Huge waves were sweeping over the deck. He felt something vital shatter below the thin planks beneath him. With a shuddering groan, the mast was catapulted into the water. Sir Roger was swept across the surface of the sea at a terrifying pace, plunging in and out of the raging waves, leaving him gasping desperately for air.

Sir Roger had never been much of a believer in anything other than a good horse, a sharp sword and his own somewhat limited wits, preferably reinforced with strong ale. He always left the obligatory penny at the shrines to the appropriate saints, more in superstition than any strong faith.

That very morning when he walked down to the harbour, he'd taken the precaution of leaving a few pennies at the small shrine to Saint Christopher.

Sir Roger felt now was the time to encourage whatever deity might be listening to lend him a hand. He shouted into the howling wind. "Perhaps we can come to some arrangement?"

The wind seemed to pick up even more, and the force of the spray felt like someone was throwing gravel into his face. Perhaps a different approach was required. Sir Roger decided to confess his sins and make amends. There was a lot to get through, and he didn't know whether he'd have enough time. He made a start by shouting at the top of his voice toward the dark sky. "It's all true, I'm afraid. I dare say you already know that. Robbed, killed, raped and grievously injured my way across Christendom for the last twenty years. I've fought for whoever's paid me the most coin and I can tell you it's never bloody well been enough."

He watched as lightning flickered between the clouds. A few seconds later and the roar of the thunder nearly deafened him. "Afraid I don't have much to recommend me. I've stopped counting the number of men I've killed, although I have to say most of them deserved it. Then there's the trail of bastard children I've fathered the length and breadth of France."

Sir Roger peered up into the gloom. If anything, the storm looked to be getting worse. "I've only just been summoned home after all this time. My older brother Hugh is dead. You'll know that already. Truthfully, I thought you were going to let the old bastard outlive me, so then what's the point in letting me drown now?"

He bawled at the heavens, "You can't do this to me damn you. I've ridden back through France as fast as I could. All you had to do was let me cross safely to England. I should be allowed to spend everything that bastard Hugh has been hoarding all these years. I deserve it!"

Spitting out a mouthful of water, Sir Roger shouted into the darkness, "I swear if you'll do me the trouble of washing me up alive on an English beach, I'll grant one of my northern manors to holy mother church. I swear it."

There was a momentary lessening of the wind. He shouted again, "So what's it to be?"

Old John of Draymouth was down on the sand collecting driftwood. Wandering the same stretch of beach every day for forty years he'd found many strange things. It was a fine morning and, after last night's storm, the pickings were sure to be good.

The hideous creature, dragging itself up the sand, caught him completely off guard. He watched in horror, rooted to the spot, as a vast mound of quivering seaweed crawled up the beach. It finally reached his bare feet, and he whimpered in sheer terror. A strange salt encrusted hand shot out from the mound. It clamped his ankle in a vice like grip. An overpowering stench of rotting fish filled his nostrils.

"Lord have mercy on me," he moaned.

The mound shuddered violently then spoke. "Help me up you old fool."

John looked down at the mound and realised the devil had not come to claim his soul. It was only a man, encased in a ball of seaweed, sand and rotting fish. "Who in God's name are you?"

The hand was released from the old man's ankle and a

figure rose unsteadily to its feet. A minor avalanche of debris fell to the sand. It revealed a man, dirty, battered and stark naked except for a ring on the middle finger of his right hand. He lurched forward and grabbed John by the throat. A salt encrusted face pressed close to the old man's ear. "The question isn't 'who am I', but how may I help you?"

John clawed at the hand at his throat. "How may I help you my lord?"

"A good question. Follow my instructions and I might let you live, cross me and I'll snap your neck, understand?"

John gasping for breath and transfixed by the stranger's bloodshot red eyes nodded as best he could.

"Very good. I'm Sir Roger Mudstone. I need some fresh clothes, a meal, a horse, the road to Draychester. In that order."

John slowly raised an arm. He pointed over the stranger's shoulder towards a shack built into a dune at the top of the beach. Sir Roger, his hand still around the old man's throat, shuffled him around slowly in the sand and studied the shack. From a crude hole, cut in the dirty thatched roof, a thin wisp of smoke rose. Sir Roger sighed loudly.

"God's teeth." His hot foul breath seared the old man's face. It didn't look promising but in the circumstances he'd take whatever the old fool had. "You live there do you?"

"Yes my lord."

"Then let us go, I've much business to attend to."

～

Sir Roger set out for Draychester in the early afternoon. He rode a donkey which he'd found tied up behind the shack on the beach. Clothes had been more of an issue and he wore the ill-fitting rags the old man had dressed in. It was an uncomfortable ride as the donkey seemed to be deliberately stepping into every pothole in the road. He missed the great warhorses he'd ridden during his mercenary years, but he'd had little choice.

The old man had owned hardly anything of value. The only things he thought worth taking from the shack were a blunt knife and the two pennies he'd found hidden under the dirty straw sleeping pallet. How the old peasant had eked out a living on the beach was beyond him. He hadn't even put up much of a fight as Sir Roger had throttled him in annoyance. Whether he'd choked to death or simply died of fright, he couldn't decide. Either way, he'd left the limp body in the burning shack.

Before he left, he'd wolfed down a pot of mussels that were boiling over the fire. His stomach was now groaning ominously. He suddenly felt the urge to dive off the donkey and seek relief amongst the bushes at the side of the road.

Sir Roger hadn't ridden the roads of England for over twenty years. Nothing much had changed. The track was dusty and rutted but perfectly passable, in the winter months he'd have been up-to his knees in mud. At a junction with a wider track, he came to a halt. Uncertain of the correct direction to take he trusted his rumbling gut and turned the donkey to the right. The animal plodded along slowly but steadily. A few minutes later a cart overtook him. He shouted over to the carter as it rumbled beside him, "Is this the way to Draychester?"

"Aye it is. Keep to the road another six or seven miles.

You'll be able to see the top of the cathedral over the hill in front of you."

Sir Roger briefly considered abandoning the donkey, knocking the carter over the head and taking the cart. He judged it too risky this close to the city. There was a time to make trouble and a time to sit on your donkey and mind your own business.

The cart rumbled off into the distance and there was suddenly nothing to hear except the birdsong and the soft plodding of the donkey's feet in the dusty soil. Here and there he passed stretches of carefully managed coppiced woodland, but mostly the road passed through massive open fields. There were no hedges or fences, only the grass strip on the roadside marking the edge of the track and the beginning of the fields. They were divided into long individual strips growing crops or lying fallow. In the distance rose a low ridge of hills dotted with white spots which could only be sheep.

Here and there a side road branched off and a small village was visible up the rutted tracks. They weren't much more than a small cluster of thatched cottages, sometimes accompanied by a small church and tower. Sir Roger pressed on along the main road, wanting to be in the city a good few hours before dusk. He slowed only once, at a windswept crossroad where he gazed at the desiccated remains of some unfortunate thief hanging on the gallows.

As Sir Roger neared the city, the road became busy. There were carts, people on foot, some on horses and a few like Sir Roger on donkeys or mules. Over the crest of the hill, the top of Draychester cathedral came into sight just as the carter had said. The cathedral dwarfed the rest of the buildings in the city which clustered around its base like tiny boxes. The central tower rose one hundred and fifty feet above the pointed leaded roof, which was itself eighty feet above ground level. It was the wonder of the county and beyond. Sir Roger had not set eyes on it in twenty years. He'd seen many sights on his travels but it still had the power to impress. The city walls seemed slight in comparison, but he knew they were a good thirty feet high. They surrounded the sprawling city and the castle that sat on its north western perimeter. There was power and wealth here.

He headed down the hill towards one of the city's great gatehouses. Two round towers, fifty feet high, were set in the city wall. Between them was a stone arch through which the road traffic flowed. On one side of the road ran a ditch in which a disgusting mix of dirty water, shit, rotting offal, the odd dead cat and dog and countless other refuse from the city flowed. The stench almost made him gag. Rooting through the thick putrid sludge that lined the banks of the ditch was a small herd of pigs. The sight brought back long forgotten memories from his childhood. He'd often returned this way with his father and his hated older brother Hugh.

A crowd of disheveled boys ran here and there among the crowd on the road as he approached the gatehouse. They called out to the more obvious travellers.

"A room master?"

"I know a good inn."

"A meal sir?"

"Let me guide you."

They didn't approach Sir Roger. Dressed in the old man's rags, astride an ancient donkey and with a face that looked like thunder, he was not their natural customer. At the great gate itself, several poles were set up either side of the road. On these sat the blackened eyeless heads of those criminals and traitors who had suffered the city's justice. He looked at the heads carefully as he passed, but he didn't recognise anyone.

There was only one bored looking watchman on guard at the gate. Sir Roger didn't even attract a second glance as he got off the donkey and led it under the shadow of the gatehouse. As he passed under the gate and into the city proper, he found himself on a wide and prosperous street that he remembered well. Some of the best inns and the finest houses in the city were here. Sir Roger realised he badly needed a change of appearance. He could hardly conduct his business in the city dressed in rags. The only money he had were the two pennies he'd taken from the old man's shack. He looked speculatively at the donkey. It was slow, cantankerous and somewhat smelly but it had got him here. He almost felt like patting it, but at the last minute he stayed his hand, it wouldn't do to get sentimental. Sir Roger knew just the place to get rid of it and gain some coin in return.

In the late afternoon sun, the main streets were still crowded. Sheep and cattle were being driven down toward the marketplace. Carts laden with eggs, milk and cheese wove in and out of the crowd. Ponies and packhorse, laden with corn, were headed towards the marketplace. Sir Roger led the donkey slowly through the throng. The merchant's houses here on the right-hand side of the street had their shops open. Under the covered fronts there were expensive fabrics on show. As he pressed on towards the centre of the city, the shops were more tightly packed together. Before he came to the marketplace he began to look for a small alleyway that he once knew well. At last he came to it, wedged between two small shop fronts. It was only six or seven feet wide. As Sir Roger led the donkey into the passageway, the sun vanished behind them.

Here the jetties of the upper storeys of the houses on either side of the passage were almost touching. The way was none too clean. There were wide muddy puddles difficult to avoid. Most were filled with the kitchen waste of the houses he was squeezing between. The rotting stench made Sir Roger cough. This area of the city was a dense warren of narrow lanes and paths. It would be easy to get lost, but he kept to the main passageway.

Eventually the way opened out to reveal a small courtyard. An old timber stable stood on one side. Sir Roger banged on a dilapidated door at its far end. He doubted much had changed while he'd been abroad. It was a place where no one asked too many questions. Especially when a stranger turned up with a decrepit donkey for sale. The beast would be meat pies at the marketplace this time tomorrow else hauling some fat friar out of the city in the afternoon. Sir Roger didn't care much either way.

A short while later and he was donkey-less and two shillings better off. It wasn't much for the animal even in its poor condition but, as he'd predicted, no questions had been asked as the coin changed hands. Sir Roger made his way back up the passageway to the main street and worked his way down to the busy marketplace. At the far end behind a high wall sat the bishop's palace and the cathedral. He could see a steady flow of people entering the cathedral precinct through a gate set in the stonework. It was open throughout the day but once the sun set, it would be firmly barred.

Sir Roger pushed his way slowly through the crowd in the marketplace. He remembered there used to be a tolerable alehouse down another side passage. With some difficulty, he found the passageway and entrance to the alehouse.

Inside it was dark and stank of stale ale with dirty rushes strewn across the floor. It was packed with a rowdy and boisterous crowd of every description. Sir Roger blended easily into a far corner. Over a wooden tankard of weak, sweet tasting ale and a simple meal of bread and cheese he studied his fellow customers with interest.

There were the usual cut-purses, prostitutes, beggars and several other obvious lowlifes. In addition there were also carters and wagoners, stonemasons and carpenters from the never ending building work at the cathedral and several weary looking pilgrims. There were also two foreign merchants arguing drunkenly with each other in slurred French. They were just what he was looking for. Sir Roger bided his time, at some point nature would take its course with the amount they were drinking.

After an hour or so the fatter of the two stumbled towards the rear of the room and out a dark doorway to the backyard. Sir Roger slowly made his way towards the same doorway. No one paid him any attention.

It was dusk outside and the rear yard was gloomy. The French merchant was lent against a wall pissing over his own feet. Sir Roger snorted, it was almost too easy and came with the added bonus that he'd never much liked the French. He walked up behind the drunken man, grabbed hold of the back of his head with both hands, and smacked it into the wall with a satisfying thud. The Frenchman went down like a sack of grain.

Sir Roger relieved him of his clothes, his cloak, a fat purse and a short sword. He quickly stripped off the rags that he'd been wearing all day and put the merchant's clothes on. They weren't a bad fit. Sir Roger almost left the piss wet boots behind but, deciding this was no time for squeamishness, pulled them on.

Dragging the now naked and unconscious man to a pile of old rushes and straw, he covered him over. Sir Roger doubted that he'd awake until the following morning. He smirked as he imagined the merchant finding himself stark bollock naked with one hell of a headache. He pushed his way out of a side gate, leaving it open behind him.

Sir Roger weighed the merchant's purse in his hand with appreciation. It had obviously been a good market day. Looking a lot more prosperous he made his way to an inn on one of the main streets leading from the marketplace. The image of a lamb was painted on a board hanging above an arch in the middle of the stone-built structure. He walked under the arch past the heavy wooden doors that would soon be closed and bolted to the street. The courtyard he entered was just flattened earth. The accommodation on either side was two-storey timber-framed buildings their roofs steep and shingle covered. There were external staircases running up to galleries on the first floor. There was nobody in the courtyard, so he made his way to the hall in search of the landlord.

The hall was high and open to the roof beams. There

was a hearth in the centre set on blackened flagstones. Smoke rose lazily from the fire and exited through a louvre in the roof far above. Down one side was a long trestle table where some guests sat eating a meal. A stout, no nonsense looking man emerged from the rear of the hall and approached him. The landlord didn't offer anything more than a polite, "Evening sir."

Sir Roger put on his best fake smile. "I'm Sir Roger Mudstone. I've come a long distance today. I need a bed for the night and a good meal."

He put his hand on the purse and jangled the coins. He generally found this approach produced the desired outcome. The landlord appraised him slowly. The local byelaw required that each innkeeper in the city offer a visitor a bed whether they arrived on foot or on horseback. Still, the landlord wasn't in the business of giving charity, there were plenty of monasteries for that. Sir Roger looked slightly dishevelled but apparently had the coin to pay. The landlord knew the Mudstone name and there was something about the man that was vaguely familiar.

"I knew a Sir Hugh Mudstone. He stayed here a few times in years past. Your father perhaps?"

Sir Roger tensed at the name. "Hugh you say? That would have been my late brother."

"Ah, then I'm sorry for your loss."

"Don't be sorry. I'm not."

The landlord was momentarily lost for a response. Finally he said, "I'll have my wife bring you some food. You can have a chamber outside on the first floor or," he looked meaningfully at Sir Roger's purse, "here next to the hall?"

The upper rooms would be cheaper, but Sir Roger had no intention of sharing a chamber and bed for the night with any of the other guests. After the journey he'd had to

Death Of The Official

get here he felt entitled to some comfort and privacy. He said, "I'll take a chamber down here."

The landlord nodded and gestured for him to take a seat at the end of the trestle table. It wasn't long before he was served a meal of ale, pottage, bread and cheese. Some of the other customers tried to make small talk with him. They soon gave up and left him to his own thoughts. Sir Rogers's fearsome stare and obvious lack of interest in anything anyone had to say discouraged even the most curious.

"Mean looking bugger. Who is he?" asked the landlord's plump wife.

Her husband looked across the room at his noble guest. "Sir Roger Mudstone. I can tell you a tale or two about that one."

She looked at Sir Roger with renewed interest. "Old Sir Hugh's brother is he?"

"The same. I didn't recognise him when he first came in. Come back to claim his inheritance I dare say. He's the last man standing now."

"What do you mean?"

"The tales well known Wife."

"Well, I haven't heard it."

The landlord's wife, sensing a good story, slipped onto one of the empty benches and pulled her husband down to sit beside her.

The landlord sighed and said, "Wife you are too curious for your own good."

She playfully jabbed a finger into his side. "You'd better tell me Cedric. You know I'll pester you until I hear it."

He smiled at her indulgently. He well knew her weakness for a good tale. "Well, there were four Mudstone brothers originally. If I remember rightly John was the oldest. Had an unfortunate childhood accident, at least that's what they called it. Found dead at the bottom of a well."

"It wasn't an accident?"

"Rumour has it the good Sir Roger over there and his brother Hugh did the deed."

The landlord's wife's eyes grew round and she suppressed a shiver. "Never. Not his own brothers."

The landlord shook his head sadly at her naivety. "You'd be surprised what the nobility get up to Wife. They found a bucket loaded with rocks on young John's head. Tossed down the shaft to finish him off."

"No one was accused?"

He shrugged. "Accusing is one thing and proving is another. Now the next oldest was his father's favourite, Harry. The other two hated his guts. Next thing we hear is that poor Harry has been savaged to death by his father's prize boar. How he came to be in with the boar is a secret only Harry and the pig keeper could tell you."

"What did he say?"

"Who?"

She elbowed him. "The pig keeper of course."

"Ah, well, the boar had been kept starved for weeks on Sir Roger's orders. Ravenous it was. Seems Harry got blind drunk and decided to sleep it off in the pig pen. Nasty business, wasn't much of the poor lad left by all accounts. The pig keeper mysteriously disappeared not long after."

The landlord's wife gazed with fascination at Sir Roger. "You think they set the boar on him?" she said breathlessly.

"Of course. Him or his brother, or maybe both together."

"So then there was just the two brothers left?"

The landlord nodded. "The father was proud to have raised two killers. Thought it was the natural order of things, keeping up family traditions and all that. That's the nobility for you lass. Can't trust them as far as you can throw-um! Problem was their old dad needed an heir and a spare."

"So?"

"So he thought they might just finish each other off. That'd leave him with neither."

"And did they do each other in?"

He nodded towards Sir Roger. "Don't be daft woman. Sir Roger is over there isn't he, and you knew Sir Hugh. The talk was that his dad banished young Roger to France. Sir Hugh inherited the lot on his dad's death. Now his brother is in the grave, Sir Roger will be back to claim his own inheritance."

"They do say blood's thicker than water. You think old Hugh left him everything?"

The landlord snorted. "Wife, there's more chance that I'll be the next bishop of Draychester."

3

SIR ROGER AT THE BISHOP'S PALACE

"Roger Mudstone arrived in the city last night my lord," said Scrivener, chewing a piece of bread. He belched noisily then continued, "Thomas was on duty on the gate and knew him for who he was. Apparently he turned up dressed in rags and riding a donkey."

The bishop grimaced and said, "Pass me the wine will you. Tell me, has he killed anyone yet?"

Scrivener slid the wine jug across the table to his master. "Well there's an old man with a broken neck down at Draymouth. Dead in his cottage near the beach. And there was some skulduggery in one of the alehouses off the marketplace last night. Mudstone went in the front dressed in rags and came out the back dressed as a merchant. Oh, and before that he sold the donkey, he got two shillings for the beast; it wasn't in the best of condition."

"Scrivener, I never fail to be impressed by your attention to detail," the bishop said sarcastically.

"Thank you my lord, you're too kind."

"It wasn't a compliment. Who was the merchant who lost his clothes?"

Scrivener shrugged. "No one important, a Frenchman. Poor sod has been arrested for offending public decency. The watch found him wandering the streets just before dawn, naked."

The bishop poured himself a large measure of wine and sighed. "Typical of a Mudstone. The whole family were cold-blooded killers and believe me Roger is no exception. His brother was a complete turd, always stirring up trouble. The only reason he's left most of his estate to the church is because he loathed Roger. We need to handle this business with care Scrivener."

"I thought you might say that my lord. Perhaps we should just have him whacked over the head and have done with it."

The bishop wagged his finger at his friend and said in mock outrage, "Really Scrivener, have you no morals?"

Scrivener gave him a wolfish grin. "I fear you've taught me too well my lord."

"Well I wish it was as simple as hitting him over the head and dropping him in the Shitbrooke," said the bishop in reference to the stinking drain that ran out by one of the city's main gates. "However, we must be seen to have observed all the legalities. Sir Roger will be at our door before the mornings out, you can be sure of that. I can't say he's going to be happy with what we have to tell him."

"And the French merchant my lord?"

"Oh the sergeant of the watch will no-doubt put him in the stocks for the day. That'll teach him to hold his drink. A man should know his limits."

Scrivener reflected that the bishop's limits ran a lot further than most.

~

In the mid-morning Sir Roger entered the cathedral precinct through the gate in the marketplace. There were a great many people coming and going, and the gatekeeper merely gave him a nod as he passed through. Here, within the precinct walls, lay not only the cathedral but the bishop's palace, as well as the choristers' school, a hospital for travellers and a chapel all within the liberty of the cathedral. The great bulk of the cathedral itself lay ahead across the green. Sir Roger turned to his left and followed a path alongside the precinct wall, which gradually led him around to the bishop's palace.

The palace stood almost in the shadow of the great cathedral on a sloping site with sweeping views over the ancient city and the countryside beyond. Over the past century and a half, the building had been embellished by the three previous bishops of Draychester. It was now complete with its own moat dug into the slope and crossed by a flagstone drawbridge. To be fair, the moat was more to impress than for any serious purpose of defence. Sir Roger was indeed suitably impressed, a feeling which slightly unnerved him.

Sir Roger had known the previous bishop well. His father and then later his brother Hugh had many dubious business dealings with old Bishop Thorndyke. In his own way 'Old Thorny' had been a greater crook than either of them.

The bishop had been killed during the great storm that had caused devastation across southern England a few years past. Sir Roger had heard the tale even in France. The bishop had been in bed with an infamous whore from the city when the wind had sent two chimney stacks crashing through the palace roof. Thorndyke and his companion had been found crushed in a deadly embrace. The town folk favoured divine retribution. Sir Roger wasn't so sure, he liked to think his brother may have had something to do with it.

This new bishop, Jocelyn Gifford, Sir Roger knew only by reputation. From what he had heard he'd soldiered with the king in his younger days and was well liked and respected at court.

Sir Roger crossed the mock drawbridge and approached the entrance. It was an elaborately decorated stone archway with a tall iron studded oak door. He was slightly unsure of how he was supposed to gain access. There was a door knocker in the form of an iron serpent and a large iron ring for the door handle. As he reached out to grasp the knocker the door opened in-wards to reveal a small man.

"Good morning, do you have business here?"

"I'm here to see the bishop. The name is Mudstone, Sir Roger Mudstone."

"Is he expecting you sir?"

"He'll know what I'm here for. He sent a messenger half way across France to find me."

The doorkeeper deliberately looked Sir Roger up and down. "Can I ask the exact nature of your business? The bishop is a very busy man. He sees few people this early in the day. If it's urgent, I'll make you an appointment for next week."

Sir Roger stuck his weathered face into the doorkeepers and grabbed him around the neck with a hand. Jabbing the man in the windpipe with the thumb of his other hand he hissed, "I suggest you go find your master right now and be quick about it you pompous little turd."

He released the little man from his grasp and barged through the doorway into the large hallway. The doorkeeper stood bent over, hands on knees, gasping for breath. Still wheezing he staggered off deeper into the interior of the palace.

∾

"Roger Mudstone is here my lord. He seems to have upset Geoffrey at the door."

"Geoffrey?"

"The doorkeeper my lord. Half strangled him."

The bishop sighed heavily. "Well, you'd better show Sir Roger into my day chamber. You and I can go through his brother's will with him. I fear he's not going to take it too well. Perhaps we should have Bernard lurking in a corner just in case things get out of hand?"

Scrivener nodded in agreement. "I'll find Bernard then fetch Sir Roger."

Bernard was part of the bishop's personal retinue. Sometime body guard, at other times a trusted messenger he was a great ox of a man with a chest like a barrel. He was immensely strong, had arms like blacksmith's hammers and was intensively loyal to the bishop. If his master ordered him to stand in the corner of the room, he would stand like a rock until ordered otherwise. If there was trouble, Bernard would positively relish the opportunity to knock the offender into the next county. The bishop took a seat behind a small table covered in a richly embroidered cloth. Bernard appeared and was soon stood behind his master, hands folded across his chest.

Scrivener arrived back with Roger Mudstone in tow. Bernard scowled at him with suspicion. The bishop forced a smile in greeting and said, "Ah Sir Roger, so kind of you to drop in. I feared my messenger hadn't found you. It's been some time since we dispatched him; he hasn't returned."

"My lord bishop," said Sir Roger, removing his hat and inclining his head. "It was a long journey. I was on the other side of France when I received the news of my brother's death. The sea crossing was difficult."

For a moment the question of the missing messenger hung in the air. Finally the bishop gestured for Sir Roger to take a seat opposite him. "Ah yes, your brother. My condolences he was…" the bishop paused struggling for the right words, "an interesting man."

Sir Roger's left eye twitched almost imperceptibly, but he showed no other emotion. They both knew that Sir Roger's late brother had been a complete and utter turd.

"Some wine for Sir Roger please Scrivener," said the bishop.

Scrivener crossed to a bench in the corner and poured two cups of wine, handed one to the bishop and the other to Sir Roger who greedily slurped it down. "So my lord, to business. I'm eager to travel to my late brother's estates and take possession." He hesitated and then continued, "First though I'd like to make a bequest to the church."

The bishop was taken-aback; This was taking an unexpected turn. He glanced at Scrivener, who gave a slight shrug of his shoulders. "Can I ask why?" asked the bishop curiously.

Sir Roger said, "I had a most miraculous escape crossing the channel. I prayed for deliverance and I was washed up safe and sound. I believe I've been saved for a higher purpose."

"Well, the Lord moves in mysterious ways indeed Sir Roger. May I know the nature of your bequest?" asked the bishop.

"I wish to grant one of the Mudstone northern manors to the church. It's called Sodham, or Sod-um, something like that, I don't recall exactly, I've never actually been there."

"That's a most generous gesture Sir Roger. Scrivener, you know the details of this place?"

"The manor is Sodham in Grimsdale my lord. It's in Yorkshire. Your brother, Sir Roger, has left you two manors in the north. Sodham and a few miles to the south Coxington. They're near the great Cistercian abbey of Ribsdale."

The bishop beamed falsely at Sir Roger. "Yorkshire, well, well". He knew, and Sir Roger certainly realised, that the manor would be practically worthless. If the nearby abbey hadn't already drained most of the manors resources, it would no-doubt have been raised to the ground by the Scots at least once a decade for the last hundred years. The great pestilence had probably decimated the place as well. If there was anything more than a decrepit hovel or two and a pigpen he'd be surprised. The bishop waved a slightly dismissive hand at Scrivener and said, "I suppose you'd better take care of the legalities."

There were a few minutes of uncomfortable silence broken only by the scratching of Scrivener's quill. Sir Roger's gaze flicked from the bishop to Scrivener to a scowling Bernard and back again. Finally Scrivener finished his writing and placed his quill down on the bench. He read from the parchment, "I, Sir Roger Mudstone, grant to God and St. John of Draychester, and to the Bishop Jocelyn and his successors for ever, the church and manor of Sodham in Grimsdale, in pure and perpetual alms, so that it may be henceforth a prebend in the church of St. John of Draychester."

He placed the parchment flat on the desk, heated some wax over a candle flame and dripped it onto the document. Scrivener gestured at the document and said, "Your seal please Sir Roger."

Sir Roger removed the seal ring from his finger and walked over to Scrivener's bench. He pressed the ring into the wax, leaving the impression of a phoenix rising from the flames. That's what Scrivener presumed it was supposed to look like. In reality, it looked like a scrawny chicken drowning. Scrivener stifled a laugh and said, "The church thanks you for your generosity. We'll pray for your soul."

Sir Roger grunted somewhat embarrassedly. He didn't really know what had come over him. "So, it's done. Moving on to my brothers will?"

The bishop looked uneasily at Scrivener. "Ah yes, your brother's will. Scrivener?"

Scrivener cleared his throat nervously and said, "Your brother was a very sick man towards the end of his life Sir Roger. He spent his last years at the hospital for lepers; St Mary Magdalen on the outskirts of the city. An institution the cathedral and bishops of Draychester have supported for many years."

A flicker of emotion crossed Sir Rogers face, pity vying with horror. "Hugh was a leper?"

Scrivener nodded. "Indeed, he was. A most curious case Sir Roger. I'm no expert but I'm told the disease normally takes it course over many years. The progress in your brother was rapid."

Sir Roger was now at the same time both horrified and curious of his brother's fate. "Rapid you say?"

Scrivener consulted some parchment notes on his desk.

"He entered the hospital at Christmas, he'd lost the fingers on both hands by Easter, his toes were gone by late spring, during the summer he lost his nose, he was dead before harvest."

All Sir Roger could summon up was an emotionless, "I see."

Scrivener continued, "As you may know, a leper can hold no property once he is admitted to the hospital. A cruel rule, but the doctrine of the church is to treat a leper as already dead. His will was executed immediately he was admitted to St Mary's hospital."

An uneasy feeling began to spread through Sir Roger. He lent forward, suddenly anxious. "Yes the will, what of the will?"

Scrivener sorted through more of the papers on the desk, found the document and began to read the relevant terms from the long text. "To my brother Roger, if he still lives, I grant my manors of Sodham and Coxington in the county of York. Also to Roger I grant within the city of Draychester the stable next to Middlegate and the chickens and hen house in the yard attached. Finally, I leave to Roger my brother, my warhorse to be found at the said stable. All my other worldly goods, estates and possessions I do freely grant to God and the Cathedral of St. John and Bishop of Draychester and his successors in perpetuity in hope and expectation that they will pray for my poor soul."

There was a long silence. Finally a shocked Sir Roger croaked, "I'm not sure I understand you? Are you saying he left me nothing?"

Scrivener looked up from the papers. "Well not quite nothing, I understand you might be a little disappointed, but the manors in the north, although you have now generously gifted one of those to the church, the stable and war horse..."

Quite unexpectedly from the back of the room Bernard added, "And the chickens and the chicken house, don't forget them," and then under his breath he mumbled, "bloody ungrateful sod."

"Yes, a very good point Bernard, let's not forget the chickens" said the bishop trying in vain to lighten the mood.

"Disappointed!" hissed Sir Roger, going red in the face and jumping to his feet. "Disappointed is a word I use when I have throttled a French knight with my bare hands on the battlefield and I take his purse from his dead and mangled body and find only a single coin. That's disappointment! The northern manors will be practically worthless as you well know. So no, I'm not disappointed, what I am is burning up inside with rage, my bile burns in my very throat all the better to spit on you and this smug turd of a clerk of yours. You deprive me of a fortune and expect me to go on my way as though it was of little consequence..."

He moved across the room towards the bishop who sat calmly, a wisp of a smile playing across his lips. Bernard slowly started to shuffle his bulk out from behind the bishop and edge around the walls of the room. Sir Roger was now positively foaming at the mouth. "I know what this is all about. That bastard brother of mine did this deliberately, to spite me, and you've colluded in this stinking, evil, illegal business. You can't deprive me of what's mine by right! I won't have it!" he roared, thumping the top of the bishop's desk. "I'll petition the archbishop, the king, whoever, I'll take it all back by force if I have to. I'll crush you, do you understand me you pair of rump-fed curs."

Bernard took a deep exception to his master being insulted. He advanced towards Mudstone with surprising speed and with one huge hand on his shoulder pulled him back from the bishop's desk. "This one has a terrible temper my lord. My old mother always told me to watch my temper. Do you want me to break his feck'in legs master, perhaps an arm?"

The bishop turned and grinned at Bernard affectionately. "I'm sure your mother was a model parent Bernard, and no, not just yet, although thank you for the offer."

Bernard dropped his hand from Mudstone's shoulder but hovered menacingly beside the angry man. The bishop lent forward in his chair and regarded Sir Roger. His eyes narrowed and went a steely blue, his stare seemed to bore into the angry man's very soul. He spoke slowly. "Let's be clear Mudstone. Don't take me for a fool. I know of you and your family. Do you think I don't know how you have whored and robbed and murdered your way through life? Your brother died a wretched, disease ridden and penitent sinner. An outcast from the city in the leper hospital. They looked him after with sympathy and kindness in his final days. A treatment that he didn't deserve but one which is freely given, whether rich or poor, to those who are admitted to the hospital. Pray someone will do the same for you someday. At least he has tried to make some reparations for his lifetime of sin with his grants to the church. I suggest you take what he granted to you and be grateful for it. Appeal all you want, good luck with that, your reputation precedes you. Perhaps you should retire to your northern manors... I should say manor... and reflect on your many sins. Be out of the city by the curfew bell. Bernard show Sir Roger out, try not to damage him."

Bernard placed a hand in the centre of Sir Roger's chest and shoved him none too gently towards the door. Sir Roger by now incandescent with rage shouted, "You treacherous, stinking…"

At which point one of Bernard's colossal fists came down on the top of the angry man's head. Bernard dragged the limp body out of the room with one hand. Sir Roger was eventually deposited next to the marketplace gate, on a little stone bench set in the inner wall that circled the cathedral precinct.

After the unconscious Sir Roger had been dragged from the room, the bishop sank back into his well-cushioned seat with a sigh of relief. "Well, that could have gone better. Mudstone's gift of the manor in Yorkshire was unexpected and that chicken clause in the will most unfortunate. You'd better make sure we know what he gets up to."

Scrivener nodded. "Indeed, I shall keep a close eye on him my lord."

4

SIR ROGER LEAVES THE CITY

Sir Roger woke with a splitting headache and a burning rage. He could feel the anger simmering away deep down in his guts. Hauling himself upright on the stone bench he sat for a moment, his head still spinning from the blow that had knocked him unconscious. He tried to gather his thoughts. One thing was clear, following the bishop's advice and reflecting on his sins wasn't an option. Turning the other cheek was for the weak. He despised the weak; they deserved to be crushed. His whole life had taught him the truth of that. It was the natural way of things. No one would take away from him what was plainly his. Heading north to Yorkshire was the one piece of the bishop's advice he would follow. He'd take the damn warhorse his spiteful brother had left him and go lick his wounds in the north. He'd plan, scheme and plot to bring down that whore's son of a bishop and his smug clerk and recover his estates and property or he'd die trying.

He got to his feet slowly, his head still pounding. He found he was just within the cathedral precinct with the marketplace gate to his left. Taking one last look out across the green to the vast cathedral and the bishop's palace he coughed up a great glob of phlegm and spat violently out into the void.

∼

Leaving by the gate, he was met by the outstretched arms and cries of the beggars who naturally gravitated there. The rich pickings from the constant stream of visitors passing through the gate supported a ragged band of variously afflicted souls, some genuine, some undoubtedly fake.

A one-legged beggar using a battered wooden crutch approached Sir Roger, his arm and hand outstretched. "Alms for a poor beggar sir? Once a solider in the king's army."

Sir Roger reached out to the beggar's grubby hand as though to place a coin in it. Instead, he grabbed the man's fingers in a vice like grip and slowly crushed them, the finger bones audibly creaking and popping under the strain. Finally he released his grip, and the beggar collapsed moaning onto the ground his shattered hand clutched tightly to his chest.

There was an angry mummer and drumming of crutches from the other beggars clustered around the gate. It was a competitive business to be sure, but they didn't like to see one of their own harmed. Sir Roger met their gaze, the crazed look on his face silencing them. He sneered once, swirled around and stomped off across the marketplace, barging aside those who weren't quick enough to get out of his way.

∼

Sir Roger's progress across the city towards Middlegate could be charted by a catalogue of injuries to anyone or anything that impeded his progress. He was still in a foul mood when he reached a run-down stable block in a back street near to the great gate. As he looked at the ramshackle wooden building, Sir Roger could picture the smirk on his brother's face. There was a rotten wooden door at one end hanging from a broken hinge. The roof, what was left of it, had once been thatched but was now a decomposing mound of straw perched on the leaning walls.

"God's teeth," he roared, "there had better be some spectacular beast in here or by God I'll torch the place myself!"

Sir Roger ripped opened the door in a fury. It tore free from its one forlorn hinge and he threw the whole thing into the stable yard, scattering a flock of what he presumed where his own chickens. He stepped into the dim interior which reeked of stale horse piss. A slender head swivelled around to regard him with evil bloodshot eyes. There was a long snort and a curious whinny. The horse, for that's what it was, was jet black and in the dim light he had trouble seeing it. The beast moved forward and nuzzled its head against his outstretched hand. Animals in general hated Sir Roger, but he could tell this one had been bred for war, taught to bite, kick and trample its opponents to death. He would expect nothing less in a horse ridden by his own brother. It recognised the same qualities in it's new owner. A genuine grin, the first for many years, spread across Sir Roger's face.

"Hello my beauty!"

There was a battered saddle hung over a beam. Sir Roger grunted in surprised that there was anything left in the stable. Abandoned buildings containing horses and saddles weren't normal in a city like this. Without a watchman it would soon be stolen. He peered into the gloom. Someone must have been feeding the horse since his brother had disappeared to the leper hospital. He found the answer at the back of the building. A dirty ragged figure was snoring away, half buried in a pile of hay. Sir Roger looked down into a face from his past. Travis, once his father's groom and Hugh's as well no doubt. Older and half starved from what he could see, but it was Travis none the less.

In a far corner he found a stagnant pale of water or it could have been horse piss, Sir Roger wasn't sure and he didn't really care. He emptied its contents in a slow stream over Travis's head. The man spluttered and coughed into life, choking on the noxious fluid. "Morning Travis, pleased to see me?"

Travis wiping his mouth and clearing his stinging eyes looked up. A familiar figure loomed over him. "Sir Roger," he said shielding his eyes from the light of the doorway, "is that really you?"

"Who else would it be, fool. On your feet man, we have work to do."

"Sir Roger, it is you! I thought you'd never come master. Sir Hugh said you would but I've almost run out of money, what with the warhorse to feed and the stable to maintain. It's been months since they admitted your brother to the hospital and…"

"Stop babbling man. You were always a babbler, surprised Hugh let you live this long!" Sir Roger slapped Travis hard across the face and dragged him to his feet. "Now help me get the horse out of here."

They got the animal out into the yard, Sir Roger nodded once and grinned again. "Hugh always did have a good eye for horseflesh. A magnificent beast, a warhorse for sure."

He ran his hands down the horse's flank in admiration.

They bred a warhorse for speed and responsiveness. They also had to withstand the short, sharp shock of the charge and clash of battle. Sir Roger had ridden many such horses in his mercenary days and he knew quality when he saw it. "What's his name?"

"Red Eyes."

"I can see why. Is there something wrong with his eyes or has he always been like that?" asked Sir Roger.

"As long as I've tended him they've been like that master. Your brother said he had a touch of the devil in him."

"He may have been right there Travis, he may have been right," murmured Sir Roger entranced by the beast. Finally he turned back to his brother's former servant. "Tell me Travis, did my late brother still keep company with that den of thieves at the ale house on the road to Codlingham? I was thinking in particular of the Bouchard twins. I need a task undertaken that might suit their particular skills."

Travis nodded."Your brother drank and plotted there often. The Bouchard twins skulk there still, evil men they are master. I think they've become crueler as the years have passed."

"Excellent, excellent. It's always nice to know how the friends of one's youth are doing. I think I shall pay them a visit. Get what's of value out of that stinking stable and saddle up the horse. I want to be away from here within the hour."

∼

Sir Roger sat down on an old upturned barrel in the yard and watched as Travis dragged various bits of tack from the stable. When the job was finally done Sir Roger hopped off the barrel and swung easily into the saddle, the horse hardly stirring as though they'd been companions for years. Travis looked up at Sir Roger mutely. Sir Roger felt he had to make some gesture, however small. The feeling disturbed him; he thought perhaps he was going a little soft. "The chickens Travis, they're yours. Let no one say I don't reward loyalty, but if I never see you again, it'll be too soon."

With that he made to move off. Travis fell to his knees and hung on with grim determination to one of the front legs of the warhorse. A move some would think suicidal. "Sir Roger, what am I to do? I've known nothing else but service to the Mudstones," he wailed.

Sir Roger looked down at him with utter contempt. "Always been the trouble with you serfs, needy, needy, needy. What about me man, I've been deprived of lands and a fortune!" He contemplated the pathetic figure below him. "I'm off to the north, a manor called Coxington, it's in Yorkshire. Get your disgusting carcass that far and I'll put you to some use, God knows what."

Sir Roger used his boot to peel Travis off the horse's leg. He spurred the beast into motion and rode out of the yard, leaving the forlorn figure on his knees in the mud. He guided Red Eyes through the narrow streets back towards the gate where he'd originally entered the city. Sir Roger was none too subtle in forcing his way through the throng and he left behind him a trail of cursing tradesman, mud splattered merchants and outraged ladies. He passed through the great gate without dismounting or even slowing, scattering pedestrians and forcing a cart to crash against the stonework of the gatehouse. The guard on duty shouted a stream of abuse after him.

As Sir Roger made his way out onto the road, he deliberately clipped the backs of two Gonfermours who were emptying barrels of night soil into the ditch. They were sent sprawling headfirst down the greasy bank into the sludge that ran there. Their barrels bounced down after them, spewing forth a froth of brown liquid.

Sir Roger set off up the hill without a backwards glance. At the crossroads on the crest of the hill he guided the warhorse to the left with a press of his knee, then headed off north at a gallop.

5

SIR ROGER AND THE BOUCHARD TWINS

About three miles north of the city lay a small cluster of buildings at a crossroads. The huddle of low wattle and daub hovels with turf roofs hardly justified a name, but at some point they had been forced to accept Codlingham. Sir Roger knew the place from his youth. It was a veritable viper's nest of unsavoury characters, most of whom were only too willing to accept money for doing violence against others. Sir Roger felt very much at home.

He stopped in front of one particular grubby and rundown looking structure. A dirty leather hide covered the main door. There was a broom hanging outside the doorway showing the place served as an alehouse and that a fresh batch had recently been brewed. Sir Roger pushed aside the hide and entered, pausing a moment just inside the doorway to let his eyes adjust to the smoky dimness of the interior. There were no windows, just a small smoke hole in the middle of the turf roof. The smoke from the small fire pit struggled to vent through it and left his eyes stinging. There were no other customers as far as he could see. Two long tables with benches were placed either side of the fire.

A single spluttering tallow candle was set in the middle of one of them. There was another open door on the opposite wall through which the alehouse keeper could presumably come and go with bowls and pitchers. The combination of smells made even Sir Rogers hardened stomach turn. It was a rich aroma of sweaty bodies, sour ale and two-day-old cabbage and onion potage.

The alehouse keeper, a stout, dull eyed woman in her thirties, emerged. She wore a heavy linen apron which was covered with all manner of old stains and encrusted food. Wiping her hands on a greasy rag she scowled at him. Before she could open her mouth, Sir Roger held up a finger to silence her. He sat down heavily on a bench and put his feet up on the table.

"Before you speak woman consider that whatever comes out of that revolting mouth of yours will be of absolutely no interest to me. I need you to do one thing only, and that's fetching the Bouchard twins to me. They're no doubt sleeping off last night's ale in one of the nearby hovels. Tell them Sir Roger Mudstone needs them for a job."

He tossed a couple of pennies onto the table in her general direction. Her mouth flapped open, she made to speak, then took a hard look at Sir Roger and thought better of it. She left via the front entrance without a word.

∼

A little while later the leather hide over the door was flung back and two men entered. They came and sat opposite Sir Roger. He slowly removed his feet from the table. They studied Sir Roger for a minute and he them. No one who'd ever met them before could be in any doubt who they were. Gilbert and Godbert, the Bouchard twins. Born within ten minutes of each other, but more unlikely twins it would be hard to find. Gilbert was the one with the brains and Godbert the brawn. They were in their mid-thirties but the similarities ended there. Gilbert was rake thin, small with dark greasy receding hair and a cunning rat-like face complete with three-day-old stubble. Godbert was a big, beefy man with broad strong shoulders and a minimal neck. He was mostly bald apart from an odd tuft of white hair on his forehead, whether this was natural or deliberate it wasn't advisable to ask. He was smooth-shaven with a large flat nose and small unfocused piggy eyes that shifted restlessly. One of his ears looked like it might once have been heavily chewed.

Eventually the smaller of the Bouchards, Gilbert, said, "Gawd's teeth it is you, on my life, Roger Mudstone. We thought you dead many a year ago."

Sir Roger nodded. "Rumours of my demise have been greatly exaggerated."

"Eh?"

"Never mind. I can see you two are as sharp as ever."

Gilbert grinned through the blackened stumps of his teeth. "That we are Sir Roger. Always ready to earn an honest penny or two from a gentleman such as yourself. What say you Godbert?"

Godbert blinked, thought hard, then hard again searching for the right answer with difficulty, "Pennies, like em a lot I do. Honest or not..."

"An honest penny," scoffed Sir Roger, "I don't think you two know the meaning of the word. Still, there's more than a penny to be made."

He took a small leather pouch from his pocket and poured its contents of coins onto the table in front of them. Godbert stretched out a greedy hand, only to be brought up short as Sir Rogers knife thudded into the table between his fingers. "Now, now don't be too hasty Godbert. You don't know what I want yet."

Godbert retracted his hand slowly. His brother licked his lips and said, "So what sort of job do you need us for?"

Sir Roger pulled his knife free from the table and said, "I want you to get yourselves to Draychester. The bishop and that greasy clerk of his will be sending some men north to Yorkshire. Not sure who or when but it'll be soon, a week or two at most. Probably no more than two or three men. I take it you still know every low life in the city Gilbert?"

"I keep my ear to the ground if that's what you mean Sir Roger."

"In that case, it shouldn't be too hard to find out who is going north and when. I want you to kill them."

Gilbert looked alarmed. "What in the city? The bishop will round up every likely suspect within thirty miles. He'll probably put this place to the torch just on the off chance it was us! You don't know this new bishop Sir Roger. He wouldn't rest until he had our heads on stakes outside the city gates."

"Calm down. Did I say you had to do it in the city? This has to be subtle. Follow them north, no need to dog their footsteps. They'll probably go via Gloucester. You can do it there. Make it look like a robbery or a drunken brawl that got out of hand and turned into a knife fight. It's common enough, you can easily disappear. There are travellers and pilgrims passing through the town all the time. You'll be no more likely a suspect than hundreds of others."

Gilbert sniffed somewhat placated. "Why don't you do it yourself if it's so easy?"

"I have other matters to attend to in the north. This is a side issue. Call it a matter of honour."

"Let's call it what it is, murder. It'll take more than the coins lying there for me and Godbert here to knife some of the bishop's men."

"Don't worry, that's just a part payment. Do the job, follow me north and there'll be more waiting. More than you can imagine Gilbert. I have big plans."

6

WILL BLACKBURNE IS ON TRIAL

Will Blackburne could hear the old woman cackling ahead of him. They were climbing the long stone staircase leading up from the under-croft of the bishop's palace. By now he knew that manic laugh all too well. Chained to the wall alongside him she'd been cackling incessantly all night. He suspected the bishop's constables had deliberately put her next to him. She was completely raving of course, he'd even felt sorry for her that first hour. By the time one of the constables released them the following morning he would have cheerfully throttled the old hag himself. Unfortunately, his hands were shackled behind his back. The staircase came out directly in a corner of the bishop's great hall. As they emerged from the stairs, the constable pushed him roughly against the wall. He forced him to sit down on the floor, his back to the smooth stonework. The old crone was gently propelled out into the centre of the hall where she came to a stop before the court. For the first time in twelve hours, her cackling came to an abrupt halt.

At the opposite end of the hall, behind a rough semicircle of benches, were the five judges of the Consistory Court in high-backed chairs. At their centre sat the imposing figure of Jocelyn Gifford, the twenty-second bishop of Draychester. Now in his early forties he still had something of the build of a warrior. This was unsurprising as he had once been a soldier in his youth. He was tall, with powerful shoulders, a weather-worn face with lively, intelligent blue eyes and a faint, mocking, wisp of a smile never far from his lips.

On his left was Robert Fitz-Herbert, the bald-headed Vicar General of the diocese. He was snoring softly, his mouth wide open. To Fitz-Herbert's left sat the Commissary General Walter Bubwith. He was obviously drunk and still clutched a half empty goblet in one hand.

On the bishop's right was a small hunched figure, Ralph of Shrewsbury. He had dull, lifeless, dark black eyes, which were likely to induce a shiver if they happened to focus on you. To the unacquainted it was most disconcerting, which was one of the reasons the bishop liked him on the bench. He was a man of very few words. In fact, the bishop couldn't actually remember him speaking these last two years which of course was another bonus. He forgot what Ralph's official title was, but he saw him creeping around the cathedral precincts sometimes. He'd inherited him as a judge from his predecessor.

To the right of Ralph sat the huge man mountain of Theobald Beaufort, dean of the cathedral. He'd struggled to get into his chair at first but had somehow jammed his large posterior onto the narrow seat. He rested his elbows on the bench in front, his head supported in his hands, the wood bowing slightly with the weight. He was content to watch the court's business from this position but generally not inclined to interfere. To one side of the judges sat the bishop's clerk, Adam Scrivener. Before him was a small bench covered with parchments, ink, and quills.

~

Not all the judges were sure of the proceedings of the court. In fact, when they were awake, some were even dubious of its legality at all. The bishop tended to run things as he wished. Not that they objected most of the time. They met infrequently and several of the members were getting on in years. Apart from Ralph, who never said anything of course, they treated it more of a social outing. As was usual the bishop had treated his fellow judges to a sumptuous meal in his private apartments before the proceedings began. He found plenty of food and wine sped the process up no end. He could count on at least two or more judges being asleep after the first five minutes or so. Those who were still awake were content to leave the actual business of the court to the bishop, ably assisted by his clerk, Scrivener.

~

Scrivener ran an ink-stained finger down a list written on a scrap of parchment. "My lord, before you is Agnes, formally a nun of the convent of St Michael's at Sandford."

The old crone gave an uncertain cackle at hearing her name. The bishop lent back in his chair mildly alarmed, even from this distance she was pungent. He studied the prisoner with some distaste. She was dressed in a collection of old rags, her hair looked like a bird had been nesting in it and she had fingernails that were two inches long. Her skin was brown with ingrained dirt and filth. "What are the charges Scrivener?"

Scrivener read from one of his notes. "That she did break her vows some twenty years ago and did run away first with a friar and then with a wandering harp-player. That she has begged unlawfully in the city these last five years, she is also further accused of witchcraft on Bradshawgate this Monday last, the feast of St Eustace, in that she did curse Edward Archer's best boar and cause it to suffer an unnatural death."

Agnes let rip with a particularly loud cackle. This threatened to wake some of the slumbering judges much to the bishop's annoyance. "This boar Scrivener, what sort of unnatural death did it suffer?"

"I believe Archer claimed it exploded in the street my lord. I witnessed the aftermath myself; it was most distasteful. Although I must say there is some conjecture that the pig in question had been lying dead in the gutter for a number of weeks, despite Archer's claim."

"I am very well aware of some of Archer's more outlandish claims Scrivener. I think we may safely discount the witchcraft charge. But what to do with this wretch? It's high time we got her off our streets. A woman of her years, I'd say another winter like last will finish her off. We'd better make her somebody else's problem. She's a nun or was, well she can do penance for her no-doubt many sins back at St Michael's convent. Have you anything to say wretch?"

Agnes started with the mad cackling again, this time at an ear shattering level. "Gods teeth! Arrange her return to the convent Scrivener, and for God's sake, get someone to give her a good bath." The bishop frantically gestured for the constables to get her back down to the under-croft.

Once Agnes had been safely dragged down the stairs, Will was hauled to his feet and roughly shoved forward to face the judges. "This is William Blackburne my lord," one of the constables said.

The bishop scrutinised the next prisoner. He was a lanky youth with a startling mop of thick red hair, under which sat a pleasant and cheery looking face. The lads good humour the bishop found surprising as he had just spent the night in the cold under-croft. The prisoner was reasonably well attired in a long cote with a wide belt and stood and looked the bishop straight in the eye with a mildly defiant air. The bishop asked, "What are the charges Scrivener?"

Scrivener unrolled a long parchment, cleared his throat, and began to read. "For telling of fortunes, for drunkenness, for vain swearing, for making water against the churchyard wall at Tedcester, for selling the bell and other ornaments belonging to the church at Ellerton, for clipping coins of the realm, for escaping from lawful custody and finally my lord, for carrying a dead man's skull out of the churchyard at Ulver and laying it under the head of an old woman to charm her to sleep. Blackburne was in the sheriff's custody when he claimed benefit of clergy."

The bishop looked at the prisoner with renewed interest. Those claiming benefit of clergy were seldom actual clergy; it was an irritating loophole in the law. Blackburne was no clergyman in the bishop's diocese for he would have known him or at least of him. It was a claim many of the more literate prisoners made. They only had to read a passage from the bible, psalm fifty-one to be precise, to claim benefit of being clergy and have any case transferred to the bishop's jurisdiction. The sheriff was only too happy to lessen his workload, much to the bishop's annoyance. In recent times it wasn't unknown for some of the more devious rogues of the city to memorise the psalm even when they couldn't read in case they were ever arrested. They knew the bishop's court was generally more lenient. "Well, well, you have been busy Blackburne. Tell me, do you have some particular grudge against the church?"

"I bear no ill will to the church my lord," Will said puzzled.

"Yet your more heinous crimes seem to resolve around the church... except for perhaps the coin clipping?"

Scrivener helpfully chipped in, "I believe my lord that the prisoner carried on his coin clipping in the crypt beneath St Etherwald's church in the parish of Ulver."

"Is that true Blackburne?"

"Err... yes my lord, it was the ideal location, being dry, quiet and near the crossroads for easy access."

"Well, I admire your enterprise, I really do," said the bishop with only a hint of sarcasm. "What age are you Blackburne?"

"Twenty-one years my lord."

"The coin clipping charge is serious. You do understand that? If you go back to the sheriff's custody, a judge could have you condemned to death if found guilty. They take a dim view of debasing the currency of the realm. Strictly speaking it's classed as treason; the sheriff should never have sent you here, benefit of clergy or not."

"Yes my lord. I'm sorry to have caused you such trouble, truly I am. Things started to go wrong after I met a likeable rogue in the Boar's Head. That's an inn, my lord. He said there was an easy way to make some money. Just snip a sliver of metal from each penny. I'd had quite a lot to drink and one thing led to another."

"I can imagine. And the skull from the churchyard?" the bishop queried.

"That would have been old Joan my lord. She's had trouble sleeping since her husband died. I got him from the graveyard and err... reunited them."

"Did it work?" the bishop asked curiously.

With a straight face Will replied, "I believe she's slept as soundly as a new-born babe since my lord."

The bishop chuckled. The boy had wit. "Truly a miracle...tell me, are you educated Blackburne? You claimed benefit of clergy, can you actually read and write?"

"I can read and write my lord. My mother had little money, but she made sure I had some education. My father was a knight. He was one of Edward of Woodstock's army fighting the men of Castile. He didn't return home. Dead before I was born."

"Castile! I remember it well, a bad business. We lost some good men on that campaign," the bishop said this with some sympathy and shook his head sadly.

Will sensing the bishop's interest continued, "When my mother died I was sent to live with my uncle, he's a tavern keeper."

"So you grew up without a father. I always think a boy needs a strong guiding hand if he isn't to go wild. What are we to do with you Blackburne, what are we to do?"

"Hang him," mumbled old Fitz-Herbert briefly waking from his slumber and uttering his normal verdict.

Will looked briefly alarmed.

"That was a rhetorical question Robert," replied the bishop turning towards Fitz-Herbert who was already snoring again. The bishop rubbed his chin. "You're still young. If I'm truthful, you remind me of myself at your age. Which is why I think you do probably deserve a good hanging."

"My lord?" said Will aghast.

"Scrivener take care of it before I change my mind. The sooner the better."

Scrivener raised an eyebrow somewhat cynically and said, "Of course my lord, I believe we can make time for young William this very afternoon."

∽

The cart carrying the condemned men left the city by a small gate behind the bishop's palace. In the back were two of them chained to the woodwork of the cart by their legs. A third man, a guard, sat with them, he was humming tunelessly.

"Lovely afternoon for it," he said eventually.

"I don't feel very talkative. In fact, I'd prefer if you didn't speak to me at all," said Will.

The guard sniffed. "Suit yourself. Only trying to make small talk, this isn't an easy job you know."

"You have my sympathy," said Will sarcastically, "but I've got rather a lot on my mind."

The man chained to the seat opposite let out a low moan and put his head in his hands. "It was a roll of cloth, that's all I took."

"Hardly a first offence in your case Rollo," said the guard. "Didn't you finish off that bloke in the marketplace last year? Stomped on his head I heard, very nasty."

"It was self-defence."

"Pity you stove his head in so we can't ask him if that's true or not."

"Do you think it'll be quick?" Will asked the guard.

"Oh, so now you want to talk."

"Just tell me."

The guard nodded to the front of the cart. "Have you met our hangman? Tom the Stretch they call him."

The man driving the cart turned around and gave Will an evil grin and said, "Don't worry lad, I'll see you right. They rarely struggle long, unless I've got the length of the rope wrong of course."

"How comforting," said Will, "does that happen often?"

The man grinned again. "Depends if I like you or not. You boy, I'm not sure about yet."

"I don't deserve this," moaned Rollo.

The guard laughed. "Course you do, you'd murder your own granny for a penny."

∾

They trundled away from the city the guard whistling cheerfully. The tune soon started to grate on Will's frayed nerves. Eventually they started up a steep hill, the horse struggling against the gradient.

"Where you taking us?" asked Rollo fearfully.

The guard said, "They call this Hangman's Hill. You're two lucky sods being hanged up here. It's the bishop's private gallows. Not long now lads and we'll get you sorted."

On the crest of the hill in a field by the side of the road stood a gibbet. The decaying remains of two corpses gently rocked in the light breeze. Tom the Stretch brought the cart to a halt. He pointed up to the fly-covered carcasses. "Looks like we'll have to make some room for you first."

He climbed down from the cart and walked over to the gibbet. Below it, partially hidden in the long grass, was a long wooden pole. He picked this up and jabbed it at one of the corpses. A cloud of flies took to the air. The two chained men watched in horrified fascination. Tom prodded remorselessly until the parts started to disintegrate and fall to the ground. He did the same to the other corpse. Soon there were just the two skulls and some neck bones hanging. Tom looked at the two prisoners with a wolfish grin and said, "Watch this."

Gripping the pole tightly he took a swing at one of the skulls which went shooting off into the field. He did the same with the other one. Both Tom and the guard hooted with laughter. When they'd dried their eyes, Tom said, "Right well that's tidied that up. Let's get you two lads on your way."

There was the sound of the steady approach of a horse coming up the hill. They all turned to watch as the horse and rider climbed the steep slope. It was Scrivener. He came to a stop next to the cart but didn't dismount.

"Not changed your mind about these two have you master Scrivener?" said Tom. The two condemned men look at Scrivener with unconcealed hope. He looked back and slowly shook his head.

"No I don't think so Tom, don't let me interrupt your work."

"It's no bother master Scrivener, we like an audience. Hardly get anyone up here these days. It's not like the sheriff's hangings down in the city, hundreds that attracts sometimes."

Scrivener nodded sagely. "Hard to get the quality of criminal to hang these days. The sheriff gets most of the good ones I believe. Still, perhaps we should start making more of a day of it. A few pie sellers, an ale stand, that sort of thing. The bishop's coffers could always do with more coin."

He took an apple from under his cloak and started to munch away.

Will shouted, "God's teeth. Can we just get on with it please? I want to get this over with."

The guard laughed. "Not often we have a customer who wants us to hurry up. I think you'd better oblige Tom."

Tom walked back to the cart and took two ropes out of an old leather bag that was tied to its side. They each had a noose on the end. He slung the ropes over the gibbet so the nooses were dangling and tied the other ends off on the post. He patted the horse on the rump. It moved with practiced ease under the gibbet. It left the nooses dangling just above where the men sat in the back of the cart. The guard climbed out and Tom climbed in. "No funny business now," he said, releasing them from their chains. "Stand up."

Will stood shakily, trying to summon up some dignity. Tom quickly tied his hands tightly behind his back with a thin leather strap. Rollo didn't move. Tom poked him in the shoulder. "I said stand up, I won't tell you again."

Rollo began to whimper. Tom hauled him to his feet and in the blink of an eye pulled one of the nooses around his neck and tightened it. He forced the terrified man's hands behind his back and tied them off. He quickly slipped the other noose over Wills head, pulled it tight, and sprang down from the cart. A thwack of his hand on the horse's behind and the startled beast jerked forward and pulled the cart away from under the condemned men's feet.

Will hardly had time to contemplate what had just happened. The noose bit painfully into his neck as he swung briefly on the end of the rope. He suddenly plummeted to the ground and fell face down into the damp grass. His hands were still tied behind his back and he struggled in vain to turn over. Someone's booted foot jabbed itself in his ribs and rolled him over. He looked straight up into the face of Scrivener. He could hear someone choking.

"Finish him off Tom," Scrivener said, his eyes still locked on Will's own.

Tom grabbed hold of Rollo's legs and added his full body weight to that of the struggling man. There was a sickening crack and Rollo went limp.

"Why would you do this," croaked Will.

Scrivener smiled coldly. "To teach you a lesson. Our lord bishop said you deserved a hanging and now you've had one. If you're wise, I'd make this your last."

Will closed his eyes and lay still for a minute, too stunned to move. Eventually he opened his eyes again. Scrivener hadn't moved an inch. "What now?"

Scrivener smiled again. "Take this as a warning, a second chance. It seems the bishop has a use for your dubious talents. I'd advise you stay on the right side of the law from now on."

7

APPOINTMENT OF THE OFFICIAL

Will found himself lodged in a warm and dry chamber within the bishop's palace. It was basic but far more comfortable than the under-croft. Scrivener had told him to stay within the cathedral precinct walls but other than that he was free to roam as he pleased. He took his meals in the great hall with the rest of the household and made good use of his time observing the business of the bishop and cathedral. He wasn't sure what he'd expected, but he found the place fascinating. The bishop was a powerful man, not just a cleric but a great nobleman with connections to the highest in the land. Throughout the day there was a constant flow of messengers, envoys, merchants and all other manner of people passing through the main gates. What seemed like a small army of clerks and clerics were employed administrating the bishop's domain and a steady undercurrent of purposefulness ran through the whole complex of buildings. For the first time in his life Will felt he could fit somewhere if given the chance.

On the afternoon of his third day within the precinct walls Scrivener tracked him down in the great cathedral itself. Will had spent a couple of hours each day within the vast structure, sometimes exploring, sometimes just standing and watching. It was by far the biggest building he had ever been in. Its proportions were simply staggering. The nave where he stood made use of massive rounded pillars. These were so huge and imposing that they almost overwhelmed the rest of the interior space. The magnificent vaulted roof seemed like an after-thought. The vaulting led your eye towards the choir where a huge east window punctuated the wall. The stained glass commemorated an English feat of arms over the French and the rich colours glowed and shimmered with the shifting afternoon sunshine. It was mesmerising.

Scrivener came and stood by him, looking up at the far ceiling and then towards the beautiful east window. After a few moments of quiet reflection, he said softly, "We have a meeting with the bishop."

"We do?" asked Will dragging his eyes reluctantly away from the stained glass.

Scrivener said, "We do. When he's made his mind up about something it's not good to keep him waiting."

"Can I ask you a question... and I mean no insult by it?"

"You can speak freely, I'm a hard man to insult, I would guess it concerns the bishop?"

Will nodded. "Tell me, what sort of man is he? If I'm to be a bishop's man I think I should hear what others think."

"I'm not exactly unbiased. I've known him many years, since we were boys in fact. My father was a steward in his father's household. We practically grew up together."

"Then you'd know him better than most?"

The older man leaned against one of the huge pillars of the nave and folded his arms. "What can I tell you? The bishop is an unusual man for someone of his high birth. You could be the lowest villain or the king himself, he's not afraid to talk to you as his equal or too proud to seek good advice from those around him either. He can be a hard man on occasion, devious sometimes when it's needed, generous with those he thinks deserve it. He's not perfect, he has many faults, as we all do, but he's always fair and he seeks out those qualities in others. If you're loyal to him, you'll have no better master in this kingdom William. One thing I'd never do is to make him an enemy. There, I've probably said far too much. We'd better go, we're wanted in the bishop's garden."

~

They left the cathedral and headed back towards the bishop's palace, entering via the monumental inner doorway of the south porch. Will once again marvelled at the size and splendour of the palace. The massive portal led directly into a wide cross-passage with arched doorways on both sides. On the right were the entrances to a buttery and pantry and access to the eastern service range, which contained a great kitchen with a brew and bake house. To the left, a doorway led via a wooden screen into the great hall. They took the archway next to this. Will found himself outside again and followed Scrivener down the side of the building. They entered the gardens via a gate in a thicket hedge. Against the back wall of the palace on a simple wooden bench sat the bishop. As they approached, he got to his feet and smiled.

"Walk with me Will. I like to take a little air to clear my head in the afternoon. Besides, the garden is magnificent at this time of year. My predecessors spent a great deal of money out here so we might as well enjoy it. It's a small indulgence which I grant to myself daily."

Death Of The Official

The bishop took the lead with Will and Scrivener just behind. The garden was a truly spectacular sight on this summer afternoon. Trellis walkways and arbors provided shade and privacy. Here and there were turf seats built against the cathedral precept walls with flowers planted in the surrounding grass. There was a special physic garden with regimented beds of medicinal herbs and a large orchard providing apples for the kitchen and for making cider, of which the bishop was famously fond. There was also a large fish pond and against a far wall stood an ornate stone dovecote that provided pigeons for the bishop's table.

They walked in silence, Will drinking in the splendour of his surroundings. After a time, the bishop guided them to a secluded turf seat. They sat with their backs against the stone wall which radiated a comfortable warmth, heated by the afternoon sun. Will sat between the bishop on one side and Scrivener on the other. The bishop leaned far back, his hands behind his head, eyes half closed against the sun.

He turned his head to Will and said, "You know Will I really should have let you hang but I hate to waste talent and as a bishop I sometimes have problems that require unusual solutions. Scrivener knows what I mean better than most."

Scrivener nodded sagely and said, "Indeed I do my lord."

Will frankly had no idea what they were talking about.

The bishop continued, "I think you could be useful and I want you to join my household. We'll even pay you, let's say sixpence a day to start with. What do you say?"

Will was young, reckless even, but he was no fool. He realised the patronage of a powerful figure like the bishop could completely change his fortunes. On the other hand he wasn't sure he enjoyed being controlled by lords who treated other men's lives like pawns in a game of chess. He'd seen plenty of those in his short life. He'd rather be a player himself, but that was for the future. For now he was content to do the bishop's bidding and in truth he had little choice.

"My lord, you do me a great honour."

Before he could say anything more the bishop thumped him on the back, "Excellent, excellent, you won't regret it Will."

Scriviner said, "We need you to go to the north for us Will; Yorkshire to be precise."

"The north?" Will spluttered. What little he knew of the north was that it rained a lot, the food was terrible and the natives unintelligible.

"Ah, you know the north?" asked the bishop only half seriously.

"No my lord. I thought perhaps I was to join your household here."

Both the bishop and Scrivener chuckled at his naivety. The bishop continued, "All in good time Will. What we need right now is someone to look into a matter in the north. We own a manor in a place called Sodham in Ribsdale. It was gifted to us a few weeks ago by a somewhat disreputable individual. We own many such manors across the kingdom Will, often gifted to us. They're partly what allows all this to function," he gestured with a sweep of his hand at the garden, the palace and the cathedral.

Scrivener took up where the bishop left off. "The monies they generate contribute to everything we do here. We sent a man to take stock and oversee the place and it seems he's had an unfortunate accident."

"What kind of accident?" Will said nervously.

"Apparently the kind involving a sharp implement to the throat. We received a message two days ago that he was found in his chambers with his throat cut."

"I can image the north to be a depressing place, he took his own life perhaps?" Will said hopefully.

"Perhaps he did," the bishop said unconvincingly, "or perhaps someone helped him. Go take a look for me Will. We need someone to take charge up there for a time and report back to us. For now you'll be my official on the ground, the official of Sodham in fact. Has a nice ring to it doesn't it, the Official. Set things to rights for me in Sodham William and who knows where fate may take you in my service."

Before Will could respond Scrivener stood up and retrieved something from his purse. "This William, is your official seal," he said, handing him a small metallic object attached to a thin leather strip. "It confirms you are an official of the bishop. You should keep it safe and about your person at all times. Let no one else make use of it or take it from you. It's yours alone. In some circumstances that seal could save your life and in others cause you to lose it!"

Will studied the seal. A somewhat crude figure he took to be an image of the bishop looked back at him. It wasn't the most flattering likeness to be honest. Around the edge of the seal was the latin inscription 'SIGILLUM : WILLELMI: OFFICIALITATIS: DRAYCASTRA: EPISCOPI'. Which he read as Seal of William, Official of the Bishop of Draychester.

"As luck would have it your predecessor was also called William. William of Wallcot. We didn't even need a new seal," said the bishop.

"It wouldn't be that you appointed me the official just because I'm called William my lord?" He asked suspiciously.

The bishop laughed and draped one arm around the younger man's shoulders. Will couldn't decide if it was a friendly gesture or an intimidating one, maybe both. "My, my, for one so young Will you have a very cynical mind."

Will smiled nervously. "I think that's why I'm still alive my lord. I intend to remain so if I can."

The bishop thumped him playfully on the arm. "You see that's what I like about you Will. Mark my words Scrivener this boy will go far with a bit of guidance."

In response Scrivener gave a thin smile. William hung the object around his neck with the thin leather strip and pushed the actual seal under his shirt so it was hidden from sight. The bishop said, "Don't worry Will. You won't be going alone. I think I'll send some traveling companions with you."

Scrivener raised an eyebrow. "Who did you have in mind?"

The bishop said, "Your nephew Osbert for one and I thought Bernard could assist."

Scrivener shook his head. "Bernard I can understand, but Osbert?"

"They could do with a good clerk. I want detailed reports. Who better than Osbert?"

Scrivener explained, "Osbert is my nephew, my sister's boy. He's trained as a clerk and he's a good one too, meticulous to a fault. He can also drag the very angels down with his gloom ridden talk. If you're in good spirits, you won't be for long! It's my sister's fault of course, spare the rod, spoil the child and look what happens…"

"You're far too hard Scrivener. It'll do the boy good to get away from here and see something of the world. I'd be surprised if your sister has ever let him more than five miles from Draychester's walls. Anyway, it's about time he earned his keep."

"As you wish my lord."

Death Of The Official

"I do Scrivener, I do. Now I think I will take a nap while this sun lasts."

With that the bishop closed his eyes, leaned back on the bench, and said no more. Will assumed their meeting was over. He got up, as did Scrivener, and they slowly began to walk back through the garden to the entrance they had entered by. At the gate, Scrivener turned to him and said, "Find me in the great hall tonight at the evening meal. I'll introduce you to Osbert, God help you, and also to Bernard." Then he was gone, striding off into the palace.

Will stood at the gate, not sure of where to go next, partly overwhelmed by the afternoon's events. He reached a hand into his shirt and touched the cool metal of the seal hung around his neck. It was real; he hadn't imagined it. He'd just joined the household of a great lord, he was the official of Sodham, whatever that might mean, and one of the bishop of Draychester's men.

∽

That evening, Will found Scrivener in the Great Hall. It was the central hub of the bishop's palace. It was rarely quiet apart from in the very dead of night. Even then it wasn't unknown to find a weary traveller snoring on a bench, there being no more room in the travellers lodge in the cathedral precinct. The hall was tall but elegantly proportioned with a fine timber-framed roof, a central hearth, and high windows. Down the length of the room were three long tables with benches either side. At the far end of the hall a table ran cross-ways across the room where the senior members of the household sat at meal times. The walls were freshly whitewashed and the floor was covered with fresh, sweet smelling rushes.

Standing next to Scrivener was a small thin lad of perhaps eighteen years with dark brown hair, a gaunt-looking face with large staring eyes and a mournful expression. Will thought he looked like a sad fish.

Scrivener made the introductions. "Osbert, this is the new official of Sodham, William Blackburne." He jabbed a thumb at Osbert and said to Will, "My nephew Osbert, your new clerk, He's none too happy with the bishop's plans for him. Mind you, you're generally none too happy about anything, eh Osbert?"

"I feel my talents are much better employed in the city than tramping the roads of the north amongst the ungodly," said an indignant Osbert.

"Well, that's one way of looking at it," replied Scrivener. "Perhaps you want to tell the bishop that yourself?"

Osbert gave him a sour look.

"I thought not," said a smirking Scrivener. "Best make the most of it my lad. The bishop is unlikely to change his plans to please you."

Osbert turned his attention to Will. He scowled at him and said, "So you're the criminal the bishop saved from the hangman. I've heard all about you. Tell me Blackburne, have you been to the north?"

Before Will could answer Osbert rambled on, "The north is a disease-ridden wasteland populated by robbers and outcasts. We'll be lucky if we don't get our throats cuts or die of some hideous disease. We're all doomed."

William raised an eyebrow sceptically, "So you've been to the north then?"

Osbert shrugged and said, "No, but it's a well-known fact. I hear things around the precinct. There're messengers going to and from the north all the time. Sodham is clearly a nest of vipers. The bishop's only sending us because we're

Death Of The Official 65

young and expendable. You know the last man sent there is dead. Murdered by all accounts."

"Perhaps it wasn't murder, there may be another explanation?"

"I've seen the signs. A week last Thursday a cock crowed before dawn, the day after there was a blood red sunrise and on the same day a pigeon fell dead from the roof of the cathedral at noon, then…"

"God's teeth Osbert!" said Scrivener in exasperation, "Can you not be a little more cheerful, just for once?"

Osbert shook his head, "Not when we are all bound to hell, especially the more sinful amongst us." He gave a meaningful look at Will.

Scrivener turned to Will and shook his head in disgust. "Well, now you've met Osbert. Let's find Bernard before I do something involving my boot and Osbert's backside…" He strode off across the hall, Will trailing after him leaving an outraged Osbert behind.

∽

Bernard's huge frame was sat at one of the long benches, a wooden tankard of cider in front of him, surrounded by a host of laughing drinking companions. He looked up from his drink as they approached and smiled with genuine warmth. "Ah Scrivener, my old comrade, come and join us. And this must be Master Blackburne, welcome my young friend. I'm Bernard, the bishop's sometimes bodyguard and more usually his general dogsbody for my sins."

He gestured for them to sit down opposite him and called to the potboy to fetch more tankards. From a large jug he poured them generous measures of the bishop's finest golden cider. "That'll put hairs on your chest my young friend. On the inside that is," he said chuckling.

Scrivener grinned affectionately at Bernard. "Don't let this old rogue fool you. He's done many a service for the bishop; he's much more than a mere bodyguard. Travelled the length and breadth of the kingdom carrying messages and escorting the bishop. A seasoned traveller is our Bernard." Bernard nodded in agreement. "That I am, but it'll be good to go journeying again. I've been too long away from the road. Makes a man soft," he said prodding his considerable girth.

Will drank from his tankard, coughing with the first sip. The stuff was potent to be sure, each gulp slipping down the throat like liquid fire. His curiosity piqued he asked, "Where are you from Bernard?"

Gesturing with his tankard clutched in a huge hand Bernard answered, "Me? I was born in London. Entered the bishop's household there when I was just a young lad with no brains between my ears. The bishop spends a lot of time on church business in London. And you young William, what's your story?"

Will shrugged. "It's a common enough one these days. My father was a knight, dead in the wars even before I was born. I was the youngest son, my mother did her best, when she died I was to live with my uncle."

"How did you end up in the bishop's court?"

"My uncle and I had a difference of opinion and I left. That was about two years ago now."

"What you argue about?"

"I got big enough to stop him beating me. He was a drunken, greedy, grasping bastard. Had me working every hour God sent in his tavern, treated me worse than the servants. Had to sleep with the dogs in the outhouse. I said I'd kill him if he raised a hand to me again."

Bernard gave a nod and raised his tankard to Will. "I know the type myself. Once nearly killed my old man when he raised a hand to my mother, God bless her soul. What you do then?"

"Had nowhere else to go. Took a horse and some money, nothing I wasn't owed, and lived on my wits. I didn't venture far; when the money was gone I fell in with some dubious characters. Got into some scrapes, before I knew it I was sitting in the bishop's under-croft chained up. The rest you probably know."

Bernard appraised him from across the table. After a moment or two he looked at Scrivener giving an almost imperceptible nod, seemingly satisfied with what he saw. He took a long swig from his tankard and said, "So Master William, are you ready for a bit of an adventure?"

"I suppose I am," said Will uncertainly. "Are we to travel all the way by road?"

"Some distance by road, some by river. If the weather holds it'll take us maybe three weeks to reach the city of York. Then a day or two more to Sodham."

"You've been there before?" asked Will.

Bernard nodded. "To York I've been twice in the bishop's service. It's a city much like this, the biggest in the north. The minster is wondrous. Of the rest of that county, I've not ventured and of Sodham I know nothing."

Will found he was getting woozy. Scrivener and Bernard grinned knowingly. Scrivener tapped the side of his tankard with an ink stained finger. "Better not drink too much, you leave in two days."

"Two days!", spluttered Will, "but I know nothing about what I'm supposed to do..."

"Oh we generally make it up as we go along. Isn't that right Bernard?"

Bernard drank the dregs from his tankard, sniffed and wiped his nose with the back of his hand, belched loudly and said, "Too right my old friend, it's the best way."

8

RALPH OF SHREWSBURY HAS A VISITOR

Ralph of Shrewsbury had been an inhabitant of the cathedral precinct longer than most could remember. He knew every nook and cranny within its walls. He was such a familiar sight that for the most part he could pass without notice or raising any undue suspicion. He blended seamlessly into the background of the life of the busy cathedral and bishop's palace. None knew him well and to those he did have contact with he was a man of few words. His death stare discouraged all but the most persistent. It was a persona he had cultivated carefully over many decades and it had served him well. He was instinctively nosey, and he had found most people were indiscreet at some stage. He overheard a lot of things as he drifted around the precinct. Over the years he had come to know a great many things that he shouldn't have known about a great many people. Old Bishop Thorndyke had liked to keep tabs on people, and Ralph had proved invaluable. The arrangement had been mutually beneficial and a certain amount of coin had changed hands regularly. Those had been good days, but nothing lasted forever. Thorndyke had been easily manipulated to Ralph's will. The new bishop was a different proposition altogether. He had his own network of eyes and ears. These last couple of years Ralph had gone nearly exclusively freelance. Which is why he stood lurking in the shadows of one of the great pillars in the dimly lit cathedral. It was an hour before the Matins service at midnight.

A figure approached the pillar in the dim light, its shadow merging with it and slithering around to stand by the side of Ralph.

"Bouchard," whispered Ralph. It was a statement not a question. How the man had got within the precinct walls at this time of night he neither knew nor cared.

Gilbert Bouchard grinned in the darkness. "I see you're still alive Ralph. How many bishops have you outlived old man?"

"This will be my fourth, of course this one may last longer than I."

Bouchard chuckled softly and said, "I need some information." There was the faint clink of coins as he pressed a small leather bag towards Ralph's leathery hand. Their fingers touched briefly as the bag exchanged hands and he recoiled at the coldness of Ralph's skin.

"Ask and you shall receive," said Ralph.

"The bishop is sending someone north to Yorkshire?"

There was a slight pause in the darkness then Ralph responded, "They leave in two days. Stand outside the east gate of the precinct that morning and you'll see them depart."

"Them? How many in the party?"

"Three men. Bernard, built like an ox, a favourite of the bishop. A red-haired youth named William Blackburne recently saved from the hangman. Osbert, a clerk, he's a thin coward of a boy. And a woman."

"A woman? Describe her..."

A soft chuckle came out of the darkness, "No need of a description for that one, you won't mistake her for another..."

There was a slight movement in the shadow of the pillar and Gilbert realised Ralph had slipped away. "Wait!" he hissed, but Ralph was gone.

9

WILLIAM THE OFFICIAL DEPARTS

"Tell me again Bernard, how far is Yorkshire?"

"It's two hundred miles Will, same as last time you asked me."

"Sorry, just seems a very long way."

Osbert trailing after them said, "And with danger and death at every turn."

Bernard ignored him with a weary ease and said to Will, "It's a good distance to be sure and we're going to need some decent mounts. I think we need to look at the bishop's stables and stores. We're looking for three good riding horses and two pack animals. First rule of the road; go well prepared."

"Not that'll make any difference, we're doomed anyway," added Osbert mournfully.

Will made a point of standing on the clerk's foot as they set off towards the storerooms next to the stables. The bishop, his household, and his various officials were constantly traveling the kingdom. The storerooms were well stocked with everything a traveller would require on the road. Not all of it was in the best of condition. The new

Death Of The Official

was mixed in with the well-used and the downright decrepit.

There was a lot to organise, but Bernard sorted through the mounds of kit with quiet efficiency and the eye of a seasoned traveller. For each of them he found a protective leather over-mantle for bad weather riding. Some were a better fit than others, but he tried to match them to each individual as best he could. Then there was some basics, a knife, a spoon, and a bowl for each of them. Also, a lantern and some candles, a comb, and a horse brush. He made sure they had some shoemakers thread a needle and a bodkin. This he explained was to allow a saddle to be sewn back together if it burst its stuffing, which he assured them would happen at some stage. Finally each man was to have a leather flask which to start the journey was to be filled with the bishop's best cider. Onto the pack horses would go their bedding, which comprised a pillow each, some linen sheets and some thick woollen blankets.

"Now we need some weapons, purely for defence you understand," said Bernard grinning.

Osbert shook his head sadly and murmured, "Those who live by the sword die by the sword. Blessed are the peacemakers."

They both turned to look at the lad. Bernard said nothing but Will thought he could see a slight twitch in the older man's eye that didn't bode well. The big man sighed deeply then gestured for them to follow him.

He led them to a small locked room that served as the palace's private armoury and opened it up with a large iron key which he produced from under his tunic. They saw a variety of weapons stacked inside. Bernard methodically started to root through the stacks and hand out weapons. For each of them he handed over a wooden cudgel, a wooden staff tipped with iron, a short dagger, and a cheap riding sword. In additional for himself, he selected a crossbow and a wicked-looking mace comprising an ash shaft with a steel-tipped head.

Osbert looked on horrified as the mound of weapons at his feet grew. "Dear God," he spluttered.

"Are we expecting trouble?" asked Will nervously. He could hardly carry what he'd been given.

"I always expect trouble Will. That's why I go prepared." He threw a small silver object onto Osbert's pile of gear. The clerk stooped low and picked it up curiously. It was a small medal of St Christopher, the patron saint of travellers. Bernard grinned evilly at him. "I'd keep that one close at hand Osbert. We may need him to intercede on your behalf before the journeys' done."

～

The following day dawned grey and overcast but there was a warm breeze and the promise of brighter skies to the north. They gathered in the courtyard ready for departure and Will heard a familiar sound. Scrivener emerged from around the back of the stable block leading a packhorse on which sat Agnes, former nun and insane cackler. As she caught sight of Will her laughter raised in pitch.

"God's teeth!" shouted Will over the din, "What's she doing on that horse?"

Scrivener smirked and said, "The bishop asked that you do him the favour of delivering Agnes to the convent of St Michael's at Sandford. It's not really out of your way, you'll be passing through the place as you head north."

There was much noisy protest from the assembled group but Scrivener grimly insisted and a short time later the party set out. Bernard took the lead. Will followed closely behind, then Osbert with a face like thunder and voicing dire predictions, and finally the madly laughing Agnes. As they passed through the east gate of the cathedral precinct the two figures of the Bouchard twins Gilbert and Godbert were slouched against a nearby wall. Gilbert watched them pass and grunted his satisfaction to his brother.

"It's them, just as described. The woman I know, a beggar, used to hang about near the marketplace gate. She's mad, surprised nobody has cut her throat laughing like that." They made no move to follow. The time and place to strike needed to be well away from the city. On that at least he agreed with Sir Roger.

10

ON THE ROAD TO GLOUCESTER

They left the city and headed north, the road was well maintained although unsurfaced. Bernard and Will soon rode side by side. Behind them rode a grumbling Osbert and the ever cackling Agnes. This close to the city the bishop and guilds ensured the upkeep of the highway to a good standard. Bernard had ridden the roads of the bishop's diocese for the last two years. This close to home he knew every twist and turn of the road and which village and hamlet each side track led to. Many of the manors they passed were owned by the bishop and he knew them well. The road was busy with carts heading in both directions and pack horses with goods traveling longer distances which they easily overtook. William noted that nothing moved faster than horse and rider. The carts and pack horses they encountered moved at little more than walking pace. Their little mounted party easily forced those on foot, the pedlars, friars and monks, pilgrims and beggars to give way.

They'd not travelled far before Agnes became a problem. Osbert cracked first. He'd been grumbling since the first moments they'd departed the courtyard at the bishop's palace.

"For God's sake woman, will you be quiet!", he snapped at her. This sent Agnes into fits of even higher pitched cackling.

"Easy Osbert," said Will, "It's not her fault that she's lost her mind."

"I'd say it God's punishment for her sins and now it's my punishment to listen to her," he said bitterly.

"Give me your cider," said Will.

"What?" said Osbert confused.

"Give me your flask of cider. Be quick, hand it over."

Osbert reluctantly reached back into his pack and handed the leather flask of the bishop's finest to Will. He held it out to Agnes and it was eagerly snatched from his hands. After five minutes she was slumped asleep in her saddle. They tied her on securely and continued in relative peace except for Osbert's grumbling.

∼

"Do you like this life Bernard?" Will asked curiously. "It must be lonely sometimes, dangerous too?"

"Truth is I've known little else Will. The bishop's not a bad master and he's better than most nobles I've met. Take my word for it, most of them I wouldn't put out if they were on fire. They're constantly scheming and plotting, makes a normal man's head ache."

Will chuckled and said, "I'll bear that in mind."

As they ambled along side by side Bernard spoke to William about his previous journeys. "The roads are good here, the bishop sees to that, but further away and you'll see the change, be lucky if you're not up to your backside in mud. No one's built a proper road since the ancients."

From behind they heard Osbert sniff and mumble, "I think you probably mean the Romans."

Bernard shrugged and said, "Them too lad, them too."

More loudly this time Osbert said, "This is the king's highway, isn't it the law to maintain it?"

Bernard turned in his saddle and said, "And do you think the king checks after every stretch himself? The local lords and churchmen are supposed to arrange the upkeep. Sometimes they do, often times they don't. A few years back I was caught in a storm on the road north of Oxford. I saw a man and horse up to their necks in a water filled pothole."

Will looked up at the sky dubiously. "Then let's pray the weather holds."

Bernard grunted his agreement. "Most of the time the locals have the sense to keep the bridges in some sort of order. There's a toll sometimes, pays for the upkeep or goes in the local lord's coffers, one or the other. If there's no bridge there's generally a ford or ferry. If the weather holds it's relatively easy passage, if the weather turns we could be delayed for days."

∼

Around noon they took a break by the side of the road for food. The meal consisted of bread and a little cheese. Bernard suggested they save the rest of the cider. He thought they'd need it later in the afternoon to keep Agnes quiet. They sat on the grassy roadside in the warm afternoon sun eating their food. Bernard and Will had gently lifted Agnes down from her horse and she lay snoring beside them on the grass.

"I knew her before she became like this you know," Bernard said with his mouth full and gesturing to the sleeping Agnes.

Osbert looked at the snoring figure with barely concealed contempt. "I imagine she was always a sinner. I hope you didn't know her in the biblical sense?"

"Watch your tongue boy," snapped Bernard. "I won't tell you again. Who knows what sort of life the poor woman's had. Don't go judging her before you've seen something of life yourself."

In an effort to keep the peace Will said, "So how do you know her?"

Bernard continued chewing for a moment then said, "She lived for a time with a blacksmith, Joe or John, don't recall exactly, but he shod the bishop's horses a few times. He had a place down by Bradshawgate in the city. Dead now I think, that sweating sickness that swept the city a couple of years back. She begged by the cathedral gate in the marketplace after. Never knew she'd been a nun, but that's life for you."

Will stared at the gently storing figure. "So she wasn't touched like she is now then?"

"No, it's her age lad, catches up with us all, eventually."

∼

Bernard called a halt in the late afternoon. They'd covered only twelve or so miles when they stopped at an inn by a busy crossroads. All of them were tired from the first day's riding. Osbert, unused to riding very far, loudly complained about his sore backside. He hobbled inside in a bad temper.

After a mediocre meal Bernard stood by the door of the inn with Will. Each held a cup of watery ale and watched the great golden orb of the sun sink below the far horizon. Out front it was peaceful but around the back of the inn a noisy cockfight was in progress observed by a scowling Osbert and a motley crowd of locals and travellers alike.

A scrawny looking man with a weasel like face sidled up to Osbert and said, "Nice looking bird that."

"Which one?" said Osbert. Both the cocks looked the same to him. He couldn't judge which if any was winning. They both appeared to be tearing bloody chunks from each other with their sharp spurs.

"The one on the left of course," said the scrawny man jabbing his finger at the mass of whirling feathers. "Jethro has been training that bird these past three months. Been hand fed the best corn it has. That's the only way to train a winner. Take the time with the bird and it'll reward you."

"You've got money on the bird yourself?"

"A penny."

Osbert snorted with derision. "A penny. What sort of wager is that!"

~

By the time Will went to find him Osbert had lost the entire contents of his purse. One cock lay bloody and lifeless on the ground, its throat ripped out. The crowd slowly slipped away, dispersing into the interior of the inn or the twilight of the surrounding countryside.

Will shook his head in disgust. "We've been on the road not even a day and you've lost your money already?"

Osbert shrugged. "It was bad luck, that's all. The cock was a born winner, that's what the man said. Hand reared on corn..."

"What man was that, the one who saw the size of your purse?"

Osbert responded angrily. "It was my own money to lose. Better I lose it as we're bound to be robbed anyway."

"Are you really this stupid naturally or have you been practicing?" asked Will exasperated. "Believe me, you're going to have to start using your wits or you'll get your wish and something bad really will happen."

"I suppose you've never lost a wager then?" said Osbert sarcastically.

Will just smiled. "Let's get your money back."

He led them back inside the inn. The place smelled of stale drink and mouldy food. Mud and horse dung trodden in from the road lay mingled with the old rushes that covered the floor. The only light came from the fire and some flickering candles made of tallow which gave off a harsh reek.

Will sat down on a bench and grabbed three empty wooden cups. He opened his leather purse and brought out an old shrivelled pea. Turning the cups over on the long table top he covered the pea with one of them. He then started to shuffle them around, faster and faster. He stopped and asked Osbert to tap the top of the cup he thought covered the pea. Osbert confidently tapped one of the cups. Will picked it up to reveal nothing at all underneath. He picked up another cup to reveal the pea. Replacing the cup, he started to shuffle the cups around again. Three attempts later and Osbert had still failed to identify the cup covering the pea, and they had also drawn a small group to their end of the table. Two more shuffles and money was being wagered.

Bernard watched knowingly from a nearby stool. He'd seen this many times on his travels. Sleight of hand turned the game known as thimblerig into a simple con trick for the skilled, which Will certainly was. Whoever had taught him had been good, very good. Will offered to double the stake for anyone who could pick out the cup covering the pea. He'd enough sense to let the players win some of the time. This had the effect of drawing in others or increasing the stakes of those already wagering. He knew not to push his luck too far. It was always a fine line between relieving the curious of some of the contents of their purses and avoiding getting lynched by an angry mob. He kept the cups shuffling for no more than a half hour, by which time he reckoned he'd made back what Osbert had lost. He bought a few ales for those at the table and they slowly drifted off satisfied with the night's entertainment. He slid the coins he'd won across the table to a slightly bemused Osbert. "Keep hold of your money in future Osbert. We may need it before the journey is done."

Bernard joined them at the table and said, "You're a lad of many talents Will. That was nicely done, I've seldom seen it bettered."

Will grinned. "Thanks, another gift of my misspent youth, I've learnt from some of the best."

～

They slept in one of the upper rooms. Agnes was propped up against the wall in the room downstairs, fed and well provided with ale and virtually comatose. Upstairs there were a dozen or more beds, each having to accommodate two or more travellers. They consisted of a cheap wooden frame strung with rope with a straw mattress on top. Will found the bed only slightly more comfortable than the floor. Osbert moaned that he wished he was back in his quarters at the bishop's palace. Bernard grunted that he better get used to it and promptly fell asleep. Will struggled to find any peace amongst his snoring companions. Throughout the night there was constant movement as folk stumbled around in the dark trying to get down the stairs to relieve themselves noisily in the backyard.

∽

On the third day after leaving Draychester they turned off the king's highway. They followed a narrow track down towards a river on whose banks sat Sandford. The village clustered around the small convent of St Michael. The convent was surrounded by high white washed walls which made it a stark, self-contained entity, amid the low buildings of the village. Agnes remained uncharacteristically quiet as they approached the main gate. Whether she remembered the place it was difficult to tell. St Michael's appeared to be a small but wealthy institution and Sandford, unlike many other villages they'd passed through, appeared prosperous.

"Been some coin spent on this place over the years," said Bernard, gazing at the spotless white walls.

Will nodded, he knew those who joined the convent or were sent there were often of high birth. It was a convenient place to get rid of a daughter who couldn't be married off easily and they might go with a smaller dowry than a husband of their own rank would demand. Perhaps Agnes might once have joined St Michael's as some knight's castoff younger daughter.

Bernard rode right up to the gate without dismounting and hammered on the wood impatiently, his huge fists shaking the great oak door in its frame.

"Osbert, what do you know of this place, who's the prioress here?" Bernard asked.

"The nuns are of the order of St Augustine, how closely they follow the rules I don't know. The prioress is Dame Sibil Papelwyk and with the racket you're making, I'm sure she knows we're here," Osbert answered.

Bernard grunted. "Well, we can't be hanging about. We have business elsewhere. I know these bloody nuns, they'll keep us waiting here all day if the mood takes them."

He increased the violence of his knocking; it was now loud enough to wake the dead.

Osbert shrugged indifferently and said, "I understand the prioress is the sister of the Bishop of Ely. He despises our own bishop and the feeling's mutual. They're fierce rivals. I shouldn't think we'll get a warm welcome or a warm bed tonight either. Bishop Gifford's sent us here to make a point as well as to return Agnes."

"Couldn't you have told us all this earlier?" asked Will annoyed.

"I don't remember you asking," replied a defensive Osbert.

Eventually a small wooden slat sat high in the gate was pulled back and two dark eyes looked out at them. A weary sounding female voice said, "What business have you knocking on our gate like the very devil himself?"

Bernard thrust his face up to the slot. "The business I have is with your prioress, we're officials of the bishop of Draychester. So be quick about it and open the gate."

Both William and Osbert visibly winced, diplomacy wasn't Bernard's strong point. The slot in the gate was drawn shut with a slam. Bernard banged on the gate again. The slot was drawn back and a long wooden staff shot out and prodded Bernard hard in the centre of his chest. It took him completely unawares and sent him sprawling from the horse onto the muddy ground in front of the gates. He struggled to his feet covered in mud and roared with anger, his face turning bright red. Will and Osbert fought hard to stifle their laughter. He pounded on the gate and kicked it viciously with his boots cursing. After a minute or two with no response he turned exasperated to the others.

Will held his hand up. "Enough Bernard, let me try."

He walked over to the gate and gave a gentle rap with his knuckles. He called up to the slot which had opened again. "I apologise for my companion, he's a little rough around the edges. My name is William Blackburne. We are with the bishop of Draychester's household. We have business with the prioress. If you'd inform her we're here I'd be grateful."

Two dark eyes stared down at him. After a moment a voice said, "What proof do you have you are the bishop's men?"

Will took out the official seal that hung around his neck and held it up to the watching pair of eyes. They scrutinised it intently. It apparently passed inspection as the voice said, "Wait." After a time there was the sound of the gate being unbarred and it slowly swung inward. A small figure dressed in a black nun's habit tied around the waist with a cloth belt stood blocking their way. She wore a wimple and veil. Around her neck hung a heavy gold cross. Will recognised the dark eyes that glared back at him.

"Follow me, talk to no one. In this place we follow the three rules, poverty, chastity and obedience. Keep your eyes and your hands to yourself."

Will nodded, his eyes fixated on the gold cross around the nuns neck. Bernard gave the nun a sour look but he had the sense to hold his tongue. Will could see that he was still seething at being knocked off his horse.

The three men led their horses and a silent Agnes through the gate into the convent enclosure. They looked about with interest. The principal buildings were grouped around an inner court. These included a small church, a refectory with the kitchen and buttery near it, and what looked to be a dormitory. There was also a small hospital building and a guest house. There were storerooms and workshops a laundry and a stable where they left their horses. Beyond the buildings but still within the walls lay a large vegetable garden. Everything was built in stone and looked in good order, this was no poor nunnery. The few nuns they saw didn't fit in with Wills idea of chastity. There were some shapely figures visible under their black habits and their eyes were most defiantly not downcast as they passed the strangers in their midst. Will saw Osbert visibly blush in embarrassment at a suggestive smile. They were led into a building which by its rich furnishings was evidently the prioress's personal lodgings. The nun stopped before a heavy wooden door, knocked softly and entered. They were left to wait in a long hallway lined with tapestries. Eventually the door opened again and the nun beckoned them into the prioress's inner sanctum.

∼

They were expecting some venerable old nun and were all shocked at Sibil Papelwyk's appearance. She was beautiful, in her late twenties, gold rings on her fingers, with a silken veil worn intentionally too high on her forehead to cover raven black hair. Round her neck on a long silken cord was a gold ring set with a large diamond. It hung below a considerable chest. She oozed an icy sexuality entirely inappropriate for a nun.

"Leave us," she said dismissing their escort who swiftly disappeared.

Osbert stood with mouth hanging open, Bernard mesmerised and Will simply intimidated. Agnes lurked in the background behind the other three. The prioress offered no pleasantries and got straight to the point.

"My, my, what interesting visitors the bishop has sent me! An old crone, a red-headed youth, a barn door of a man and a gormless fool. Close your mouth boy I can see your tonsils... so what do Jocelyn Gifford's men want of me?"

There was a tongue-tied silence before Will found the nerve to speak. "Reverend Mother, we are on the bishop's business, a journey to the north. I'm William Blackburne, this is Bernard and Osbert. As our route takes us past St Michael's, we've been asked to return a nun to your care, she was once of your convent. She's been living in Draychester many years."

The prioress fiddled seductively with the gold ring hanging at her breast and said, "Your bishop has a nasty habit of shifting his problems on to others. I know him of old, he and my brother have a long-running feud." She gave a bitter little laugh. "Men and their games. If the world was run by women things would be very different." Pointing a slender, manicured finger at Agnes she said, "You woman, what's your name?"

Agnes grinned toothless at the prioress but said nothing. Will took a step forward. "I'm afraid the woman has lost her mind, she's known as Agnes"

The prioress studied Agnes with obvious distaste and drummed her fingers on the desk. "Well if she was ever a member of the community here it was before my time. Let me send for our librarian. She's as old as the books she looks after. If your story is true sister Juliana will know her."

She picked up a little brass bell and shook it gently. A door opened behind her and the nun who had escorted them before reappeared. Without turning around the prioress said, "Ask Sister Juliana to come to me and to bring the register of the convent with her."

The nun scuttled off without a word, leaving them once again under the piercing blue-eyed inspection of the prioress. She made no further effort to talk to them or to offer them a seat. They stood in an increasingly embarrassed silence which she seemed to enjoy. Bernard took to a tuneless, barely audible whistle between his front teeth. Osbert's gaze seemed fixated on the prioress's chest.

Eventually Will could stand it no longer and tried some small talk. "The season has been pleasant madam. We've made good time."

"Has it, did you?" she said with that mocking smile again.

"You know the bishop well madam?"

"Well enough."

This was sheer torture thought Will. Was the woman purposely trying to embarrass them? They were the bishop's men, not to be belittled, they didn't deserve this treatment and he was on the verge of telling her so. He was saved when the door behind the prioress opened. A stooped-backed elderly nun entered carrying a heavy leather-bound book which she placed on the prioress's desk.

"Ah, Sister Juliana."

"Reverend Mother how may I help?"

"Tell me, do you know this woman? Take a good look now."

Sister Julian crept forward and studied Agnes carefully. A weak smile broke on her lips. "Why yes Reverend Mother, although my eyes are failing, I do believe this is Agnes Montague."

"She was a nun here once?"

"She was Reverend Mother. Given to the church by her parents, she was probably around eight when she arrived. I was just a novice myself then. She'd just taken her vows when she disappeared with a friar if I remember rightly. She was a young woman by then."

"She will be in the register?"

"Oh yes, old Revered Mother Helen was very strict about record keeping."

"Are you implying my predecessor was stricter with records than I Sister Juliana?"

"Of course not Reverend Mother. Perish the thought!"

"Indeed."

The prioress began to slowly turn the pages of the leather-bound volume. It took some time but she eventually found an entry. "Here it is. Agnes Montague, youngest daughter of Sir Henry Montague, under sheriff of the county no less. A very small dowry was given. Satisfied she snapped shut the volume, "Well it seems that you have returned a lost sheep to the fold. You must give my thanks to bishop Gifford. He's always... most helpful. Now if there's nothing else?"

They looked at each other. "She's had a hard life these last few years. She will be well cared for?" asked Bernard.

The prioress looked suitably offended. "Rest assured a place will be found for her however much she has fallen from grace. There is always work to do here. After suitable penance perhaps a place will be found for her in the laundry or the bakery. Does she never speak?"

Will shook his head. "No Reverend Mother, the only noise she makes is laughter when agitated."

"She laughs?"

"Manically Reverend Mother."

"Well we seldom have time for laughter here. So, if that's all? I'm sure you want to be back on the road and we have our own duties to attend to." They were clearly dismissed. Mumbling their thanks they were swiftly shown out of the prioress chamber by the librarian. She led them back to the gate, Agnes trailing after them.

They mounted up, the spare horse tied to Osbert's saddle. Agnes stood forlornly looking up at them beside the librarian.

"The prioress was wrong about one thing," said the librarian. "Agnes brought a valuable dowry to the convent. That ring around the prioress neck was a part of it, a pretty thing. I remember it well, handed over by her father the day she first came to the convent."

Bernard looked around at his companions, sighed heavily, and said, "Well lads, she'll be better off here than begging on the streets of Draychester. What more can we do? We've done the bishop's bidding, let's be on our way."

∼

They swiftly left St Michaels and Sandford behind, although not without a few twinges of guilt about leaving poor Agnes. Soon they re-joined the main road and once again began to head north. The intention was to make Gloucester before nightfall. As they pressed on the weather turned. The sky became overcast, a wind started to rise and a light drizzle became a heavy rain. They stopped to put on their leather over-mantles, which were designed to keep the worst of the weather out. After less than ten minutes Osbert complained loudly his was already letting the rain through.

Death Of The Official

Will's was just as bad but he held his tongue. They plodded on through the rain somewhat dispirited by the day and slowed by the weather.

"It'll be dark soon. Are we far off Gloucester?" Osbert asked Bernard anxiously.

"Another hour or two at least. We'll not make the town tonight. There's a place on the road not much further on from here, Painswick. I stopped there once at an inn. We can rest for the night."

Bernard had an uneasy feeling. He peered back down the road they'd travelled. He saw no one but he couldn't shake the feeling they were being followed. There was no logical reason, some would call it a sixth sense, all he knew was that it'd served him well in the past.

Despite Bernard's misgivings, within the half hour and in the gathering gloom, they safely entered the village of Painswick. There was just the one rundown looking inn. They were all tired and glad to be in from the rain at last. The place was packed with travellers who'd been caught out by the turn of the weather. In the flickering light of candles and the fire there was a confusing din of voices, noise and smutty jokes. Will thought they were in for a long and uncomfortable night.

They managed to secure some food. Dinner began with a cup of thin sour wine, bowls of pottage followed, interspaced with soups. Next came some roast meats which were offered sparingly and were quickly whisked away by a serving girl.

Bernard beckoned the landlord over. "Why the hurry landlord, I've barely tasted the food and you're taking it away?"

"Lot of travellers in tonight, we've no time for playing the good host."

"You've no objection to our coin though?" said Bernard angrily.

The landlord gave a bad-tempered shrug. "There's only one inn in this village. If you don't like it you're more than welcome to spend the night out in the rain."

Will and Osbert instinctively grabbed Bernard's arms before he could do any damage to the surly man.

There was little room left in any of the upper chambers, and they opted to sleep in the main room rather than share a bed with strangers. No one got much rest. It soon became cold once the fire had died down and the benches they lay on were hard and uncomfortable.

∼

They left just after dawn, tired and achy from the previous days ride with their clothes still damp. None of them had been inclined to stay any longer than necessary in the place.

A thin drizzle drifted down from low cloudy skies as they made their way along the road heading northwest to Gloucester. The roadway became increasing well maintained. At Saintsbridge they came across a chapel with a grubby little hermit collecting alms for the road repair and they left a few pennies. About an hour and a half after setting off from the inn they were finally on the outskirts of the town. They entered at Eastgate where a porter collected another toll from them, this time for the upkeep of the walls.

When they passed into the town Bernard finally grinned. "Cheer up lads. Tonight we will have the best bed and grub between here and York. We stay as guests of the abbey, so make the most of it. Walter, the abbot, is one of the few monks our bishop likes, they're good friends."

The abbey of St Peter lay on the north side of the town. They entered the abbey precinct by the gate on St Mary's Street. There were two porters on duty. Bernard said they were Bishop Gifford's men, showed his seal, and they were admitted at once and emerged into the great courtyard of the abbey. Two stable boys came running over to take the horses. On one side stood the abbey guest hall, a large newly built structure which looked all too inviting to the weary travellers. They soon found the hosteller, Brother Luke, an old acquaintance of Bernard. He was a stoutly built, jovial figure who welcomed them into the hall with a ready smile and friendly clap on the back for Bernard.

"Welcome Bernard and company. You look tired my friends, come sit awhile and take some wine with me. Let's sit near the fire, dry yourselves off, you look like three drowned rats! If you've come with messages for the abbot, then I'm afraid you've missed him. He's been gone these two days past, off to the see the Bishop of Worcester. I'll have to do instead."

Bernard laughed and grasped the other man's arm in welcome. "It's good to see you brother. No messages this time Luke, although you can be sure of Bishop Gifford's best regards. We're passing through, heading north, and all the way to York. These two youngsters, newly made bishop's men I might add, are William Blackburn and Osbert Frampton."

"York! Well bless my soul, a journey indeed. Better take your ease while you can my friends."

11

GLOUCESTER

Sitting beside the fire in the great hall with Brother Luke, they slowly dried out, drank some wine and ate bread and cheese. Eventually Bernard said, "Why don't you two take in the sights, make the most of it. We leave first thing in the morning. I'll reminisce a while longer with my good friend Luke."

As they left Brother Luke shouted after them, "Go see the new cloisters in the abbey, the abbot has spent a small fortune, the roof is magnificent. Don't miss old King Edward's tomb either."

Will was all for finding the nearest alehouse but Osbert insisted he wanted to see the abbey. Will felt obliged to keep him out of trouble and reluctantly agreed. Brother Luke had been right. The cloisters in the abbey were magnificent. It was clear they had spared no expense on the new building work. Osbert and Will looked up open-mouthed at the fan-vaulted roof. "Bishop Gifford will be jealous when he sees this," said Osbert marvelling at the workmanship. "I fear even his coffers won't be deep enough to pay for something like this in Draychester. Of course old King Edward's tomb brings in the pilgrim money here."

Will said, "Well, maybe our bishop should acquire a saint's bone or two to boost our own cathedral's coffers."

Osbert gave him a glare. Will just grinned back. "Come on, let's take a look at King Edward."

They entered the main body of the abbey. There was a crowd of pilgrims clustered around the tomb. It was so popular there were niches cut into the pillars on each side so the crowds could walk round it. The tomb itself was startling. Surrounded by flickering candles, a lifelike alabaster effigy rested on a high plinth covered by an ornately carved limestone canopy. At the king's feet lay a stone lion. Will could see how the tomb would draw the crowds and the pennies of the pilgrims. He was impressed with the ingenuity of it all

∽

They left the abbey precinct by the south gate and met a steady stream of pilgrims coming the other way. Most of them wore a collection of crude pilgrimage badges on their outer clothing and hats or around their necks. Just outside the gate clustered several rough stalls where the badge sellers set out their wares. Will presumed the abbot took his cut of the proceeds. They stopped at a stall and the seller quickly began to run through his pitch.

"A souvenir of your pilgrimage to take home young sir? A bell sir, or a King Edward? Perhaps an ampulla of holy water?"

Will looked at the crude metal badges, no doubt cast in their thousands. The allure of buying such trinkets eluded him but apparently not the hundreds who daily tramped past the stalls here outside the abbey gates. At a neighbouring stall Osbert had already been persuaded to part with several pennies for a selection of badges. As Will turned away from the stall the seller made one last pitch.

"Perhaps something a little special can tempt you sir?"

"It'll have to be good to tempt me. So what have you got?" he asked with good humour.

From underneath the bench the weaselled faced man brought out a little wooden box with a sliding lid. He opened it and handed it to Will. Inside was a small length of ancient looking wood. The seller looked around furtively and said in a low voice, "A piece of the true cross, brought back from the holy land by a crusader. Are you interested?"

Will chuckled. "I've seen enough of these to make a whole forest let alone a cross! Do you take me for a dunce?"

The seller snatched the box back with a scowl. "You can't please some folk."

Will still laughing re-joined Osbert who was now proudly wearing several badges about his person. "Happy with your purchases Osbert?" he asked.

Osbert gave him his usual scowl.

Will sighed. "Right, how about a drink and some food?"

As the pair left the stalls they were followed at a discreet distance by the Bouchard twins. A short walk later and they were soon sat in an alehouse known as the Bell on Westgate Street. The Bouchard twins entered some five minutes later and took a bench facing them on the other side of the room. It was market day, and the place was busy and a little rowdy but in a good-humoured way.

Will started his ale and was about to sample a meat pie when he became aware of a hostile stare from the opposite side of the room. Osbert, sat across from his companion with his back to the rest of the room, noticed the pie stop

Death Of The Official

just in front of Will's mouth. He said, "I've not started my own pie yet, don't tell me it's off? I feel like I've not eaten for a week."

"It's not the pie that's off. There's an ugly looking character across the room giving us looks that mean trouble."

"I for one don't know anyone in Gloucester. Perhaps it's one of your former partners in crime."

"I don't think so, believe me I'd have remembered this ones face."

Osbert made to turn around. Will reached across and grabbed his arm. "No don't turn around. Let's try and not antagonise anyone, at least until I've finished my pie. He must have mistaken us for someone else."

Godbert and Gilbert got up and moved to a free table less than ten feet away and directly behind Osbert.

Gobert glared at Will directly. "You stinking turds," he hissed at them through his pudgy lips. Gilbert just sat forward half slumped on the tabletop and smiled at them maliciously. Will avoided eye contact, pretended he hadn't heard and started eating his pie. The last thing he wanted was trouble. Godbert hissed at him again, "You, Ginger Top, I can smell your stink from here. And that streak of piss with you, I can smell him as well."

Will carefully put down his half-eaten pie and said slowly, "I think you've mistaken us for someone else. We've been in Gloucester but a few hours."

"Think I care. You and your bum boy still stink."

Will picked up his pie again and regarded it rather sadly. He made to eat it but suddenly lobbed it with some force at Godbert. It flew across the short distance between them trailing a stream of rich brown gravy. It hit Godbert square in the face with a satisfying splat.

Godbert slowly wiped the greasy mess from his face

then went red with rage. He sprang up with a roar, grabbed the table by its edge, and sent it flying to his right. Even Gilbert was surprised by the turn of events and ended up flat on his back as the table was pulled out from under him. There was pandemonium as the airborne table ploughed into a group of nearby drinkers. Godbert grinned evilly at Will. In a split second he lurched forward, grabbed him by the throat and forced him backwards to collide with a dull thud and gasp of breath against the wall. With one hand still clamped around Will's throat Godbert swung a huge fist at his head as though hammering a fence post. Will's legs gave way, and they left him dangling limply from Godbert's left hand. "You spineless little turd. I'm going to gut you like the pig you are." As if from nowhere a wicked looking dagger appeared in Godbert's other hand. He drew it back and aimed it directly at Will's guts and said, "I'm going to enjoy this. Bet you're a squealer. I can tell, little runt like you, I like it when they squeal..."

Suddenly a wailing banshee jumped onto Godbert's back and the dagger went flying. The screaming figure clamped two hands around Godbert's face, thumbs gouging at his eyes. He released Will and half blinded he flailed about madly trying to shake his attacker free from his back. He staggered across the room knocking over more tables and scattering drinkers to the left and right and starting the beginnings of a mass brawl.

Will could hardly believe it. Godbert's attacker appeared to be Osbert. Eventually the clerk was shaken loose from the big man's back and flew across several tables back towards Will. He landed in a groaning heap at Will's feet who promptly grabbed him by the scruff of the neck and hauled him upright.

Godbert turned his murderous gaze on Will, his eyes

bulging with rage. He tried to make his way back across the room but the brawl had now taken on epic proportions. The alehouse was in an uproar with brawling men occupying every square foot. Try as he might he couldn't make headway against the tide of fighting figures.

Will started to push Osbert towards the entrance. "We need to leave. By the way, you have my thanks, he was about to gut me."

Osbert giggled like a child, high on adrenaline. "I've never been in a proper brawl before."

Will pushed him harder this time and said, "Let's go!"

They elbowed their way to the door and staggered out into the street. The cooler air outside revived Will but left his head throbbing. "Listen Osbert, we don't have to tell Bernard any of this. If he finds out, he'll never let us out of his sight for the rest of the journey."

Osbert nodded. "I agree. Still, it would have been nice to tell him how I saved you."

Will threw an arm around Osbert's shoulders, both in appreciation of his companion's efforts and to keep himself on his feet. "You did well my friend. I didn't think you had it in you, I really didn't. You never cease to surprise Osbert."

Osbert grimaced in embarrassment and simply said, "Umph."

They found their way back to the abbey's main gate. As far as they could tell nobody had followed them but it had been difficult to see in the crowded streets. They looked a little disheveled, but the porters waved them through without any comment. They found Bernard dozing by the fire in the guest hall. He regarded them through sleepy eyes. "You two are back early. Is there nothing in the whole of Gloucester to hold your attention?"

Will glanced at Osbert and said sheepishly, "Ah, we've seen the sights. One town is much like the next."

Bernard looked at them suspiciously. "Well if you're not going out on the town, I suggest you get some rest. You look bloody rough Will. I won't ask what you've been up to. Osbert, go find one of the lads in the courtyard and get him to show you our chamber. I've got some errands to do the rest of the afternoon. Just try to stay out of trouble."

∽

They were allocated a small whitewashed chamber on the second floor of the guest house next to the main hall. There were four comfortable beds, a table and a wooden chest. A window seat overlooked the great courtyard of the abbey and there were two heavy shutters that could be closed at night.

Osbert was soon sitting at the table with his quill and ink. He began to scribble away. Will lay down on one of the beds his head still pounding, he thought he might be mildly concussed. He asked wearily, "What are you writing Osbert?"

"I need to keep the bishop updated on the journey. I can send the report back easily from here, there'll be regular messengers going to Draychester."

"What have we done so far that would interest him? He's a busy man."

"You'd be surprised. You forget I've trained with the diocesan clerks. As the bishop's men we need to keep him updated. It's expected of us. Information we pick up on the journey is always of use. My uncle Scrivener says knowledge is power."

"I hope you aren't going to tell the bishop we got into a brawl in an alehouse?"

"I am always quite thorough in my reports."

"Yes, I suspect you are...God's teeth, this is going to be a long journey."

⁓

That night they dined in the great hall and Brother Luke once again joined them. As they ate, the talk inevitably turned to tales of the previous journeys the older men had made over the years. Luke said, "You'd do well to travel with a larger group if you're going via Tewkesbury and Worcester."

Bernard looked up sharply from his food. "There's been trouble on the road?"

"Just this last month. They robbed two of our messengers on the highway north of Tewkesbury. One of them lies in the abbey infirmary there still, his skull stove in. He's not expected to live."

"And the other?" said Osbert his eyes wide.

"Beaten black and blue, stripped naked and left tied to a tree. He'll not ride far ever again. The sheriff's men have been making regular patrols ever since, but they can't be everywhere. I've heard other reports of robberies on the road, but these are the worst injuries. The outlaws seem to be getting bolder."

"They would prey on a larger group?" asked Will.

"I think not. Still, it's always safer to travel in numbers if possible."

"Is it known who these outlaws are?" said Will.

Brother Luke shrugged. "The usual I would suppose. The hungry, the disinherited, runaway apprentices, cattle thieves, the plain evil. There's many who try to survive on the wrong side of the law and their reasons are as numerous. Don't be unduly panicked just take good care on the road, that's all I ask my friends."

Bernard nodded. "It's good advice nevertheless."

"So, you leave in the morning?" asked Brother Luke.

Bernard nodded again. "Yes. We need to be on the road early."

"Then travel with some others. The master stone mason here, Peter is his name, and two of his apprentices are traveling to Worcester tomorrow. I'm sure they'll be glad of your company."

"We're doomed, " said Osbert sadly.

"Oh shut up," said Bernard and Will in unison.

12

THE ATTACK

By the afternoon of the following day they were on the road north of Tewkesbury. They had stopped only for an hour in the town itself, around noon, to eat. Bernard was eager to keep moving. The great tower of the abbey church was a constant presence behind them for some miles after they'd left the town. The master mason and his two apprentices had proved amiable company. They were keen to get to Worcester and start work on a new project. The master mason himself was a big man and sat uncomfortably on his horse. His two apprentices were equally well built with faces heavily tanned by weeks working outside. Will felt secure in their company, sure the sight of the six of them would put off any but the most determined robbers.

Bernard didn't feel as comfortable. His sixth sense made him keep glancing at the road behind them. The hairs on the back of his neck rising. He felt sure they were being followed but try as he might he could see no one. Which made the attack when it came all the more surprising. They were in a dip in the road, passing through a small copse of trees. Two men stepped out from the tree line directly into the road in front of them, causing the master mason's horse to rear. Bernard cursed himself for not being more vigilant, especially after Brother Luke's warning.

Their small party came to an abrupt halt. One robber, for that was surely who they were, grabbed the reins of the master mason's horse. The other man levelled a crossbow directly at the centre of Will's chest.

Keeping his eyes fixed on Will he said, "All of you get off your horses now. Tarry and I swear I'll put a bolt right through this one's chest."

The riders looked at each other uneasily then dismounted slowly and stood by their horses.

"I knew this journey was doomed from the very start. We're all going to die," hissed Osbert at Will.

Bernard was itching to grab his own crossbow which sat hanging from his saddle. Behind them half a dozen more men emerged from the bushes bearing an assorted array of weapons.

Bernard calmly said, "You're making a mistake here my friend. We're bishop's men. Harm us and I guarantee you'll hang before this month out. Let us ride on and nobody will be any the wiser, I give you my word."

The crossbow was turned towards Bernard. "Shut your mouth big man. Say one more word I'll drop you where you stand. That goes for all of you. Search them lads and get the horses off the road."

Two of the robbers, daggers drawn, began to search them one by one, removing weapons and purses and anything else of value about their person. The haul taken from Bernard was a veritable arsenal. From all three of the bishop's men they retrieved their seals and letters of authority. They led the horses off into the bushes. One searcher piled up the loot, except for the seals and letters, at the side of the road. The man with the crossbow, who appeared to be in charge swiftly passed it to another. He held out his hand for the seals and letters.

He studied them intently for a few seconds. "These three are bishop's men all right. The documents I can't read but these seals I've seen before."

"Could be trouble Tom?" said the man now holding the crossbow.

"There's always trouble. You think this is some kind of game? Now shut your mouth and get that stuff off the roadside before someone else comes along."

He gestured to the mason and said, "Who are you?"

"Peter, master mason. These two are my apprentices."

The man nodded slowly and turned his attention back to Bernard. He looked him up and down. "Your boots big man," he pointed at Bernard's feet, "I want them. Take them off and hand them over."

Bernard's face turned from one of simmering anger to dark thunder. They eyed each other for a few moments. Then Bernard advanced a few steps to stand by Will. He placed one arm on Will's shoulder for balance and slowly started to take his right boot off.

The leader of the robbers smirked. "That's a good boy."

Bernard slipped a hand into the top of his boot as though to pull it free. He withdrew his hand and for an instant Will saw something metallic flash there before Bernard expertly flicked the small dagger, for that's what it was, towards their smirking captor. It took him completely by surprise, embedding itself deeply into the man's right shoulder. He fell to his knees with a gasp, rich red blood spreading in a dark stain across his tunic. Bernard pulled himself and Will downward as the man with the crossbow, with a muttered curse, let fly a bolt. The projectile passed over their heads and thudded into the trunk of a tree behind them.

"The knife!" bellowed Bernard thrusting Will towards the injured robber while he turned menacingly to the man with the now useless crossbow. He took two huge strides and wrenched the crossbow from the terrified man and used it to club him to the ground mercilessly.

Will stumbled forward and with a grimace extracted the knife from the injured man who promptly collapsed face first onto the ground with a groan. There was blood everywhere. In the confusion, the master mason and one of his apprentices had the good sense to grab for the pile of weapons and valuables. He grabbed two wooden cudgels and flung a short sword towards Osbert who stood back just in time to save it taking his legs off. In the scuffle that followed, the master mason took a long raking wound down his right arm. They edged back in a ragged line beside Bernard on the opposite side of the road to the remaining robbers.

Bernard, his eyes fixed with murderous intent on the disheveled men facing them, pointed a finger towards the sword on the ground and said, "Osbert, hand me that."

A trembling Osbert gingerly picked the weapon up by the blade and handed it hilt first to Bernard. The big man tested its weight and tossed it between hands expertly. "So who's first, anyone feeling brave?" By his side one of the mason's apprentices started to smack the head of a cudgel into a palm. No one stepped forward. Bernard said, "Walk away now before anyone else dies. I swear if I have to I'll gut each one of you. You've had your chance and I won't ask again. What's it to be?"

One of the robbers turned and slipped into the undergrowth, then the rest turned and followed without a word. They were soon lost to sight.

Will walked over to where the man lay face down in a pool of blood. He gently turned him over. He stared up at Will and his lips moved without any words being audible. "He's still alive," said Will.

The man coughed, a thin trail of blood leaking from the corner of his mouth. Will knelt down beside him. Bernard came over and crouched down beside them. The man's eyes flicked between them and came to rest on Will. He said, "I'm dying?"

"I won't lie to you. The wound looks mortal."

The man nodded his head in acceptance. "I've done some bad things. Didn't set out too, just the way it turned out," he croaked.

Bernard looked down at him, a hard look in his eyes. "Save your breath man, we're not priests we can't hear your confession."

The man gave a humourless chuckle. "I knew you were the one to watch big man. My own fault, I always push it too far." He suddenly gave a sharp gasp and slipped away from them into death.

Bernard got to his feet, "Better dead here on the road than at the end of the sheriff's noose."

Peter the master mason shuddered. His arm was a bloody red mess and he held it close to his side. "A bad business. God has shown us mercy today, we should all be thankful for our lives."

"What do we do with this one?" asked Osbert poking with a toe the man Bernard had clubbed.

Will walked over to the man. From what he could see he wasn't breathing. "I don't think we have to worry about him. Bernard appears to have stove his head in."

Bernard said, "If I'd been more alert this would never have happened. Two is poor, we've let at least five or six get away."

Will shook his head in disbelief. "Bernard, two is plenty. I think we need to let the sheriff have his chance with the rest. We're bloody lucky to be alive!"

Bernard grunted and turned to the master mason. "How bad is the wound Peter?"

"Painful. I don't think I'll be laying any stone for a while."

"Looks nasty. First things first. We need to see if they left the horses." He gestured towards the trees. "They must be back there."

"Osbert, let's take a look, they can't be far," said Will.

Osbert looked horrified. "You want me to go into the woods with you, after we've just been robbed and nearly murdered?"

"Do you want to walk the rest of the way? The robbers are long gone."

Osbert reluctantly followed him into the undergrowth. The horses were tied to some branches in a small clearing just out of sight of the road. They soon led them back to the others. Will removed one of the packs from his horse. He found his bedding within and tore some of the linen into strips so they could bind the master mason's arm. When it was done he asked Bernard, "Is there somewhere we can get this cleaned up? He can't travel far in this state."

"We'd better press on. We're nearer to Worcester now anyway. There's a hospital there, Saint Wulfstan's just outside one of the city gates."

Will nodded. "And the dead men?"

"We need to report this to the sheriff. Let's drag these two to the side."

Death Of The Official

They dragged the bodies of the two dead robbers over towards the ditch at the roadside. It somehow seemed wrong to leave them there in the dirt but there was nothing for it but to carry on. They repacked their belongings and set off, the master mason wincing in pain with every jolt from the road.

∼

The rest of the way to Worcester was uneventful although Bernard kept his weapons close to hand and was constantly looking back the way they'd come. It was a long day in the saddle and the earlier events led to a sombre and mostly silent journey. Just outside the city walls by a gate known as Sidbury, at the junction of three main roads, stood Saint Wulfstan's hospital. They arrived at dusk, just as the main gates to the city were closing. Bernard rode on into the city, taking Osbert with him to report the day's incident to the authorities. He said, "We'll be back tomorrow morning. We must get back on the road as soon as we can. There's a long way to York yet."

Will and the injured mason and his two apprentices sought aid at the hospital. It wasn't strictly for the care of injuries. Once they'd entered the large red roofed building, they saw it mainly catered for giving the poor and infirm a roof over their head if they hadn't made it through the city gates before dusk. An elderly attendant hobbled over. He took one look at the mason's blood stained arm and shook his head.

"That's nasty that is. You'd be better off at the priory's infirmary within the walls."

Will shook his head. "Maybe we'll go there tomorrow morning. For now, find whoever you need to tend him. I'm on the Bishop of Draychester's business. I'm sure we'll make a more than generous donation before we leave."

The man scuttled off. He returned with another equally ancient man who squinted at them through bleary eyes. "This is John, he used to be a lay brother at the priory, worked in the infirmary once."

John nodded in greeting and said, "Come sit at one of the tables. Let me have a look at that wound son."

The mason took of his tunic and stretched his arm out on the table top, wincing in pain. The old man untied the blood-soaked linen revealing a deep wound that ran for a good three inches down the Mason's arm. "Looks like you've had a run in with a blade? Best way is to seal it with a hot poker. Hurts like hell mind you. Done it a few times, but it's been some years, my eyes aren't what they used to be."

Will turned to the mason. "We can just bind it again if you want? It's pretty deep though, risk of it festering like that. I've seen it happen..."

The mason shook his head. "Find me something for the pain old man, then you can use the poker. Seen plenty of injuries in my time, it's the best way."

The old man shuffled off into a back room and returned with a small stoppered bottle. "Opium from poppy seeds. It's powerful stuff, just a drop or two taken with a measure of honey and water. You won't feel a thing."

The mason looked sceptical but gave his consent. "Let's get it over with."

The old man carefully mixed the drug with honey and water. The mason downed the lot in one gulp. After a few minutes he was barely awake. Will and both of the mason's apprentices took up position and held him down while the old man applied a red-hot poker to the wound. The mason howled like a trapped wolf. As the hot poker did its work the injured man's flesh smoked and spluttered and gave off a sickly sweet stench like burnt bacon. It was all Will could do to hold down what little he'd eaten that day. When the job was done they carried the exhausted mason to a simple cot in a back room. He fell into a deep, drug induced sleep.

The old man said, "He'll be in bad pain for a day or two but the wounds closed now. He should rest for a few days if possible and he won't be working any time soon."

∼

The following morning and the mason could barely move his arm. It was red and inflamed. When Bernard arrived, he took one look at him and said, "Let's take you to the priory infirmary. The monks will look after you there; the bishop's name will see to it."

The master mason spoke to his apprentices, "Listen lads. I'm going to be laid up, no idea how long. I've a plan if you're agreeable. My brother John is the master mason at the minister in York. I'll get young Osbert to draft me a letter you can give to him. You can travel to York with our good friends here. I'm sure they'll be glad of the company and you'll be guaranteed work for the summer."

Will nodded. "It's a good plan and better for us if we travel as five rather than three. What say you Bernard?"

"The more the merrier and your master's right, there's no shortage of work for masons in York."

The two apprentices readily agreed although they insisted that they take their injured master into the city first. Will got Osbert to draft a letter to the prior on Bishop Giffard's behalf asking that the mason be cared for at the infirmary until he was well. Osbert used his own official seal to authenticate the document. He then wrote a letter for the mason to his brother asking that he take the two apprentices for the summer whilst he recovered from his injuries. The mason added his own seal to the bottom.

"My brother will know for sure that's mine," he said approvingly.

They waited at the hospital while they escorted the injured man into the city. After leaving a generous donation at the hospital, the party of five were back on the road by late morning.

13

THE TWINS ARGUE

To the south, on the outskirts of Gloucester the Bouchard twins were trying to make up time. Gilbert was flogging his horse relentlessly with a thin stick, whilst Godbert was digging two wicked looking spurs into his mount's sides. They had spent a night and a good part of the following day in a lock-up along with most of the regulars of the Bell alehouse. The brawl had finally been broken up by half a dozen of the city watch swinging wooden clubs. Godbert sported a black eye and Gilbert now walked with a bad limp, the result of a brutal rap across a kneecap. Both men were in a foul mood. The whole business was turning into a disaster. They'd killed none of the bishop's men and they'd had to hand over nearly half their money as a bribe to get released from the lock-up. God alone knew how far ahead the bishop's men were now. Gilbert was seriously contemplating turning around and forgetting the whole thing. "I'm tired of this brother. Let Sir Roger do his own dirty work. Why not head back to Gloucester? We could get drunk for a week then head home."

His brother turned to look at him. "Think I'd let them

walk away from us like that. I'm going to carve 'em up. Go back if you want, I don't care."

Gilbert knew his twin might be short on brains but once he got something into that thick skull his determination knew no bounds. If needs be, he'd follow the bishop's men to the very gates of hell.

∽

North of Tweksbury they came across two dead bodies lying at the side of the road. They slowed and came to a halt. "Not any of 'em is it?" grunted Godbert.

They were the first words he'd spoken in two hours. Gilbert slid off his horse and studied the two figures. "Nope. Never laid eyes on these two. Been dead a day, maybe a little longer. Nasty wound in the shoulder of this one, the other looks like someone stove in his skull. Pity it wasn't some of them, would have saved us a job."

Godbert spat on the ground, the green glob of spit just missing Gilbert's feet. "Don't want nobody else touching them. That red-haired bastard, I want to do him myself."

Gilbert sighed heavily. "In that case we'd better get a move on." He climbed back into the saddle, as he did so the rain started to come down heavily. He was thoroughly depressed. Godbert just looked at him with a slightly blank gaze that Gilbert knew only too well. He was difficult to control when he got like this and could become dangerous even to his own brother. They needed to catch up with the bishop's men and fast before Godbert's temper got them into serious trouble.

"Horses are getting tired. We can't keep this pace up all day."

Godbert shrugged. "Then we get new horses. Buy them or take them, I don't care…"

With that he dug his spurs viciously into his horse and it bolted off up the road with him hanging on tightly. Gilbert shook his head in defeat and urged his own horse to follow.

∾

Just as the light began fading, they arrived at Saint Wulfstan's hospital outside Worcester's walls. The city gates were closed. "You think they're in the city or travelled on?" asked Gilbert.

Godbert peered at the city gates. "Don't know. My gut tells me they've pressed on. Going to need fresh horses whatever."

"Then let me do any talking brother and try not to hit anyone."

They dismounted and led their horses around to the back of the hospital where they could see a stable. The simple wooden lean-to that comprised the stable was crowded with various horses. Presumably they belonged to those staying the night at the hospital. They dismounted and led their animals under the roof, tying them up. Nobody emerged to question them and after a minute Godbert walked down the row of animals and chose one he liked the look of. He rapidly transferred his saddle to the new beast. Gilbert, alarmed, looked around, but still saw no one. "This isn't a good idea," he hissed.

Godbert glared at him. "Choose a horse brother. Hurry up before someone comes and I have to kill 'em!"

Gilbert hurried down the row of tethered animals after his brother and ten minutes later they were heading north again on their stolen mounts.

14

BURNING THE INN

Will and the other bishop's men stopped at an inn on the road between Lichfield and Derby. The way had been wet but passable. They would have made better progress but that afternoon Osbert's horse had gone lame. Bernard looked at the injured beast and declared they would stop and rest Osbert's mount for the night.

The inn was a one story wattle and daub construction with a newly thatched roof. Inside it was basic but comfortable. The riding party was soon settled at a long bench with food and ale. A welcoming fire burned in the central hearth and cast a cheerful glow over the interior of the inn. As the evening progressed, the ale flowed freely and even Osbert seemed more cheerful than usual. The gloom that had overshadowed them since the attack on the road seemed to have lifted.

"Osbert's horse, you think we need to rest it longer than just tonight?" asked Will. The prospect of a full day's rest in the convivial surroundings of the inn was inviting.

Bernard shrugged his shoulders. "We'll look at the horse again before we set out in the morning. We'll not press as hard tomorrow, give the horses an easier day of it."

An hour later and the inn was crowded with travellers and locals alike. A party of pilgrims had arrived on their way south to Canterbury. There were at least twenty of them and they seemed intent on drinking the night away. They were boisterous but not rowdy and their good humoured banter and joke telling even conjured a smile from Osbert. Soon two of the party had started to play a popular ditty with pipe and lute and the evening got livelier still.

∼

The Bouchard twins had arrived just after dark. It wasn't clear to them if the bishop's men were still ahead or not. Even Godbert conceded they couldn't keep up this pace indefinitely. In any case it was as likely a spot for weary travellers to stop for the night as any other.

Godbert said, "They may be inside even now. If not, they can't be far ahead."

Gilbert put a hand on his brother's arm. "Have a care brother. Even you can't murder in plain sight and get away with it."

"Accidents happen all the time brother, although I'd rather use my knife."

They slipped inside and mingled with the happy crowd. And there across the crowded room they saw the red-haired youth and the thin, lanky one they had encountered at the alehouse in Worcester. Gilbert also recognised the familiar bulk of Bernard. They'd crossed paths often enough in the past and he knew him as the lead rider of the party they'd watched set out from Draychester.

Godbert pulled his brother back to the door and they

went outside again. He grinned evilly. Gilbert knew that look, "What have you in mind brother?"

His twin tugged some thatch from the low roof of the inn and rubbed it in between his hands. "New thatch. Nice and dry. Accident waiting to happen. I'd rather gut them, but I'll burn them just the same."

Gilbert stared back at him aghast. "Even for you that's evil. There must be fifty people in there Godbert."

Godbert shrugged. "If it bothers you that much we'll wait until later when they're asleep. The locals will've left by then, should only be travellers in there. Find me a couple of branches or something, we'll need to jam the doors, front and back." He rubbed his hands together and said, "Let's roast the bastards."

~

It was late into the night when the main room of the inn finally became quiet. Most of the revellers had either passed out where they had sat and slid to the floor or had made themselves comfortable on the tables and benches. The bishop's men had spread their sleeping rolls and packs up against the back wall of the room. They were soon sleeping soundly in the muggy warmth.

In the dead of night Will awoke hot and bothered. He rubbed his face hard, his eyes still closed. For some reason he found it difficult to breathe. He turned on his side to get more comfortable and soon threw off the rough blanket he had over him. It was still too hot and now he thought he needed a piss. He half raised his head to get up, but his face was immediately enveloped in a thick choking smoke. He gasped, breathed in the thick smog, which made him half retch and pressed his head back down onto the floor. The place was on fire.

Now fully awake he bellowed as loud as he could, "Fire!"

He kept bellowing at the top of his voice and crawled over to Bernard who was sleeping nearby. He grabbed him and began shaking him violently. "Wake up! The place is on fire! Wake up!"

His cries woke up several of the others and soon the room was full of frightened shouts and cries and people coughing as the smoke grew thicker. Bernard tried to struggle to his feet, but Will pulled him back down to the floor where there was still air. From overhead they could see a dull orange glow and bits of burning thatch had dropped into the main room itself. In the few seconds that had elapsed since Will woke a frightening roaring sound had grown as the fire took hold.

Will shouted again, "It's the roof that's on fire, we have to get out now."

All their party were now awake and crouched low on the floor trying their best to avoid the worst of the smoke. Bernard started shoving them towards the back wall. "Make for the back door and let's be quick about it. Grab your packs."

Osbert was the first to the wooden door at the rear of the inn. He shoved hard, but the door remained stubbornly shut. Will pushed him out of the way and shoved the door himself, to no effect. A crowd of anxious travellers were pushing in behind them. Angry shouts started.

"Open that bloody door."

"It's jammed shut!" Osbert cried.

"Let me try," said Bernard elbowing his way through the crowd.

There was screaming from the front of the room as

burning timbers started to crash down. From what Will could see, no one was making their way out the front. They were trapped. The screaming suddenly increased in pitch to a terrifying wail. A burning figure could now be seen flailing about and stumbling into the benches across the room. His hair and clothes were on fire. Will turned away unable to look.

Bernard's great bulk smashed into the back door, the door buckled but held fast. He turned around a desperate look on his face. "My pack. Where's my pack?"

Will hauled it forward across the space between them. Bernard ripped open the top of the leather bag and pulled out a wicked looking axe. "Stand back!"

He started furiously battering the door down. The wood splintered after the first couple of strikes and Bernard finished it off with a shove from his great booted foot. Will heaved their packs through the opening and then there was a mad rush towards the narrow doorway as people fought to get through. They crashed out into the backyard, Will gulping in lungful's of clean air. He was soon lying in the mud, coughing his guts up.

Eventually he struggled to his feet to see his fellow travellers dotted around the yard staring back at him with blackened faces. By now the inn was fully ablaze, the heat was becoming intense, and they had to move further away from the burning structure. He looked back at the orange opening where the door had been. No one else would come out of there alive. He caught Bernard's gaze. The big man nodded grimly towards the left of the doorway. A thick broken branch lay half embedded in the muddy soil of the yard. It had been used to jam the door shut. Bernard's meaning was clear; this had been no accident.

Around the front of the building, the Bouchard twins had retreated to the tree line on the opposite side of the road. The burning building lit up the countryside for what seemed like miles around. Red-hot embers were shooting high into the air and an unearthly screaming came from the interior. Godbert looked on with grim satisfaction. "That's it, squeal little piggies."

Gilbert looked at his brother in horror. "You've the devil in you brother, always had, always will."

Godbert just grunted in reply his eyes fixed in fascination on the scene of devastation playing out before them. Gilbert watched on in horror. Eventually he whispered, "Think anyone got out alive?"

Godbert shook his head. "No one came out the front. I had a log against it. You secured the back tight shut?"

Gilbert hesitated a moment before replying, "A branch, big as I could move, wedged against the door tight."

His brothers red-rimmed eyes turned away from the fire and towards him. "Then the jobs done brother. Might as well head north, join Mudstone if we can find him."

As they rode off, Gilbert glanced behind at the burning wreck of the inn. He thought he saw some movement against the flickering flames. He hoped someone had lived; the branch had been tight against the back door, but not that tight. He thought maybe he was going soft. Whatever the reason there were days when even he couldn't stomach everything his brother was capable of.

At dawn, Will and Bernard stood looking at the smouldering remains of the inn. The rest of the party were trying to get a little sleep in the stables. Bernard looked at him speculatively. "What sort of trouble did you get up to in Gloucester?"

Will shrugged his shoulders and looked sadly at the charcoaled timbers. "What's that got to do with the fire?" he asked.

Bernard sighed. "You know this wasn't some accident Will. Someone tried to burn us to death in there. Bloody lucky we're still breathing. You got into a fight in Gloucester that much was obvious when you came back."

"The afternoon you spent talking to Brother Luke, Osbert and I went to take in the sights of Gloucester. We got into a fight with some locals in an alehouse called the Bell."

"I know the place well and it's not known for its fights. It's generally quiet and believe me I've been in a few alehouses in Gloucester. These locals, what they look like?"

Will thought for a minute and said, "There were two of them. The first a big fellow, piggy eyes. The second thin as a rake, rat-faced. The big one made all the noise, said he'd enjoy gutting me like a pig. Almost like he singled us out."

"This big man, you say he had piggy eyes?"

"Yes and sort of unfocused, got into a mad rage within a heartbeat. Had me pinned up against the wall by the throat."

Bernard's eyes narrowed suspiciously. "Tell me, was he bald apart from a tuft of white hair and maybe it looked like one of his ears had been chewed off?"

"Yes! You know the man?"

"I know both of them and they're not local to Gloucester. The big one goes by the name Godbert, the thin one is his twin brother, Gilbert. The Bouchard twins. The dregs of

Draychester. You were lucky to get away. It's not mere chance they attacked you and Osbert."

"You think they've followed us all the way here?"

Bernard gestured to the smouldering heap that had been the inn. "Believe me they're more than capable of doing this. I've had the feeling all along that we've been followed. I didn't see them last night, but that doesn't mean they didn't see us in the inn. Any of the pilgrim party survive?"

"A few came out the door behind us. As for the rest, they're somewhere under that," Will said, nodding to the burnt heap. "Want me to ask if they saw these men, twins you say?"

Bernard nodded. "Yes they're twin brothers, obviously they're not identical, bloody spawn of the devil that's what they are."

It was hard to get any response out of the surviving pilgrims. They were too shocked to make much sense. One said they remembered two men, one big, one thin, that had entered the inn and then swiftly left again. It wasn't much to go on but it seemed to convince Bernard.

Will asked, "But why attack us? I swear, I'd never clapped eyes on them before Gloucester. What have we done to them?"

"It's not what we've done to them boy. It's who we are. We're the bishop's men. Whoever paid them, and I have a good idea who that treacherous bastard is, has a quarrel with our master."

"They'd burn men alive for a quarrel?"

Bernard laughed without humour. "For far less boy, far less. You're a good lad, smart with it, but you've a lot to learn. Life is cheap boy and for our masters it can all seem like a game. Remember that lad and you might stay alive a bit longer. I won't always be around." With that he threw an arm around Wills shoulder and said, "Come on, let's get away from this place. The main thing is we're still alive. I need to get this stink out of my nose and there's nothing more we can do here. Let's get the horses, we're leaving."

15

THE BRIDGE HERMIT

It had been a busy day collecting tolls for the bridge hermit. Early in the morning, there had been a large party of pilgrims going south. Then, from the other direction, had come a steady stream of travellers crossing the bridge heading for the local market town. By mid-afternoon he was tired. The sun was warm on his back as he rested against the parapet in the middle of the narrow stone bridge. The money belonged to the local abbey who had long ago granted him the right to collect a penny from each traveller who crossed the single stone span. It was supposed to be used to keep the bridge in good repair, but in reality most of it went straight into the abbot's coffers. He didn't really mind, and he took the little he needed to sustain his frugal existence. The rest was collected by one of the fat monks who came each evening to return the spoils of the day to the abbey. The hermit lived in a low thatched hut, which was situated at one end of the bridge.

The previous night it had rained hard and the water that had collected on the hills some miles upstream had swollen the river. The water flowed fast underneath the single arch of the bridge. He was looking down into the muddy water when he heard a horse approaching along the south bank of the river. The rider turned the horse onto the narrow bridge and approached the hermit who leaned on the stone wall in the middle.

"A penny if you please sir. Alms for the upkeep of this good bridge."

The rider looked down at him and sniffed dismissively. "A penny eh? Been a good day has it? Many travellers crossing?"

"A fair amount of traffic sir. This morning was busy, not seen anyone this last half hour or so."

The rider looked around. There was nobody else anywhere in sight. "Good, good, glad to hear it. You'll have plenty of coin then?" Sir Roger didn't wait for an answer. He shoved his foot into the middle of the hermit's chest and sent him tumbling over the side of the bridge. The man didn't even have time to scream as he plunged into the muddy water head first. He disappeared without a trace, swept away by the torrent of water passing under the bridge. Sir Roger hardly gave him a second thought as he gently urged the war horse onwards across the bridge. He came to a halt outside the hermit's hut and leisurely dismounted.

The door was a stout affair but stood half ajar. He pushed it fully open and entered the dim interior. It smelled musty and damp. There was a rough table, a bed with some grubby looking blankets, some simple cooking utensils and not much else apart from a small wooden chest secured by a chain to the back wall. It was bound with two strips of hammered iron. It also proved to be locked. He took a short dagger from inside his boot and expertly picked the lock. The bottom of the chest was covered with two or three layers of pennies. He grunted with satisfaction and went back outside to get a leather bag out of his saddle bag.

Back inside the hut he quickly filled the bag with the money. He left a thin spread of coins across the bottom of the chest and re-locked it with his knife. This way it didn't look like the hermit had been robbed. Who was to say how much he'd collected that day and after all the chest was still here. When they eventually began to wonder, they would probably think the fool had simply fallen in the river. Which he had of course, with a little help from Sir Roger's boot. The bag was heavy when he picked it up. Enough to finance a good part of the trip further north and if he came across any more hermits, well, he could always top it up.

16

THE BEAST

Gilbert was more tired than he could ever remember being before. They had been riding for days, stopping only briefly along the way, sometimes sleeping by the roadside. The farther north they went, the worse the weather seemed to become. This last day it had rained constantly. His clothes clung wetly to his body, and he thought he had caught a chill. His forehead was burning, and he was shivering violently. More than anything he was miserable. Godbert seemed unaffected by the journey. The rain just seemed to run off his broad shoulders as he plodded on. They'd skirted York two days ago. They could see the city walls from some distance away and Gilbert had urged his brother to enter the city. He longed for a warm fire and a cup of ale. They still had enough coin to get blind drunk and go whoring for a week. What was the hurry?

Godbert had just shrugged. "Find this bloody village of Mudstone's first. The city can wait."

There was no reasoning with his brother when he was in this mood. Gilbert had silently cursed Mudstone. Why on earth had he agreed to this crazy trek halfway across

England? Now in the God-forsaken wilderness that was the moors beyond York he needed to stop, get dry, eat and sleep or he'd drop from the horse. "Godbert I can't go on like this. I'm not built like you brother. I'm ill God damn you, I need rest!"

Godbert looked around at his brother, seemingly waking from a stupor. He looked around at the windswept, sodden moors in surprise. "Best find some shelter then."

At a bend in the road, a track led off to the left downhill into a wooded valley. They were about halfway down the hillside when Gilbert spotted what he thought was a cave in the rock face high above the track. "Up there brother," he shouted and gestured at the opening.

An hour later Gilbert was finally starting to get warm in front of a fire that Godbert had built in the cave's mouth. It wasn't exactly comfortable lying on the hard rock floor but with his thick riding cloak over him he could finally feel his hands and feet again. "Wake me up in an hour or two brother." Godbert as usual merely grunted at him and poked the fire with a stick.

∼

The beast of Togmoor was mildly irritated. He'd been sleeping for some time when he'd been rudely disturbed. Somebody was making a hell of a lot of noise in his lair not to mention heat and light. It was bloody well not on. He opened one sleepy eye and found there was a fire crackling away not twenty feet in-front of his nose. One of those annoying man things he occasionally ate seemed to be tending it, his back towards him. Another one seemed to be lying down on the other side of the fire asleep.

To be honest, he preferred sheep, maybe the odd cow

now and again for variety. He only ate the man things when they irritated him. There was a time when they would occasionally come up to the cave and leave him offerings. In his youth, it had been a young female tied to a wooden stake at the entrance to his cave. Very considerate they'd been, twice a year without fail, why they did it he could never work out but he'd be a fool to turn down a free meal. Things had changed though. There seemed to be more and more of the things and no one had any respect these days. Coming up here at all hours of the day and night, lighting fires and making noise. It was getting to the point where a respectable beast couldn't get a minute rest. A year or two back a whole crowd of them had come up onto the moors. Thrown actual rocks at him and they carried those little fire things on the end of long sticks with them. Running all over they'd been. Sticking the fire down holes and into caves. In the end he'd had to eat a few before they would leave. It had been purely defensive you understand, given him terrible indigestion for days. And now here were two in his actual home and they'd lit a fire on his own bloody doorstep!

He slowly got to his feet, opened his huge jaws to their maximum extent and moved forward until his hot wet breath was tickling the back of the man thing's neck. Now he thought about it; he was quite hungry. He couldn't really remember when he'd last eaten.

The man thing turned around and found itself staring into two eyes glowing like red-hot coals and a gaping hole filled with rows of razor-sharp teeth. The beast stuck its tongue out and slowly licked the man thing's face, savouring the meaty flavour.

Before the thing could scream, or even twitch more than a terrified eyebrow, he bit its head clean off in one fluid

Death Of The Official

motion. The head was crunchy but not unpleasant. The man thing's body fell with a heavy thump into the middle of the fire throwing a shower of burning embers and a spurt of thick red arterial blood onto the one lying down.

The beast fished the headless torso out of the fire by spearing it with one of his massive tusks. He found the brief heat had nicely crisped the meat. The one that had been asleep jumped to its feet, made a blood curdling scream and exited the cave at a surprising pace.

He give the man thing five minutes head start. The beast decided he'd got lazy sleeping in here all winter and half the summer. He needed the exercise and there was nothing he liked better than a good chase. Not that it would last long.

∽

Gilbert had never known terror like it. He'd seen and done things that would make many a man shudder, but the thing pursuing him down the track was a terror beyond his wildest nightmares.

He'd gone hoarse screaming, not that it'd done any good. He ran faster than he'd ever moved in his life, but he could feel the hot breath of the beast on his neck. He made it back up the valley to the end of the track where it joined with the main road. The beast was always just a pace behind, seemingly toying with him.

As he emerged onto the road, with one massive swipe of a claw it raked down his back. It was like taking a scythe to a side of prime bacon. With a vicious thrust Gilbert was impaled on a sharp tusk, lifted clean of his feet and then noisily consumed head first.

It was all over in less than a minute. His boots turned

out to be particularly tough eating. The beast spat them out and left them lying there in the road. Each contained a complete foot and a long shin bone sucked clean of flesh.

TRAVIS'S JOURNEY

How Travis had got this far he was hard pressed to remember. His journey had been one set of traumatic events after another.

He'd stumbled out of the gates of Draychester in Sir Roger's wake. Having no idea in which direction Yorkshire lay, where Sir Roger went north, Travis had hobbled off south. At night he slept in ditches by the side of the road and ate turnips he stole from the fields. He shunned the small villages along the way, fearing he'd likely be locked up or worse.

Completely exhausted, he found himself at a small harbour on the seacoast of Dorset. That night he slept on the quayside behind piles of old nets and rotting fish heads. The following morning he was dragged to his feet by two of the crew of a cog anchored in the harbour. He became the newest and mostly unwilling member of the motley crew.

The ship was carrying a cargo of wool to Flanders. Travis had never even seen the sea before let alone travelled across it. He was violently ill for the three days the trip took. The crew declared him useless and threw him down into the hold. They'd intended to throw him overboard but the mate, in an uncharacteristic moment of pity for the pathetic figure, suggested that they could sell him to another ship when they got to Flanders. Instead they tossed him up onto the quayside in disgust, not considering him worth the effort.

He crawled alongside the cobbled quay until he heard English voices and dropped into a ship loading barrels of wine. He lay there exhausted, staring up at the sky whilst the vessel took him back to England.

The ship made its first port of call at Gravesend near the mouth of the River Thames. Here he was found and hauled, half dead, from the hold. A priest from a nearby chancery chapel took pity on him and he found himself well cared for. It took over a week to recover his strength.

Travis, unwilling to give up on his last remaining link to his past, was determined to join Mudstone in Yorkshire. He took passage north on a ship returning to Newcastle. The priest, shaking his head in bafflement, had agreed to pay the few pennies cost.

~

He left the ship when it called in at Kingston upon Hull. He hoped to find his master in York so he spent two-and-a-half days trudging the forty miles. He was wandering aimlessly down Petergate in the city when he was suddenly hauled backwards out of the street into a narrow passageway.

"God's teeth, Travis! I thought it was you. You've lost weight man, you look like a skinny rat. What took you so long?"

"Sir Roger! You've no idea what I've been through to find you, I took a ship..."

Sir Roger shut him up by grabbing him roughly round the throat and then cuffing him across the head. "Don't whine Travis, you're mistaken if you think I'm remotely interested in your babbling. We've work to do. While you've been idling away I've been busy. Pick up those two sacks and follow me."

There were two heavy looking sacks placed against the narrow wall of the alley. He opened one and found it full of curled lengths of heavy rope, the other was full of hand-made iron nails. In his enfeebled state Travis could barely lift them. With a sack draped over either shoulder he shuffled off after Sir Roger into the crowded streets of York.

Minutes later they were sitting in a small chamber Sir Roger had rented at an inn near the city's heart. Sir Roger had a large flagon of ale which he didn't offer to share.

"I'm not sure your feeble mind is capable of understanding all of this Travis but I'll tell you anyway. I went out into the God forsaken wasteland that lies to the northwest of the city, looking for my brother's manor. It's a horrid and vast solitude. The moors stretch for miles. The manor my brother left me is as worthless as I imagined it would be. It consists of a large dung heap and four or five run down hovels. The inhabitants are frankly inbred sheep worrying simpletons. I can tell you I was not happy, and I gave some of them a damn good thrashing."

"The manor is worthless my lord? Then what are we to do?"

"It's not totally worthless Travis. It has one redeeming feature. I was leaving in disgust and rode up over the hill and what do you think I find in the next valley?"

Travis shook his head. If Sir Roger was still here, it had to be worth his while.

"What I found Travis was a bloody great monastery.

Huge building, lots of well-fed monks, apparently they own half the grazing rights in the county. More sheep than people out in those valleys. And like most monks Travis they're greedy. Which is a good thing for us."

"It is?"

"It is! I rode down there and had an interesting conversation with the fat abbot. He's a pompous ass named Thomas Burley. Lives in splendour, his chambers wouldn't disgrace those of the king. They're supposed to be Cistercians but they've long abandoned any pretence of living by the rule. When I got back to the city, I made discreet enquiries as to his character. Which means the first thing I did was trawl the taverns and whore houses. He's the kind of church man I can do business with Travis, totally corrupt and utterly depraved."

"A disgrace to his order my lord. You'll sell the manor to them?"

Sir Roger shrugged dismissively. "That was my first thought, but no, in the end I offered the abbot my special talents."

"If you're to become a monk my lord, what will become of me?"

Sir Roger cuffed him over the head. "Always thinking of yourself Travis! Don't be an idiot. I'm no more becoming a monk as you are becoming pope. I'm going to steal and kill for the monks and make a fortune in the process. To start with, we need to solve the problem of the Beast. Apparently it ate a dozen of the abbot's quarry men only last week."

Travis licked his lips nervously. "The Beast?"

"Yes the Beast. You're going to be of great help there Travis…"

Death Of The Official

A little over two days later and Travis found himself tied and nailed tightly to a wooden post. He struggled in vain to rock the post free. They had hammered it deep into the mud at the bottom of the quarry in the remote north Yorkshire valley.

Sir Roger sat on a stone ledge about thirty feet above and whistled softly to himself. Beside him was a huge block of stone balanced finely on the lip of the ledge. Any sudden movement would undoubtedly send it crashing down on the unfortunate man below. They were, as Sir Roger had happily put it when lashing Travis to the post, "Beast hunting" and Travis was the final bait.

Throughout the afternoon there had been a series of blood-curdling screams slowly advancing down the valley towards them. Sir Roger wasn't in the least surprised by the screaming. It marked the progress of the Beast though several villagers he had staked out at convenient intervals down the track.

The men from his newly gained manor had taken some persuading. He'd had to wallop several of them over the head before roping them together and hauling them off down the valley. Still, the hard work had been well worth it. As far as he could tell the Beast was right on schedule, he could hear it now, chewing on its latest victim just out of sight.

Even he was impressed when it finally came into view around a bend in the track. "What a magnificent creature Travis, look at those jaws and it's almost the size of a donkey!"

Travis's only response was to let out a terrified scream at the gore splattered horror galloping towards him.

Sir Roger shouted encouragingly from above. "Keep calm Travis, not long now and we're done,"

The abbot had said they had been having a spot of trouble and seeing the Beast he could well believe it. Every time the monks had come up here to do some quarrying for the ever growing abbey, the Beast had picked off some unfortunate soul. He'd implied the Beast was the last wolf in Yorkshire. Sir Roger wasn't sure the description was entirely accurate. There may have been some wolf ancestry but if so it had cross bred with a five foot tall wild boar which was now poking Travis in the foot with a large tusk.

Travis was screaming at the top of his lungs. This set off a round of excited grunting and squealing from the Beast as it ripped off the left leg of his hose. It seemed to Sir Roger to be unwrapping Travis before tucking in. The noise was deafening. He was enjoying the spectacle, but all good things must come to an end. Just before the Beast had finished stripping Travis, Sir Roger, with exquisite timing, gave the rock next to him the gentlest of pushes. It rocked back and forth on the edge for a second then fell without a sound, straight down.

The beast had just moved around to Travis's side and was directly under the falling stone slab. The huge mass of rock hit the animal dead centre on its back. It disappeared, squashed flat and pulverised into the valley floor. Travis, semi naked and whimpering was still tied to the post, the stone block no more than six inches away from him.

"Well, I think that worked out rather well. You all right down there Travis?"

18

IN YORK

A tense party of the bishop's men and the two mason's apprentices were on the road for another week trudging across England. Bernard always watchful, Will mainly silent, Osbert uttering prophecies of doom at regular intervals. Derby, Chesterfield, Doncaster and the smaller villages and towns in between rose before and fell behind them as they headed north.

Finally the party rode through one of the gates of the great city of York, second only to London in size and importance in the kingdom. The mason's apprentices headed straight for the minster and the others made their way through the crowded streets to the castle.

Sir Thomas de Pokelyngtone, Sheriff of Yorkshire, was hung over. He sat slumped at the table in the chamber he used to conduct his day business. The shutters of the room were closed tightly against the bright sunshine flooding the castle courtyard. His tolerance for daylight was directly proportional to his intake of wine. A small flickering beeswax candle cast a golden glow over Pokelyngtone's dishevelled figure.

There was a knock on the rough wooden door of the chamber. The sheriff lowered his head onto the table and placed his hands over his ears. The knock came again.

"Bugger off and leave me be," he groaned.

A muffled voice came from the other side of the door. "There are three men here seeking an audience with you my lord. They are Jocelyn Gifford's men."

"For pity's sake man, can't it wait until later?"

The door opened a crack and the sheriff's clerk stuck his head through. He blinked in the dim light. "They are Bishop Gifford's men my lord."

The sheriff sighed. "Yes, yes. You've told me once already. I know who Jocelyn Gifford is. I might be a drunken old sod but I haven't completely lost my wits."

He suddenly felt quite nauseous and belched ominously.

"Can I show them up my lord?"

"No you bloody well cannot!"

He belched again, staggered over to the window, threw open the shutters, half blinding himself in the process and projectile vomited into the courtyard below. He lay slumped over the windowsill for a minute, his head hanging over the ledge. Eventually he opened his eyes and saw three men stood at the doorway to the tower below. They were looking up at him.

"Now you can show them up clerk."

~

"My lord, we're here on the Bishop of Draychester's business. The bishop's official in his manor of Sodham has been found murdered. You and the coroner will have made some investigation my lord? We hope you may be able to enlighten us of the circumstances?"

The sheriff looked at Will blankly. He shuddered and belched noisily suddenly feeling sick again. He leaned against the wall as the chamber swayed around him. "Enlighten you of the circumstances... have you lost your wits man? Do you even know where Sodham is?"

Before Will could reply, Osbert said, "To the north of the city my lord."

With some difficulty, the sheriff focused his bloodshot eyes on Osbert. "And what, pray tell, are you boy?"

Osbert bristled. "I am a bishop's clerk my lord."

"Ah, another bloody clerk, just what I need. Can you tell me how many people reside within the walls of this city clerk?"

Osbert opened his mouth to reply, but the sheriff held up a finger to silence him. "Never mind, I'll tell you. Damn near seven thousand. I wager there's no place more populous in the realm other than London itself. Day after day I have to deal with a river of theft, thuggery, wife beating, mob violence, general mayhem and murder. And that's just within the walls of the city let alone the county, and you ask me about Sodham! Do you know how I cope boy?"

Osbert shook his head slowly.

"I drink boy, I drink to excess. I'll be blind drunk by noon today. That's if I'm lucky."

Bernard cleared his throat and said, "And Sodham my lord?"

"Sodham? What of Sodham! It's a decaying dung heap in a valley set in the middle of a God forsaken moor. It's desolate, lawless and of no consequence I can possibly think of. I haven't set foot there for about twenty years and I have no intention of doing so again. I know your man is dead. It's been properly recorded, and I even sent a message to Gifford informing him so. It was more than it warranted but I felt obliged because your master has the ear of the king. To the best of my recollection, your man was reported to have had his throat cut. Wouldn't be surprised if he actually did it himself, the poor bastard must have thought he'd been exiled. I suggest you go there yourself if you want to know more. Good luck."

The sheriff slumped down onto a stool at the table.

Bernard tried again, "Surely the matter was reported to the coroner my lord?"

In exasperation the sheriff turned to his own clerk and said, "Show them to the coroner's quarters, then bring me some wine. On second thoughts bring me the wine first and don't bloody well disturb me for the rest of the day unless I specifically call you."

With that the sheriff put his head down on the table.

"Yes my lord," said the sheriff's clerk.

He found a half empty wine jug on the floor, placed it in front of his master and then ushered them out of the chamber.

As they made their way down the stairs Will asked, "Is he like that a lot?"

The man shrugged. "It's a great responsibility being sheriff."

"A lucrative one no doubt as well," said Bernard.

"My lord carries out his responsibilities as he sees fit. Not my place to question his methods. Now if you follow me I'll take you over to see the coroner, William de Newby, if he's here."

They made their way across the busy courtyard, through

a gateway across a smaller courtyard and through a doorway at the base of another of the castles many towers. They climbed the stairs to the first floor. The door of the chamber was open and they could see a grey-haired, studious looking man sat before a table covered with documents.

He looked up in annoyance. "What is it?"

The clerk gestured at the bishop's men. "I am sorry to disturb you my lord. These are officials of the bishop of Draychester. The sheriff has asked if you would speak to them relating to the death at Sodham. The manor belongs to the diocese of Draychester."

"In that case I suppose you'd better come in. This time of the day I've no doubt my friend the sheriff was not in a good humour. I'm William de Newby, coroner. Please gentlemen, take a seat and I'll tell you what I know."

They pulled up some stools and made themselves comfortable. "So can you tell us anything about the death of the bishops official? You held an inquest?" asked Will.

"There was no inquest, nor will there be."

Osbert said, "Surely the law requires it?"

The coroner gave them a weary smile. "You have to understand the situation there. The moors are sparsely populated, lawless, and always dangerous. Sodham itself has been in decline since the great pestilence and it's half in ruins. I'd be surprised if there were forty people in the whole parish. We seldom venture into those parts, even if we hear of a death. To the north of Sodham the great Abbey of Ribsdale controls most of the land for miles around. Abbot Burley looks after his own affairs and we have no jurisdiction there."

"But your writ and the sheriff's does include Sodham?" asked Will.

"Theoretically. You've seen how the sheriff is. Don't be

deceived, he's a good man, but he's worn down by his duties. There's more than enough to occupy him here in the city. He's not going to tramp across the moors on what will probably be a worthless exercise. Men die all the time. We investigate what we can, the rest we leave to God's justice."

"You didn't think to go yourself?" demanded Bernard.

De Newby gave a humourless laugh. "Only if I'd wanted my throat cut. I'd need the sheriff and his men to guarantee my safety and even then I'd doubt any of the locals would be willing to give evidence."

Bernard said, "So what you're saying is no official ever goes there? It's beyond the law?"

"I didn't say that. You must understand we have other priorities here in the city. I visited the abbey of Ribsdale on official business three years ago. The party was myself and five of the sheriff's men as an armed guard and on the return journey we came back via Sodham. There was little to recommend it. There's a church and a priest of sorts if he's still alive. The only other building of any size is the inn run by a man the name of John Taverner. He comes into York for supplies once every couple of weeks or so. He reported the death of your man to the sheriff, claimed the dead man's throat had been cut. As I haven't seen the body, nor likely to, I can't comment on what killed the fellow. I recorded the bare facts, and that gentlemen, is as much as I know."

Will nodded. "Then we'll need to ask the questions ourselves. Our bishop has sent us to investigate the state of the manor and to find out what happened to the first official he dispatched. We'll be leaving for Sodham as soon as possible. Will the sheriff provide an escort do you think?"

The coroner shrugged. "The only thing I can promise you is that I'll ask him. If you come to grief, he'd be a fool to report that he'd offered no assistance."

Osbert's face turned even grimmer than usual. "I knew it! We're doomed. God alone knows who or what's lurking up on the moors. I've heard rumours of a giant beast."

The coroner chuckled and said, "Don't believe everything you hear young clerk. It's outlaws not mythical beasts you need to worry about."

They made their farewells to the coroner who promised to send word to them if he could persuade the sheriff to assist. They left the castle and headed towards the mighty York Minster to seek lodging within the precinct. As bishop's men they would be assured of a bed for the night.

The liberty of Saint Peter's had sturdy walls twelve feet high separating the minster from the town. They entered via one of the four guarded gates and found a grassed and cobbled area lay within. Dotted around were the various residences and official buildings, all dwarfed by the minster itself. Within the hour they were resting in a comfortable chamber of the archbishop's guesthouse.

∽

Early the following morning there was a knock on their chamber door. One of the guesthouse boys had brought some visitors to them. They were three of the sheriff's men. The coroner had evidently persuaded the sheriff to provide an escort to Sodham. There was a dark-haired, sturdy looking man in his mid-thirties and two others not much older than boys. They entered the small chamber and the two sets of men looked at each other dubiously.

The older man introduced himself as David Padget, a sergeant in the sheriff's service. The two younger men were newly recruited to the city watch and Padget had borrowed them for this duty. Finally Bernard said, "Well three of you is better than nothing! Don't suppose you're too keen on us either eh?"

Padget's face broke into a grin. "We've had more promising duties, but the sheriff commands and we obey. I for one don't mind getting out from under the sheriff's eye for a week or two."

Bernard grinned back. "You may live to regret that statement my friend. Any of you been to Sodham before?"

"I have," said Padget.

"You know it well?"

He nodded. "I did once, I lived there for a couple of years when I was a lad."

"The coroner has told you the reason for our journey?" asked Will.

"He has. The coroner knows I lived in Sodham. He recommended the sheriff send me with you. The truth is I left Sodham some fifteen years and what seems like a lifetime ago. I haven't set foot in the place since."

19

RIBSDALE ABBEY

Sir Roger Mudstone sat on his horse atop the ridge that separated his own, rather pathetic manor, from the splendour that was Ribsdale Abbey. He gazed down with envy at the power and wealth that lay below. The abbey precinct was huge, it enclosed acres of land all set behind a stone wall almost ten feet high. Within the wall the precinct had been divided into separate compounds. He marvelled at the industry of these monks hidden away out here. The entrance was via a large stone gatehouse set in the outer wall. From this a walled lane led to an inner gatehouse, which had two gateways, one led to an outer court, the other to the inner court. Even from this distance he could see the outer court was a hive of activity. There were industrial buildings, a forge, mills, and tanneries, as well as workshops. He could see barns, stables, orchards, dovecotes and fish ponds. The inner court contained a bake-house and brew-house. He knew the infirmary, the abbot's lodgings, stores and a guest house were also located there. At the very core of the site lay the church and cloisters.

A short while later and he was sat opposite Thomas Burley, Abbot of Ribsdale in the dining chamber of his sumptuous lodgings. Burley tore a chicken wing free from the carcass of the roasted bird set before him and crammed it into his mouth. Speaking with a mouth full of food he said, "So Mudstone, the Beast is dead, yes?"

Sir Roger delicately cut a piece of chicken with his knife and regarded the man across the table. Sir Roger was many things, most of them obnoxious, but he knew his table manners. He thought Burley was a disgusting oaf, but he held his contempt in check. "Squashed flat my lord. Great big boar, a pity, it was a magnificent animal."

The abbot crammed more chicken into his already overflowing mouth and spluttered, "A man-eater though."

"Yes indeed my lord. Ate half the villagers from my own manor. A terrible thing to see."

The abbot waved a chicken drumstick at Sir Roger dismissively. "Don't worry about it. I'll lend you some of the lay brothers. Soon get your manor in order. I'll even find you more serfs for the place."

"You're most generous my lord," Sir Roger said dryly. He glanced at one of the serving girls refilling the abbot's cup. She gave him a saucy wink. "You don't follow closely to the rule then my lord? I see there's no shortage of female company for the good brothers."

The abbot gave the girl's rump a firm squeeze. She giggled. "Got to move with the times you know Mudstone. I tend towards a more, shall we say, liberal interpretation of the monastic rules. I see no reason not to enjoy some pleasures of the wider world."

Sir Roger nodded sagely. "Well I must say I admire your enlightened vision, I really do."

An extremely large black dog slunk into the room through the open doorway and lay down in front of the fire, its huge bulk blocking out much of the warmth. It wasn't a breed Sir Roger was familiar with. He thought perhaps it was another moors mutant. It turned its head, looked directly at him, and growled menacingly. He looked back impassively.

"Be quiet Beelzebub. Here have some of this." The abbot tore a leg bone from his chicken and threw it to the dog. It snapped the meat from the air with a sound like a mantrap closing. "Don't mind the dog Mudstone. One of our tenants up on the moor breeds them for us. Still got the sister of this bitch up there with him. What do you think of her?"

"Very impressive my lord." He said it without much enthusiasm. He didn't get on well with dogs and this one looked decidedly dangerous.

"They make tremendous guard dogs Mudstone, bloody temperamental though. She'll take your arm off if you're not careful and she comes and goes as she pleases."

The abbot took a noisy slurp from his cup that left a thin red dribble of wine down his chin. He belched noisily and said, "You're a useful fellow to know Mudstone. You get things done, a rare quality these days. I plan to extend the abbey's land and influence to the south. You can be a great help to me Mudstone. The rewards will not be inconsiderable."

Sir Roger summoned up one of his very rare smiles. It was a strain, but he felt the moment deserved it. "I would be only too happy to assist my lord. May I suggest we start with the manor of Sodham?"

The abbot raised a quizzical eyebrow and said, "Ah yes,

Sodham. I hear you granted it to the Bishop of Draychester?"

Sir Roger's eye twitched uncontrollably for a few seconds. "That was a misunderstanding which Gifford took advantage of. I intend to have the manor back."

"It won't be easy. Bishop Gifford is a formidable man. He has friends in very high places."

Sir Roger viciously speared a chunk of meat with his knife, "Never the less..."

The abbot said, "The place is a ruin. Almost worthless in its current state. Maybe he can be persuaded to sell? The abbey would be happy to buy it."

"I think not my lord. He's one of those stubborn types. I don't believe we can change his mind with coin."

20

THE MOOR

Two days north of York and the party of riders were on the high moors. It was a windswept landscape of open skies and miles of heather-covered peat moor. The road was little more than a rutted track, hard to follow in places. Across the vast open hillsides could be seen grazing sheep. Will rode beside the sergeant, David Padget. He said, "I don't see any villages up here. The sheep, who do they belong to?"

"They all belong to Ribsdale Abbey. Most of the moor belongs to the monks, gifted long ago. As far as you can see, it's all theirs."

"And Sodham? The manor has no moorland rights?"

David shrugged and said, "Some. The manor is situated in a valley. It's good land in the valley bottom but the monks control most of the moorland grazing."

"There's ill feeling over it?"

David gave a sour little laugh. "Believe me, there's no love lost between the good brothers and what's left of Sodham's parishioners. Over the years the abbey has acquired more and more of the surrounding land. That and the great pestilence have strangled the life out of the place."

~

Sometime in the early afternoon they came across a low-slung stone building with a turf roof. It was set back from the road down a short muddy track. A thin trickle of smoke rose from a ragged hole in the roof. Bernard brought his horse to a halt and rubbed a weary hand over his face. "Will, Osbert. Be good lads and take a look who's home. We could do with some respite."

"You know this place David?" asked Will.

"No, but it's been a long time. I'd advise caution. The strangers they get out here usually bring trouble."

Will got down from his horse. Osbert sat motionless on his. Will said, "Come on Osbert, let's take a look."

The clerk grimaced. "There could be anyone down there, robbers, murderers, this place is cursed. Can't we just ride on?"

"No we bloody well can't," snapped Bernard. "It's gone noon and I for one wouldn't mind a rest in the shade and out of this bloody wind. Get your backside down that track and seek some hospitality. You need to learn we're bishop's men not mice." Quick as a flash he used his booted foot to tip Osbert off his horse. The others laughed as a red faced Osbert extracted his head from the roadside heather.

Will pulled him to his feet. "Can't you stop looking for the worst in every situation?"

~

As they approached the building the rough leather sheet

that served as a door was pulled back. A small, mean looking, potbellied old man emerged. He stomped over to them and from the distance of about three feet bellowed, "What the hell do you want?"

His breath smelled like rotting meat and they both stepped back hastily. Will put on his best smile. "Just some travellers on the road my friend. Bishop's men. We're only seeking an hour's rest out of the sun and wind."

"Travellers eh... where you heading?"

"Sodham."

The man spat disgustingly into the mud at their feet. It wasn't quite the hospitality they were hoping for. "There's nothing for you here. Move on," said the man, then glanced over his shoulder and shouted, "Ripthruckle."

The two looked back at him bewildered. Will thought it might be some peculiar Yorkshire curse. Then out of the corner of his eye an enormous black shape slunk from around the corner of the building to stand shoulder high at the man's side. The old man spoke slowly, "This is Ripthruckle, and she's hungry."

Ripthruckle was a huge black hound of indeterminate breed. Its black, lifeless eyes bored into them, saliva dribbling from its mouth and it began a low-pitched growl that continued to increase in volume. It was straight out of Osbert's worst nightmares. He stood rooted to the spot, his mouth hanging open. Will slowly backed away. He grabbed hold of Osbert by the arm and pulled him along. "Very sorry to have disturbed you. We'll be on our way."

About ten feet away from the nightmare they turned around and started to walk and then to run. From behind they heard an unearthly howl. Glancing back Will saw Ripthruckle was following, stalking them slowly. Will put on a spurt of speed and Osbert quickly outdid him. They raced up the track back to the road with the monstrous hound loping along behind. The others had already seen the beast following the pair up the track. The horses were becoming nervous at its approach. David drew his sword and shouted, "Christ's bones! Look at that thing. Prepare to ride."

Osbert arrived first and was hauled back onto his horse by Bernard lifting him up off the ground by the front of his tunic. Will managed to half climb half jump onto his mount and they were all on the move down the road with the hell hound chasing after them. The horses were spooked and broke into a gallop A good half mile later and the hound, with one last baleful howl, finally gave up the chase and they fought the horses down to a more manageable pace.

～

An hour later and David brought them to a stop at a crossroads. To the left a track led up to the crest of a hill and vanished over it. "I know this road, we go to the left here. Sodham is over the ridge and down into the next valley."

A cry disturbed the otherwise silent moorland making them all jump. In the far distance a figure on a mule appeared on the road. It headed towards them slowly. A faint cackling could be heard. "What is that?" asked Bernard.

"It can't be. Surely not here," said Will.

"What you babbling on about lad?"

Will held up a hand. "Quiet. Just listen."

They heard the sound again. Bernard squinted, trying to bring the figure into focus. After a moment he said, "God's teeth. It's not possible!"

"It's her," Will insisted.

Bernard shook his head, "It can't be."

Osbert said, "It's her all right. I'd recognise that cackling anywhere."

David shaded his eyes from the sun and gazed at the approaching figure. "You know who it is?"

Will nodded slowly, "We left her a hundred and fifty miles south of here at a nunnery. She's the last person I'd ever believe I'd lay eyes on again."

A minute later and the party were subjected to wails of mad cackling as Agnes greeted them in her own unique way. Around her neck she wore a gold ring set with a diamond. Will knew it well, he'd last seen it had hung between the not inconsiderable breasts of the Prioress of St Michael's Sandford. Osbert shuddered. "Only the devil could get her to this place. It's not humanly possible that she could have made her way here unaided. The old hag must be a witch."

Bernard smiled wryly and said, "Shut up Osbert. You know I had the feeling someone was following us. Thought it was the Bouchard twins again. Maybe it was just you, eh Agnes? The nunnery wasn't to your liking? I see you took back a little something from the prioress?"

A wave of cackling was the only response. Bernard nodded. "And I see you're as talkative as ever old girl."

"Is the old crone mad?" asked David.

Will, still gazing in astonishment at the woman, replied, "She's probably got more wits than the rest of us put together."

"Does she ever shut up?"

"Oh you'll get used to that," said Bernard.

Will turned his horse to the left and said, "So are we going to Sodham or not?"

21

SODHAM IN GRIMSDALE

"It doesn't look too bad," said Will, trying to convince himself more than anyone else.

Osbert's voice trembled. "We're all doomed, it'll be a miracle if we ever leave this valley."

"If you don't stop moaning, it will be a bloody miracle if I let you leave," said Bernard sarcastically.

Looking down into the valley it was true Sodham in Grimsdale held what could only be described as a desolate attraction. The Grimsdale valley was green and fertile after the high moors they had crossed. It was well wooded and a small river flowed along the valley bottom. A now ruined bridge had once crossed the water and what remained of the village sat on the opposite bank. The place had been much bigger in the past. David had said as much, the great pestilence had accounted for the death of over two-thirds of the population in his father's time. Will said, "Can't see anyone about. Maybe they're all in the inn?"

Bernard grunted and said, "Sun is still up, its bit early to have stopped for the day isn't it?"

They started down into the valley, eventually coming to

the ruined bridge. At some point a flood or maybe just the passage of time had undermined one of the stone piers. The central arch had fallen leaving a pile of stone in the middle of the river. The water was shallow by the bridge and they crossed with relative ease. With heavy rain or snow Will thought the crossing would be a different matter. Even now it would be difficult to get a cart across.

The village had shrunk back to its core around the bridge and a little church built of rough stone. At some stage one of the side naves of the church had been pulled down, the building too big to serve the surviving population. There was a single long street. They passed the remains of abandoned houses, roofless and little more than bare shells now. The surrounding plots overgrown in a tangle of weeds. One may have been the original manor house it was hard to tell. There didn't seem to be a soul about. Behind the houses were fields, pasture and meadows all looking neglected.

They came to the only other substantial building in the village, the inn. It was clear Sodham had been wealthy once. The building was large and stone built and would have done justice to a place three times as big. It was badly maintained, there appeared to be several patched holes in the roof and the window shutters were warped and ill fitting. There was a faded sign hung over the door depicting a man with a scythe. From inside came the sound of raised voices and the occasional laugh.

Will placed his hand on the door. "Well someone's alive in there at least."

Bernard looked at Agnes. "Agnes love. Do us a favour. Think you can look after the horses awhile?" He got a high pitched cackle in response. "Just wait here for a bit old girl, we don't want to frighten the locals. Try not to get into any trouble."

As Will pushed on the door Osbert whispered, "Looks like the sort of place they all go quiet when you walk in."

Bernard barged past him. "Osbert you're a bloody fool sometimes."

~

A fire burned in a central hearth and reflected on white scrubbed tables and flagstone floor. The walls were thick stone that wouldn't disgrace a castle. The newcomers looked around at a mixed company of locals, sleeping dogs and the odd chicken. The conversation diminished to a murmur, intelligible to the regulars alone and then subsided into a profound silence. Every eye in the place turned on the intruders.

"Hello," said Bernard to the room in general. No one said anything.

There was an ever more awkward silence which Will broke by saying, "We've come from York."

From behind them a voice said, "So that'll make you strangers then. You'll be wanting the abbey guesthouse, its further up the valley, long time since we took in abbey visitors here."

They turned around to find a scowling man, his face the colour of an old grey sack, looking at them. David looked at the man closely. "I'm no stranger friend and we're not looking for the abbey. I lived here once. Its John isn't it, John Taverner?"

From behind them another voice said, "What's your name son?"

They turned around again. The voice could have been from any of half a dozen old men sat hunched around a table cluttered with drinking cups and scattered with a handful of pennies. Their ages were hard to judge, but the weather-beaten faces suggested years spent outdoors in all seasons. "My name is David Padget."

A sudden outbreak of whispering rippled around the old men's table.

"You look like your grandfather," croaked one of the men.

"You knew my grandfather?"

"Worked alongside him some thirty years. Hard man was Tom."

Bernard said, "We need to speak to the bailiff and the reeve."

A voice said, "You'll have to speak loudly then, they've been in their graves these three years past."

Bernard looked around. "Then I'll state plainly our business. David and his two companions here are the sheriff's men. I'm Bernard and this is Will and Osbert, the Bishop of Draychester has sent us. This manor came into the bishop's possession not long ago. He sent a man here, William Walcott?" There was no response from the room. Bernard continued, "That man is dead. There are things here that need resolving. One way or another they will be resolved. Now if this is still an inn we could do with a bloody drink."

One of the old men gave an almost imperceptible nod to the man stood at the door who David had called John Taverner. He walked over and began clearing a table in the centre of the room. "You'd better sit down," he said with little enthusiasm.

As they took their seats around the long table the room slowly came back to life. One of the old men opposite leaned forward and regarded them with a critical one eyed gaze. He had a wrinkled good natured sort of face, old as he undoubtedly was, his eye was bright and had a roving commission. "Not often we get visitors these days." He looked around at the rest of his companions before continuing, "We were a lot more hospitable once."

Will smiled. "No offence taken. Can we buy you a drink?"

The old man pointed at the tankards scattered across the table. "Aye you can put a drop in these young fella."

John Taverner moved to fill the old men's tankards from a flagon and then came back and stood in front of the table. "So the bishop's men have come to claim his manor. Nobody's given a damn about this place in years, now you can't keep away. Well I hope you've more luck than your last man."

One of the old man said, "Twenty years and I never even laid eyes on our last lord of the manor. Now I hear he's living over in Coxington."

Will asked, "This man in Coxington, you say he was lord of the manor here?"

"He was. The Mudstone's owned this manor and Coxington for generations. Not that I ever clapped eyes on a single one of them. Now your bishop owns this place and next thing a Mudstone has turned up over in the next manor."

Another voice piped up, "I hear he's already whoring it up with the Abbot of Ribsdale."

At the mention of Mudstone Bernard's face had reddened in anger. He slammed his hand down on the table. "I knew it. That bastard Mudstone is already here. There'll be trouble, the man is deranged and sadistic with it. You already know our problems on the road here were no accident."

Will held up his hand. "One thing at a time Bernard, one

thing at a time," he turned to the old men, "The bishop's official, what happened to him?"

The room suddenly became silent again. Bernard said, "Come speak up. One of you had the sense to inform the coroner in York."

John Taverner stood back and rested against the whitewashed wall. Eventually he said, "That was me as reported it. Your man must have got himself in some trouble, ended up dead for it."

Bernard said, "John, come sit with us, have a drink, tell us what you know."

It was more an order than a request. Taverner reluctantly came over to them, topped up their ale, poured himself one and sat down. The background noise in the tavern slowly returned to normal. Will was impatient for more information. "So tell us, he didn't take his own life then?"

Taverner snorted. "Hardly. I'd not wager that any man could slit his own throat in such a way. But then who am I to say. Not my place to play coroner and no real coroner will venture here these days."

"It was you that found him?"

Taverner nodded and pointed at the ceiling. "He'd taken the small chamber above. Been here about a week. Then he was ill for two days, bad guts so he said. Stayed in the room. The evening of the second day I took some food up."

"And?"

"And he was laying there in his bed. His throat was slit ear to ear, like a butchered hog. The bedding was soaked in his blood, it's ruined."

Osbert visibly shuddered. Will said sarcastically, "Your concern for the bedding is touching."

Taverner shrugged. "I didn't ask him to stay here. The

man was a fool, strutting around the valley asking questions. He upset a lot of people in a short time."

Will pressed him. "Enough to get him murdered? He was the bishop's official, there were sure to be consequences?"

"These are dangerous times and the consequences are you're here. I doubt anything will be the same again."

"Why do you say that?" asked Bernard.

"I'll be plain with you. There's been no over-sight of this manor for years, the place is finished and a bishop's official is dead. I imagine you're here to prepare to sell the manor to the abbey. Why else come out here?"

Bernard smiled. "Don't be so sure my friend. The last thing the Bishop of Draychester would do is sell the manor to a bloody monk. He famously hates monks!"

Will nodded in agreement. "I'm sure the bishop has other plans for this place. We've no instructions to sell the manor. I'd say he'd like it to stand on its own two feet."

"Then I hope your bishop has plenty of coin to spend."

Osbert asked the question they all wanted to know, "If not by his own hand then who would murder him in such a brutal fashion?"

Tavener said, "He was up at the abbey the day before he took ill, came back in a foul temper. It's unwise to upset the monks. Draw your own conclusions. I wasn't his keeper, he came and went from here as he pleased. Not my business to know what sort of trouble he got into."

"The body, where is it now?" asked Bernard.

Taverner used his thumb to point at the door. "Long buried. He's across the road there in the church yard. We did the best by him that we could."

Will said, "The room where he was murdered, you can show us?"

"Not much to see. As I said, it's above us here. I'll show you if you wish."

Bernard said, "David you stay here. Have a chat with the old men and see what they have to say about our late colleague." David nodded and he and his two lads went over and sat with the table of old timers. Bernard pointed a finger at the ceiling. "So then, let's take a look."

∽

Taverner led the way. He took them through a door at the rear of the lower room. This led to an outside stairway of stone steps. They climbed to the upper chamber. It ran almost the full length of the lower room. It was empty of furniture.

Will said puzzled, "He was found here?"

Taverner shook his head and pointed. "No, the room through the far door."

They walked across the empty chamber, their footsteps echoing and entered the small room at the far end. It contained a chair, a rough wooden table, and the frame of a bed made of rope webbing. Will pushed open the shutters and let the late evening sunlight into the room. They all noticed the dark stain on the floor near to the bed. On the table was a short dagger, some scattered papers and a pot of dried up ink. "Was anything taken, money, papers?" asked Will.

"There was a purse found on his body, money still in it. The priest stripped the corpse, he may know more if you can find him sober. As for papers, as far as I know they are as he left them. I took his seal and gave it to the coroner in York."

Will nodded. "Don't worry about the seal, it found its

way back to the bishop. Did you see anyone come up here the day he died?"

Taverner shook his head. "I didn't see anyone but then I wasn't here most of that day. Anyone could climb the steps without coming into the inn itself."

Will looked around at the room. "Is that the blade used to kill him?"

Taverner shrugged. "It was on the table when I found him. There's no blood on it. I suppose it could have been wiped clean."

Will walked over and picked it up. It was a short dagger, and the blade appeared clean as Taverner had said. It was a common enough weapon in these troubled times. He placed it back on the table. Will gestured to Osbert to come over. "Have a look through these documents. See what he was making notes about."

Bernard looked at the dark stain on the floor. "So it wasn't a robbery then? At least in the sense it wasn't money they were after."

Will sighed. "I'm not sure what to think this long after the actual event. Perhaps we should speak with this priest."

Bernard nodded thoughtfully and turned to Taverner. "We'll be staying for a few weeks at the very least. We're going to need accommodation and somewhere to work. I think we should use the big chamber out there. We'll pay of course. What's the room used for Taverner?"

Taverner face brightened at the prospect of paying guests. "Nothing much these days. Storage when I need it. We used to hold meetings of the four and twenty in there at one time. I can bring a table up here and some benches, you'll have to sleep on the floor. I've not enough beds for you all and I don't suppose you'd want to use Walcott's bed?"

Osbert shuddered. "I'd rather sleep on the bare boards."

Will said, "I imagine that the sergeant and his men won't be staying more than a day or two. We'll be comfortable enough. Oh and we'd better find somewhere for Agnes."

"Agnes?" asked Taverner.

Bernard chuckled. "Yes Agnes. A former nun, amongst other things. Make sure you find room for her somewhere."

Before Taverner could ask any more questions about Agnes, Osbert said, "The four and twenty, what is that, some sort of court?"

Taverner hesitated then said, "Yes and no. We're a long way from anywhere out here. We've always had to take care of our own affairs, things are run differently."

Osbert said, "How so? It's a manor like any other."

"Not out here on the moors. The four and twenty administer the legal affairs of Sodham. Four and twenty men of Sodham, including the reeve and bailiff, plus the priest and the lord of the manor's official."

Will said, "Are there even four and twenty men in the manor?"

"You've seen the place, we've not met in over five years. Both the reeve and bailiff have grown old and died. This last year two families have packed up and left for York."

Osbert said sharply, "Without the lord of the manor's permission?"

Taverner gave a bitter laugh. "You still don't understand. We haven't had a proper lord in my lifetime. The Mudstones never came here, it's the arse end of Yorkshire, why would they?"

Will said puzzled, "From what you're are saying, I don't understand how the inn has survived this long?"

"It's the abbey. Five miles up the road and you'll come to it. Before the abbot built his new guesthouse we'd have travellers staying here all the time. Sodham would have been deserted years ago if it wasn't for their custom."

Osbert had been scanning through the various papers on the table. "These seem to be rough notes on the manor. List of the inhabitants, land they rent what they pay. Nothing unusual, things the bishop would surely want to know about his new manor. The questions might annoy but nothing that would justify a murder."

Will rubbed his tired eyes and said, "I need some air."

He walked back through into larger chamber and over to the open door. He stood on the top of the stone steps and looked out over the half ruined village of Sodham and the wider valley beyond. He felt completely out of his depth. Whether it was simply to investigate a murder, find a killer or save a manor, which or all were they supposed to be doing here? He didn't feel qualified to do any of them. Bernard came up behind him and put a hand on his shoulder. "Don't despair lad. Things will become clear, they usually do. We just have to stir things up a bit."

Will looked around at him and said, "To be honest I'm not entirely sure what task we've been sent here for. Is the bishop's business always like this?"

Bernard laughed. "Of course it is. If it were straight forward he wouldn't need men like us would he? I hardly ever know what the bloody hell I'm doing. The best advice I can give is to always start with a full stomach. And right now lad I'm bloody famished, anything else can wait."

∼

Later they sat at a long table in the inn's lower room with the sergeant and his men. Taverner had provided a hot meal that was filling if uninspiring. He'd also found some space for Agnes in one of the rooms at the rear of the inn. At Bernard's prompting he'd left her with food and two flagons of ale. Hopefully she was comfortable enough and more importantly out of earshot. What they were to do with her would have to wait for another day. Bernard poked at his teeth with a toothpick. "Catch up on old times David?"

The sergeant shrugged. "To be truthful, there aren't many folk left that I remember. It's been a long time. From what I gathered your man Walcott hadn't been here long enough to make many enemies."

Will said, "If there's anyone who knows what goes on in a place like this it'll be the priest. I'm surprised he hasn't put in an appearance yet."

David nodded. "The priest I know, Father Mathew. Over educated to end up at a place like this. Came here under some sort of cloud. I was only six or seven then but I remember him well. Banished by his bishop I would think, why else would he be sent out here? I'm not sure what he did to deserve it and, as far as I recall, he never said and no one dared ask."

Bernard said, "So where is this priest? I'm sure news of our arrival is all around the manor by now."

"Apparently he's taken up drinking. Heavy drinking that is. By all accounts he's half pissed most of the time. He has a little shack where he sleeps. It's around the back of the church."

22

OLD BONES FOR A PRIEST

Mathew Slaidburn, priest of Sodham and habitual drunk, was on the moorland road high above the valley of his decrepit parish. It was early evening, and he was making his way home on unsteady feet. Most of the day he'd sat beside old Meg in her tumbled down hovel on the moors. She'd been ill for a long time, thin as rake she'd been. This last year had been particularly hard on the poor. If she'd eaten one good meal this month he'd be surprised. During the morning he'd sat there watching her struggle for breath, slipping in and out of consciousness. She'd finally given up the fight around midday. His priestly duties done, he'd said a muted farewell to her malnourished family, and left with as much haste as decency would allow.

On the road and out of sight he drank his fill from a wine skin kept hidden within his cloak. Only the drinking now dulled his senses enough to allow him to get through another day in this godforsaken place. It had been a long time since his bishop had banished him. Condemned to live out his days ministering to those who called this valley home. He'd done his best to serve them but the drink had always been his downfall. Over the years it had become his master, one who couldn't be denied.

~

It was at the turning that led down to the old quarry that he came across a grisly sight. Two leather boots lay in the road. From the top of each, a long shin bone protruded. He stumbled to a stop in front of them. He knew the reputation of the side road. No one in their right mind would venture down there on their own. There were things that lived here on the moors that no one down in the soft lowlands would believe. Things that were best left alone if you knew what was good for you. There were deep set animal prints in the soft mud leading up to the boots. The tracks led back down the side road. God alone knew what thing had stood here and dropped those bones. He looked around nervously. He made to walk on but had only gone a yard or two when he turned around again, his conscience too strong. Whoever this poor soul had been deserved better from him. Taking off his cloak he used it to pick up and then wrap the two gruesome items. He bundled it under his arm and stumbled off towards home.

23

THE CHURCH

Father Mathew slept through most of the following morning. He lay on his bed in the little wooden structure that rested against the rear of the church. It contained only the most basic furniture; a bed, a table, and a small chest. He lived a simple life with little need for possessions. An empty wine skin lay on the floor where it had fallen from his grasp. Just before noon he was awakened by a pounding on the flimsy door of the hut.

An unfamiliar voice said, "Father Mathew, are you in there?"

He grunted. The pounding continued. He heaved himself upright and said, "Who is it?"

"Officials of the Bishop of Draychester," came the reply.

His heart shot into his mouth. He got to his feet unsteadily and kicked the wine skin under the bed. He ran his fingers through his hair. There was nothing he could do with his rather grubby shirt. He opened the chest by the bed and pulled out an old woollen cloak and flung it around his shoulders. He knew he must look pretty rough but there was nothing else to be done. He forced a smile on his face, opened the door and stepped out, a blast of sour wine fumes exiting with him.

Will, Osbert and Bernard stood just outside. Father Mathew looked at each in turn and said, "Welcome my friends. I rather wondered when the bishop would send someone else."

There were some brief introductions and then he led them back around to the front of the church. He pushed open the stout oak door and led them inside. The building was narrow with a tall roof and the interior was dim, cold, and damp. Inside, the walls were covered with whitewash on which at some point a rather inept artist had attempted to paint a series of biblical scenes. The pictures were faded and discoloured with damp. It was plain there had been a side aisle at some point which had been pulled down and replaced by a rough stone wall. Will looked about with some dismay, he'd expected something better but the church was just as run down as the rest of the place. "Times are hard Father Mathew," said Bernard, somewhat stating the obvious.

Father Mathew looked at them uneasily and eventually said, "They've been better my friends. These last few years have not been kind to Sodham. It's a struggle but with God's help we survive." He pulled his cloak around him in the damp air. "I'm sorry I wasn't here yesterday to welcome you. I was out on the moors, a sick parishioner."

Will got straight to the point. "The bishop's official, William Walcott. What do you know of his death?"

"I was called across to the inn by Taverner. He was half out of his wits with fright. It was not a pleasant scene."

"I can imagine. Have you any knowledge why anyone would do such a thing?"

"The man had been here less than a week. We hardly had the time to get to know him."

"You spoke together?"

Father Mathew nodded. "Yes, briefly, on the day he arrived. He asked me some things about the parish, which I told him gladly. No one has shown any interest in this place for years."

"The day he died where were you?"

"I was asleep in the hut behind the church. Taverner barged in crying out that I had to come across to the inn as something terrible had happened. I couldn't get any sense out of the man."

"You went at once?"

"I did. I followed him up to the back room. Your man was lying in the bed. Blood everywhere, his throat was slashed, ear to ear."

"You must have seen a lot of death in your time Father, is there any possibility it could have been self-inflicted?"

Father Matthew's face was grave. "None. Whoever inflicted such a wound has committed a mortal sin. They will answer to God for it."

"They may answer before the justices in York first," said Bernard sharply.

Father Bernard nodded in acknowledgment and murmured, "If that be God's plan."

"Was there any sign of a struggle?"

He shook his head. "I think he was taken in his sleep, the room was undisturbed."

Bernard was getting frustrated. He thrust his face in the priests. "So at whose hands did he meet his death? A grudge with somebody, an argument with Taverner that went wrong, a woman scorned? Can you not assist us at all, have you not at least speculated? You know these people better than anyone."

Father Mathew took a step back. "I can't bring myself to think it was any of my parishioners; none would do such a thing. I believe your man had been up to the abbey in the days before his death. That's a place of wickedness and sin. Perhaps your answer can be found there."

Will grabbed hold of Bernard's arm and pulled him back. He said, "So Father, I take it you're not on friendly terms with the Abbot of Ribsdale?"

The priest laughed without humour. "He dishonours his own order with his behaviour. His abbey is a house of sin and wickedness. It's a disgrace. I have written to the Archbishop of York to complain, alas to no avail."

"You think him capable of arranging a murder?"

"Who knows what he's capable of. His hand is behind many things that happen here in Sodham."

Bernard said, "It's dangerous to accuse a powerful abbot. Aren't you afraid?"

"I fear God more my friend and I'll answer to him for my sins one day, as will the abbot."

"And William Walcott, where does he lie in the graveyard?" asked Will.

"Out through the door and to the left, you'll see the grave. We buried him the day after his death."

∽

On their way out, they came across a cloak just inside the doorway. Will bent to pick it up and recoiled in horror as out flopped two boots complete with shin bones. He gasped.

"My God, what is that?" said Osbert shocked.

Even Bernard looked taken aback. Father Mathew

rushed over. "I found these up on the top road yesterday evening, by the turn to the quarry. Some poor unfortunate soul caught out on the moors. He's probably been undiscovered since winter. The bones have been scavenged by a wild animal. I nearly left them lying there, but it troubled my conscious. Every man deserves a decent burial."

"They look quite fresh to me Father. Do you know if anyone is missing?" asked Will.

Father Mathew shook his head. "Not that I know of, but it's not uncommon for travellers to go astray up on the moorland roads. There was only these on the path, nothing else to give a clue to who it could have been."

Osbert gestured to the grisly pile. "What do you plan on doing with them?"

"I'll get old Tom to bury them this afternoon. It's as much as we can do."

Bernard said, "Well one death is enough for us to investigate Father. I can't imagine the coroner would be interested in this one either. There's not really a body is there? We'll have trust in your judgment. You'd better bury the poor sod or what's left of him." With that, they left the priest inside his church.

∼

Bernard seemed genuinely unsettled by the priest. "I can't read him at all, and those bones! We've learned nothing we didn't already know or could have guessed. There's something more to this, a man's butchered not twenty yards from his church and he hardly seems surprised."

Will nodded grimly. "He was economical with the truth that much is certain. I suppose this means we'll be paying the Abbot of Ribsdale a visit."

Osbert pointed to a freshly dug mound of earth. "That must be Walcott."

They walked over and all three stood looking down at the freshly covered grave. Osbert poked his foot at the edge of the mound. "I've a bad feeling about this place."

Bernard looked at him and said, "You've had a bad feeling about every place we've been so far."

Osbert nodded. "That's true, but I have an especially bad feeling about this one."

24

A PLAN

They were in the upstairs chamber of the inn. Bernard was lying the full length of one of the benches, his hands behind his head. Osbert was at the table writing his reports for the bishop although there was no immediate prospect of them being dispatched unless someone went to York. Will was sat opposite on a small three-legged stool. He said, "I'd give this place a few more years at best and it'll be abandoned. I've seen what happens to places like this. In the years after the great pestilence scores of villages were abandoned."

"It's true, I've seen a few deserted villages in my time," said Bernard.

Osbert looked up from his scribbling. "Well in that case the bishop may as well sell to Ribsdale Abbey."

Will shook his head. "It doesn't have to be that way. I have a plan. It starts with re-forming this local court, the four and twenty I think Taverner called it? Actually, we might have to change the name depending who we can round up to serve as members. We might struggle for numbers, but you get the idea."

Osbert looked puzzled. "I'm not sure I do, and on who's authority?"

Will shrugged. "I'm supposed to be the Official of Sodham aren't I? Surely I have the authority?"

"He's right you know," chipped in Bernard, "he is the Official. He can do what he wants within reason."

"And what exactly will be the purpose of this court?" asked Osbert.

"To start with they will be carrying out our instructions. If things go to plan I hope they can be left to get on with things and we can get out of this godforsaken place and return home. I've been thinking while you've been scribbling away. I told you, I have a plan."

"You have a plan?" said Osbert without much enthusiasm.

"Surprising as it may seem Osbert I do." Will got up from his stool and began pacing up and down the long chamber. "This place is dying. Nobody comes here anymore and those that do live here don't want to stay here. When a place loses its reason to be, it dies."

Bernard nodded his agreement. "We're in the middle of bloody nowhere. Why would anyone want to come here?"

Will halted by Bernard's bench. "Exactly! There's no reason to come here, we need a reason and if one doesn't exist, we need to invent it."

Osbert held up his hands in exasperation and said, "I'm still struggling to follow you. What reason can we possibly invent?"

Will turned to face him. "In a word Osbert, bones."

"Bones?"

"Old bones, not to mention hair, fingernails and various other bits of the body, but bones will do for a start. I am talking pilgrims and saint's shrines. The possibilities are endless."

Bernard looked at him shrewdly. "I think I can see where you're going with this. I do though see a flaw in your plan"

"Which is?" said Will.

"I don't believe Sodham is renowned for having any saints deceased or otherwise."

"I beg to differ." Will jabbed his finger in the air to emphasize the point. "Those bones the priest found. Grisly and mysterious, complete with old boots, just the kind of thing we're looking for."

Bernard half sat up on the bench. "True. They could do I suppose. We'll need a miracle of course, to get things going."

Osbert look at him aghast. "You're not seriously going along with this?"

Bernard shrugged. "Why not? It sounds like a good plan to me."

Osbert shook his head. "The bishop would not approve, you can't just invent a saint."

Bernard laughed. "You're mistaken my young friend. The bishop will be delighted! I hope you're going to write all this down. It'll make his day when he reads it."

Bernard slowly got to his feet and rubbed his hands together with glee, warming to the plan by the second. "How about a saint who miraculously heals bad feet, having lost his own so horrifically?"

Will grinned. "Now you're thinking along my lines. Who hasn't got a touch of rheumatism in their feet? What better than to pray and give generously for relief from Saint Traed."

"Saint Traed?" asked Osbert.

"It's Welsh for feet," said Will.

Bernard chuckled. "Ah a Celtic saint, even better. Perhaps the pilgrims can touch the saint's bones with their own feet. Perhaps they can even dip them in the healing waters down at the river…"

Will clapped him on his back. "I like it. We're going to need some sort of wooden casket, possibly with holes in its side so the afflicted can put their feet through to touch the bones. Oh and we're going to need a lot of candles. It'll be expensive but worth it for the effect."

Will sat back on his stool, a myriad of thoughts running through his mind. Finally he felt he could put his talents to use and achieve something to justify the bishop's trust. And there was something else he could do. He said, "By the way I've also had a thought about Agnes."

Osbert said, "On our return we should take her back to the priory. That's where she belongs, to be punished for breaking her vows."

Bernard gave him a sour look. "Have a heart boy. You'd really send her back there?"

Osbert hesitated and reluctantly said, "Well if not there then somewhere she can contemplate her sins."

Will said, "Don't worry I have just the place; the far side of the bridge."

Osbert looked at him puzzled. "I don't understand you."

"We've got a bridge, or we will have when we put it back together. What we need is a bridge hermit. She's perfect. You've got to think of the future here Osbert. Sodham has no income, we need to find some revenue. Every pilgrim is going to have to cross that bridge to get to our new shrine, why not relieve them of some coin for the common good of Sodham. Money brings people and commerce and more people. It's infectious."

"It's blasphemous is what it is," said an outraged Osbert.

At this Bernard laughed out loud. "The bishop was right about you Will. He said you had hidden talents and our master is rarely wrong."

Osbert, as usual managing to bring the mood down, said "You're forgetting that we still have a murder to solve."

25

THE ABBOT

The Abbot of Ribsdale was taking an afternoon nap. The business of running the abbey was tiring and the years of excessive alcohol consumption and sumptuous feasting were beginning to take their toll. At this hour he was normally fast asleep, but a voice had been whispering in his left ear for some time. It was most persistent.

"My lord, wake up, wake up."

He opened his eyes. There was a slim, naked girl next to him in the bed. He vaguely recognised her. He thought she could be the daughter of his cook. Or was it the carter's wife again? "What is it girl, is the abbey on fire? Has the king decided to pay a visit? Think carefully now."

"Neither my lord."

"Then I'll resume my sleep. Don't disturb me again girl."

"It's the prior my lord. He's at the door, he says it's a matter of urgency."

The abbot sighed. The prior was generally a fool. "What is it Robert?" he shouted at the closed door of his chamber.

A muffled voice said, "I'm sorry to disturb you my lord. I got the girl to wake you..."

"Yes, Yes, Robert, get to the point, what is it?"

"Three of Bishop Gifford's men are here my lord. They were most insistent with the gatekeeper that they needed to see you."

The abbot sighed again, rested his head back on the pillow and closed his eyes. "What have you done with them Robert?"

"They are waiting on the seats just inside the inner gatehouse my lord."

"Go and collect them and take them through to my day chamber. I will be down shortly."

"At once my lord."

"Help me up girl. And Robert, go find Mudstone, put him in the room behind the day chamber. Show him the viewing panel, I want him to see and hear the meeting."

"Of course my lord."

∼

Will, Bernard and Osbert sat on the hard stone seats in the passageway that led out of the inner gatehouse towards the abbot's private lodging. A stout oak door sat between them and any further progress. "I don't know about you but I'm bloody uncomfortable. My backside is numb sat here," said Bernard. "I thought hospitality was a part of the monastic life."

"Perhaps it's a deliberate insult?" said Osbert.

Will chuckled. "I'm not sure we're important enough for that Osbert."

The inner door opened and a middle-aged man in the dark robes of a monk emerged. "Abbot Burley will see you now. I'm the prior, Robert. If you would follow me please."

"About time too," said Bernard. "We've been sat here for

an age. We're officials of Bishop Gifford, here on important business. A drink and some food wouldn't have gone amiss."

Will shot him a warning glance. This was no time to make a scene. Prior Robert turned hurriedly without answering and disappeared back through the door. They had to half run to catch up with the cloaked figure as he swept up the passageway. He led them into the heart of the sumptuous lodgings of the abbot. They passed through several rooms and finally into a larger chamber. It was abundantly clear that the abbot didn't skimp on his personal comfort.

∼

Burley was dressed in a silken robe. It certainly didn't look like any monk's robe Will had ever seen. The abbot sat at the end of a long table in a high-backed chair. He was a large man with a pale, unhealthy looking complexion and who carried his weight badly. He had long jowls, watery blue eyes and a bald head. As they entered the room, he got up from his seat with some difficulty and waddled over to greet them.

Mudstone watched from the adjacent room through a secret viewing slot set in the wall just behind the abbot's chair.

He recognised Bernard as soon as the bishop's men entered the chamber. He hissed a muffled, "God's teeth!" Did he have to take care of everything himself? He'd given Godbert and Gilbert simple instructions to kill the bishop's men yet here they were still breathing and interfering in his plans. The Bouchard twins had better hope they didn't run into him anytime soon.

The abbot said, "Welcome to Ribsdale, I'm Thomas Burley, abbot of this place."

They made small talk, the abbot insincerely asking after Bishop Gifford's health. The bishop's men equally insincerely asked after the wellbeing of the abbey. Neither gave a damn of course, the bishop famously loathing monks. Mudstone sneered at the hypocrisy of it from behind the wooden panel. How he wished he could get his hands around the neck of that oaf Bernard and throttle him.

Will steered the stilted conversation towards the events in Sodham. The abbot said hesitantly, "Ah yes, your man. I hear he's suffered some misadventure?"

"You mean he's dead," said Bernard bluntly.

"Ah dead is he?" There was no surprise on the abbot's face.

"Let's not beat about the bush. Someone..." Bernard said slowly, "...slashed his throat with a ruddy big knife."

Osbert winced. Will merely smiled nervously. The abbot seemed unruffled.

"Most unfortunate, I'm sure."

Will took a softer approach than Bernard. "The dead man, William of Walcott, he came here to see you?"

"I seem to remember he did, what of it?"

"You may have been one of the last people to see him alive."

"Well I have to say he was rather an unwelcome visitor."

"In what way my lord?"

"He was most undignified in his conduct. He also made some allegations against the abbey."

"What sort of allegations?"

"He claimed some of the abbey's flocks appeared to be grazing on land that belonged to the manor of Sodham."

"And were they?"

"The abbey's lands cover thousands of acres. Sometimes incursions occur onto land that doesn't belong to us. I passed the information on to Brother Allard. He looks after those sort of things with the lay brothers. You can appreciate I don't know every detail of our business, it would be impossible for one man. It's a heavy enough burden as it is being abbot."

"Is that all you talked about my lord?"

"No. I think the allegations were just a pretext. He really wanted to talk about Father Mathew, the Sodham priest. God knows why. He seemed somewhat agitated about him."

"You know Father Mathew well?"

"I've met him a few times. He's been at Sodham many years, our paths have crossed. Walcott wanted to know where he'd come from originally and what I thought of him. I may have been somewhat dismissive of his questions. I don't have time to reflect on every parish priest I come across. By all accounts he drinks too much, but who wouldn't if they had to look after Sodham. The villagers are frankly a bunch of inbreds, as I'm sure you've discovered."

"They speak equally highly of you too my lord," said Will.

The abbot ignoring Will's sarcasm said, "I've offered to buy the whole manor you know. I'd urge you to recommend the offer to Bishop Gifford. We've had our disagreements in the past but I'm sure our mutual interests would coincide over this matter."

"I think it most unlikely the bishop would sell my lord, the parish has only just been gifted to Draychester. I believe my lord has other plans for the manor."

"Really? I can't imagine what he wants with the place. Better for me to raze it to the ground and turn the valley over to our sheep. You've got to change with the times. Wool is the future up here on the moors."

"And what of the villagers?"

"What of them? None of them are of any standing and the village is half in ruins. The inn had its uses in the past when our own guest accommodation was overcrowded. As you've probably seen we've built a splendid new guesthouse."

Will tried to bring the conversation back to Walcott. "Tell me my lord, did Walcott reveal why he wanted to know more about Father Mathew?"

"He didn't say and I couldn't enlighten him with any more details. I hardly know the priest. I bid him to carry the same offer for Sodham to your bishop as I've asked you. He left in a foul mood."

"Can you think of any reason why Walcott would be murdered?"

"The moors are a dangerous place, and these are dangerous times. Violence is common among the lower sorts up here. Perhaps he insulted someone or looked at another's woman, who can say."

"Well that narrows it down," said Bernard.

"There's a knight, Sir Roger Mudstone, he has a manor nearby, Coxington. Do you think he could be involved? He has a terrible reputation and I believe he had no love for our own bishop," asked Will.

The abbot nodded. "Yes, I know of him. A dreadful fellow by all accounts. He's newly inherited Coxington. Arrived up a here a few weeks ago. Perhaps he could be the culprit."

There was a loud muffled nose from outside the room. It appeared to come from behind the abbot but he didn't seem to hear it.

Death Of The Official

∼

When the bishop's men had safely left the room, the abbot said, "You can come in now Mudstone. You didn't by any chance kill the bishop's man did you?"

Mudstone entered the room and said, "Unfortunately I didn't have the time my lord. Somebody had already finished him off before I'd even arrived in Yorkshire."

The abbot looked mildly puzzled. "Strange, if you didn't do it and I certainly didn't arrange it, who else had cause?"

"He's dead my lord, I care not, but what of these other men of Gifford's and of Sodham itself?"

The abbot rubbed his hand together slowly. "I think it's high time there's an unfortunate incident in the village of Sodham. Borrow some of the baser of the lay brothers to aid you if you wish. I've no doubt you can be very creative, I don't need to know the full details just so long as Gifford's men and Sodham cease to be an issue."

26

THE FOUR AND TWENTY

The meeting took place in the upper chamber of the Man and Scythe. The room was packed. Where half of the crowd had come from Will wasn't entirely sure. A few days before he'd announce that the four and twenty would be reconvened and that everyone would be welcome to attend. As the bishop's officials, they could have compelled all to attend, but he knew what he needed was for them to want to come.

The bishop's men emerged somewhat nervously from the back room. Will had deliberately had the main room set out with two rows of benches to the right and four stools and a table to the left. The back of the room contained every other stool, bench and spare box they could lay their hands on. "God's teeth," said Bernard apprehensively, "Where did this lot come from. Are you sure you know what you're doing lad?"

"Trust me Bernard, I've put a lot of thought into this."

"That's what's worrying me," he muttered. "Osbert you're prepared to take notes?"

Osbert nodded his readiness. Bernard said, "You'd better start then Will."

∼

Will was in his element playing to the assembled crowd. He opened the meeting dramatically by slamming his hand down on the table and shouting, "It's a miracle!" This had the effect of silencing the general chit chat. In all their years, the good folk of Sodham had never seen an official like this one. He continued, "You heard me my friends, it's a miracle. I'm going to talk a lot about miracles tonight. The first miracle is that Sodham is still alive, barely. Its lifeblood is bleeding away, year by year. I'm here to tell you it's time to draw a line in the sand. Decide to do something about it or have somebody decide for you. You know who we are. This place belongs to the Bishop of Draychester now. He's not a man who leaves assets to rot and one way or another this place needs to pay its way."

A voice called out, "Somebody else always decides, it's never us, what say have we?"

He jabbed his finger at the crowd. "I say you have a say." He pulled the seal out from under his cloak and let it hang round his neck. "I'm the Official of Sodham now and I'm reconvening the four and twenty. I'm chairman, Father Mathew has a place, Osbert here is the clerk and I suggest, actually I insist, Bernard acts as chief adviser. The first decision you get my friends is to elect the rest of the members. For those of you who can't count that's twenty of you. You've got ten minutes, I'm sure you know the traditions better than me."

There was a collective intake of breath than all hell broke loose. There was uproar. Bernard pulled a cudgel from under his stool and brandished it in front of him fearing a brawl. Will waved him back to his seat. "Trust me," he mouthed, "give them some time."

Slowly and at the prompting and cajoling of Taverner the villagers of Sodham put forward a motley collection of twenty souls to represent them. Taverner, Bryce the Blacksmith and old Tom seemed the most comfortable in their new role. The rest were the reluctant willing. There was a hasty and bad tempered shuffling around of seating arrangements to push the chosen to the front row of benches. Will banged the tabletop to bring the meeting back to order. "So then, let's continue. Father Mathew has found the bones of Saint Traed in the graveyard."

There was a nervous coughing and shuffling of many feet. Eventually a voice from the crowd said, "Never heard of no Saint Traed."

Father Mathew just looked bewildered and made to say something. Bernard gave him a warning glare which effectively silenced him. Will leaned against the back wall and said, "Well I say it's miraculous that he's turned up here, in our hour of need."

"What sort of saint is he?" asked another voice.

"He's the healing sort, feet I believe," said Will straight faced.

A crinkled old woman sat on the second row of benches said, "Well dear, my feet have been killing me for years, got arthritis in my toes I have. Never been the same since my old dad had us picking stones from the top fields in winter. Bloody freezing it was."

A ripple of laughter erupted from the crowd and a voice shouted, "We don't want to hear about your smelly old feet Rose."

The old woman turned around and shook her fist at a

young lad behind her. "You cheeky young sod. I'll have you know these feet are bathed at least once a year."

There was more laughter and from the back of the room a female voice shouted, "Like a pair of old cheeses they are. Maybe Saint Tread can take away the smell." The crowd roared this time.

"Ladies, please! Can we get back to the saint," said Taverner exasperated, "I take it this miraculous appearance of the bones is a good thing?"

Will nodded. "It is if you have bad feet. A lot of people have bad feet don't you think?"

Taverner nodded slowly. He had half an inkling of what was going on here. Taverner had successfully kept the inn going for the past twenty years in a slowly failing village. He knew how to keep his wits about him. If his brain wasn't misleading him, the bishop's man was putting forward a quite devious scheme. He liked it a lot, but he wanted to hear more. The majority of the newly formed four and twenty sat looking bewildered. Whatever they had been expecting to hear at the meeting, this wasn't it. Taverner rubbed his chin and said slowly, "These bones. Found in our graveyard were they?"

"Father Mathew has them safe," said Will not answering the question directly.

"How do we know they're a saint's bones?" asked old Tom.

With a straight face, Will said, "It's a well-known fact Saint Traed lost his legs in a battle around here. Long time ago of course. The legs were last seen miraculously walking off the battlefield on their own. These bones were found still wearing boots. Who else's could they be?"

Osbert started spluttering but Bernard placed a warning hand on his shoulder. There was a collective "ohh arrr" from the crowd. The revelation of the boots evidently gave additional authenticity to the audacious claim. Taverner gave Will a cynical smile. He had to hand it to the lad, he was putting on a good performance. Will said with as much sincerity as he could manage, "I've had a suggestion put to me that we hand them over to the abbot of Ribsdale. The abbey could no doubt attract a good number of pilgrims to see them." There was an angry response from the crowd just as he'd anticipated.

"Not bloody likely."

"They're ours, found here, I say they stay here."

"Saint Traed wouldn't have wanted them to leave the parish."

"Bloody cheek that abbot has."

Will let it rumble on for a minute or two. Now he'd planted the seed of the idea he wanted them to suggest the solution themselves.

"Suppose we could put them on display in the church. We might get the odd pilgrim or two," said Old Tom. "How they going to get across the river though? It's alright now but soon as it rains you'd be buggered."

"We need to rebuild the bridge," said Will.

Tom lent forward. "Fix the bridge lad? Who's going to do that, there's not the skill here or the coin. We had some bad floods, must be about ten years ago now. The main pier collapsed, it'll cost a fortune to put that right again."

"I'm not talking about building London Bridge. Just getting something basic in place at first, wide enough for a pack horse to cross. The stone is still piled up there in the river and on the banks. There's two apprentice masons I know. They've just arrived in York, they owe our bishop a favour. I think I can get them here for what's left of the summer. With some labouring help for them I think it could be done."

"They'll want paying, apprentices or not," said Tom.

Will nodded and said, "Osbert how much has the good Bishop of Draychester entrusted us with?"

Osbert licked his lips nervously and shuffled his papers around on the tabletop. "Two pounds, ten shillings and sixpence"

"Well that's a start. The bishop can pay."

Even Bernard looked a bit startled at that. Old Tom leaned forward again, looked Will in the eye and said, "And the bishop would be willing to do this?"

Will met his gaze and with more confidence than he felt and said, "I'm the Official of Sodham, at least for now. As the bishop's representative, it's my decision to use the funds wisely. I can't think of a better use for now."

Tavener ran a hand over his stubbly chin. "Say the bridge is made passable. Then what of the bones of this Saint Traed?"

"Put them in the church, inside a simple reliquary for now. We'll get the carpenter to make us a box. Open sides so the bones can be touched by the pilgrims seeking a cure. The church will need cleaning up. Its cold and damp. Roof probably wants fixing and the plasterwork and paintings need doing again. Oh, and we'll need candles, lots of them. Can't have a shrine without candles."

There was an outbreak of murmuring as the possibilities started to be grasped by some of the other members of the four and twenty. Taverner nodded slowly and said, "It just might work. It'd give some reason for people to start coming here again. Be good for the inn, people will need food and accommodation."

Father Mathew who had been mostly silent said, "Pilgrims would be good for the village and the church. God, my friends, helps those who help themselves. Perhaps Saint Traed's presence in the graveyard has blessed the little well behind the church. The waters may have curative properties?"

Taverner's cynical smile returned and Will could hardly contain his laughter. He said, "I think you may be onto something there Father. Of course we can't possibly keep this miraculous news to ourselves else how will the afflicted learn of Saint Traed bones and the holy well."

David, the sheriff's sergeant, had been watching the proceedings with amused interest. He said, "I might be able to help you there. My work in the city brings me into contact with all sorts." He looked at Will and Bernard pointedly and continued, "I know a few afflicted souls in York who could be persuaded to pray to Saint Traed. I'm sure he'd do his miraculous work, and they'd be cured. I'm also sure they'd be only too willing to spread the good news."

Taverner nodded knowingly. "I think I know the type. I take it these afflicted souls would maybe need their, shall we call it, expenses, met?"

"That would be a generous gesture on Sodham's part I'm sure," said David.

Will said, "I'll need to visit York to collect some supplies and talk to the mason's apprentices." He turned to the sergeant. "You'll return with us David?"

"Yes, it's time the lads and I got back. I don't think you're in any danger here. Not from this lot at least. Better if we all travel as one party, safer that way."

∽

When the meeting had broken up, and the crowd had

descended to the main room of the inn to drink, the bishop's men questioned the priest again. "We went up to the abbey yesterday Father Matthew. We spoke to the abbot," Will said.

"You have my sympathy my son. The man is an insult to his order."

"That's as may be," said Bernard, "What he did say was Walcott seemed to be interested in what the abbot knew of you. Now why would that be?"

The priest shrugged. "That I couldn't tell you. As I said, we spoke little before his untimely death. I'm always busy with my duties, this is a very poor parish and there's much to do."

Will said, "Tell me Father, you seem an educated man. If you don't mind me saying this seems an odd parish to be given to you, you're not the kind of priest I would have expected in a place like this."

The priest gave a weary smile. "My son it was God's will that I come here. Who are we to question his wisdom? It was many years ago, half a lifetime in fact, I went where I was commanded to."

"I'm not sure I understand you Father. You were sent here against your will?"

"No my son, I didn't object. I suppose you could call it fate, besides Sodham wasn't as run down then. The last few years have been hard for us all."

Will could see he wasn't getting anywhere with this line of questioning. The man was frustratingly vague. Bernard was more blunt. "So you have absolutely no idea who murdered Walcott or why? Are you afraid of somebody Father?"

All Father Matthew said was, "Only of God my son, he knows all."

27

RETURN TO YORK

Hik Wyndull was a professional beggar. His specialty was to play a paralytic, and he spent most weekday mornings being pushed around in a battered wheelbarrow by a young lad with a withered leg. They tended to prowl around the front of the great minster along with a gallery of similar unfortunate and wretched individuals. Between them they were afflicted by a bewildering number of ailments including gout, piles, manic itches, fevers, toothaches and hernias. Many of them had a limb missing or were crippled by some terrible accident either real or make believe. They presented a formidable obstacle to the pilgrims making their way into the minster. What self-respecting Christian would not grant a few pennies to such a pitiful array of humanity? By noon Hik had usually earned enough to spend the rest of his day in more pleasurable activity. Today he had the lad wheel him out of sight down a side street. Before he could leap from the barrow, having miraculously recovered the use of his limbs, he was hauled out of it by David Padget. "Afternoon Sergeant Padget. Bit abrupt today aren't you?"

"I need a word with you Hik," said Padget holding him by the throat.

"You know me Sergeant Padget, always happy to assist the forces of law and order."

"I do know you Hik. I know every little devious trick. How did you get on this morning?"

"Can't complain, the rain held off. The coin flows easier when the suns out, makes for happier pilgrims."

"How much do you make of a day Hik?"

"You can't be asking me that Sergeant Padget, it's a professional secret. I'd be breaking my professional oath."

"Professional oath! You'd sell your own granny if the price was right."

"Now I just feel insulted."

"How would you like to earn a guaranteed shilling a day for let's say three days? Half now half in three days."

Hik smiled nervously and said, "And what do I need to do for this shilling a day. I hope it's not something against the law."

Padget grinned. "All you need to do is use your dubious talents to spread a message."

~

On the morning of his return to York, Will made his way directly towards the great minster. His letter and seals once again granted him swift access into the precinct. He asked directions from the gatekeeper as to the whereabouts of the two apprentice masons and their new master. The man gave him a toothless grin and pointed at the roof of the minster itself. Will could see the tiny figures of men labouring at the top of a network of scaffolding. It rose from the base of the minster walls all the way to roof level. The gatekeeper said, "The two lads are way up there. Unless you've got a head for heights, I'd advise you to seek out their master first. I saw him descend not long ago. You'll probably find him in the mason's loft."

The mason's loft within the minster was found above the vaulted passageway of the chapter house vestibule. A door located behind the main entrance into the chapter house provided access to a narrow, steep staircase that led to the upper floor.

Will found himself in a well-lit loft consisting of two open rooms at right angles to each other with an elaborate wooden roof. At first he had thought the master mason was elsewhere, but he found him around the corner, sat regarding an elaborate design traced out on a plaster drawing floor. Will was immediately fascinated by the drawings and the mason, John, turned out to be an affable man happy to explain a little of his craft. He bore a striking resemblance to his injured brother who they had reluctantly left behind in Worcester. Eventually Will got around to the point of his visit. "Do you think you could let me make use of the two apprentices who accompanied us to York? You would be doing Bishop Gifford a great service. I'm reluctant to ask but I could do with your help."

The master mason rubbed his chin and said, "Well I suppose I could. The two are after all my brother's apprentices not mine. I am in your debt on behalf of my brother. There's always plenty of work here, but tell me, what exactly have you in mind?"

"I need to repair a bridge if it's possible. Do you think the two of them are up to it?"

The older man rubbed his chin again and regarded Will with bright intelligent eyes. "This bridge is at Sodham?"

Will nodded. "Yes, it's in very bad repair."

"I suppose you'd better describe it to me then. When you say it's in bad repair, how badly damaged is it?"

They were soon stood at a trestle table in the far corner of the room. Master John sketched on some scraps of parchment as Will described the ruined bridge in Sodham. After a few minutes the master mason declared that he had enough details. Brandishing his sketches he said, "I'll have a chat with the lads about what can be done. It won't be easy mind. Still, I think if I give them a bit of direction, and based on what you've told me, they can make a repair. Give them a few weeks and I might take a trip out there myself and take a look. That's if my own bishop agrees of course."

Will grinned. "You've been very kind Master John that bridge is going to be vital."

"Aye well, they're decent lads and my brother has been a good teacher. About time they took on a job themselves."

∼

Will took his leave and followed the master mason's directions to the chief archivist. He wanted to know how Father Mathew had first come to Sodham. The priest had arrived under some cloud there was no doubt of that, but why he'd been sent to Sodham Will could only speculate. What he needed were hard facts that only the Church's records could reveal.

The archivist listened to his request, examined his letter and seal, and said, "Please take a seat here at my desk. This may take some time. I'll need to go and take a look in the court records." He vanished into the depths of the cathedral archives. He was gone perhaps fifteen minutes and returned with a large leather bound volume. Setting this down on the desk opposite Will he leafed through the pages until he came to a stop and smiled. He said, "I thought I'd heard that name before."

"You know him?" asked Will.

"I know of him. It was quite a scandal at the time. I was a young clerk in training in those days. The bare facts are here in the records but I can tell you what I remember myself?"

Will nodded. "Please go on, anything you can remember I'll be grateful of."

"Your priest, Mathew Slaidburn, was a student here some twenty-five years ago. He shared a chamber with two other students within the minster precincts. One summer morning a young serving girl from one of the local taverns was discovered with her throat cut. She was found in his chamber and in his bed by all accounts."

Wills mouth hung open in shock. He managed to croak, "He murdered her?"

"He claimed not. It's a sordid tale. Apparently he and the girl had been lovers for a few months. The other two had come back one night drunk. They found her there asleep with him in bed, tried to rape her and when she resisted knocked him senseless and killed her in a drunken rage."

"What happened to him?"

"All three ran. They didn't get far. If I remember rightly they never even made it out of the city. They were to be tried for murder but all claimed benefit of clergy to avoid the hangman's noose or worse. A nasty tale, but not that uncommon then or now."

"Are you saying they simply walked free?"

"Of course not. No bishop could be seen to tolerate such an outrage. He wanted them out of the city as fast as possible. There was a lot of ill feeling in the streets. A case like that, he would naturally put them all as far away and out of sight as he could arrange. A lifetime's penance to be paid.

That's how Slaidburn ended up in Sodham. I dare say the bishop at the time thought it an ideal place to forget about him."

"So he's a murderer then?"

"Who's to say? Maybe he told the truth and it was the other two. It was all a long time ago."

"And the others, what of them?"

"According to the documents one was sent to a parish in Wales. The other went to Draychester."

Wills mouth was as dry as a bone. "Draychester?" A feeling of dread was building in him. "What was the man's name?"

The clerk looked at him curiously, consulted the ledger again, then said, "Let me see, it was William, William of Wallcot."

28

SODHAM BURNS

Sir Roger felt a soft, warm body next to his own. He yawned but didn't open his eyes. He couldn't remember taking any of the abbot's serving girls to his bed the previous night. Still, finding her lying there next to him was a pleasant surprise. What he did recall of last evening was drinking a lot of the abbot's fine wine. His head still felt a little fuzzy.

He hung a lazy arm over his bed companion. Maybe she could be persuaded to indulge in some early morning fun. She was surprisingly hairy. These country girls were strange, possibly due to inbreeding in the remote moorland valleys. Suddenly he felt a wet tongue move slowly down his exposed arm towards his wrist. Ah, a frisky one. He moved his leg over her thigh, which turned out to be even more hairy. There was a curious musky aroma about her. He couldn't quite place it. When she let out what could only be described as a thunderous fart, he thought perhaps he should be getting more choosy. He decided to open his eyes.

"God's teeth!" He found he was sharing the bed with the huge black dog that he now recognised as the abbot's hound

Beelzebub. His attempt to remove his leg from the beast's thigh resulted in a deep, guttural growl. He froze and lay there unsure of what to do. With infinite care, he slowly lifted the blanket and eased himself out of the bed. His bedfellow growled another warning and suddenly heaved itself onto the floor on the opposite side from him. It gave him a last baleful look and then slunk away through the open door.

Sir Roger looked on bemused at the freshly deposited turd that sat in the middle of the bed. It lay there steaming in the cold morning air of his bedchamber. The smell suddenly became overpowering.

Travis, who usually slept just outside his master's door, stumbled in wiping the sleep from his eyes. He said, "You're up early master, I know you had a late night. I'm barely awake myself." He caught sight of the giant turd, gagged at the appalling stench and asked anxiously, "Are you ill master, was it something you ate?"

He couldn't understand why Sir Roger immediately started cuffing him over the head. "Imbecile! What have I told you about making sure my door is closed."

∼

Sir Roger was in a foul mood. To appease his anger, his first thoughts had been to gather some of the lay brothers as suggested by the abbot and immediately ride into Sodham. They'd butcher whoever could be found and burn the place to the ground. It was true the plan lacked a certain finesse, but it appealed to his bloodthirsty nature. However, even he understood that such direct action might not be the best approach. The act had to have deniability. If it wasn't exactly clear who was involved then perhaps it could be blamed on the Scots. Weren't they always raiding across the border even as far south as Yorkshire? He finally decided on an attack at dusk. The approaching darkness would mean it would be impossible to say exactly who the attacking force were. The terror inducing sight of his raiders carrying burning torches would also be magnified tenfold in the gloom.

During the day he and Travis had prepared. They had collected together around twenty torches made of rough hessian soaked in wax and wrapped around the end of four foot long wooden staves. Sir Roger was fond of an impromptu lynching, for the terror inducing effect, so they gathered several short lengths of rope. They could also be used to drag down the walls of the flimsier hovels. Sir Roger had a large collection of fearsome weapons that he never travelled without, but the lay brothers would have to be well armed as well. He sent Travis to look for suitable weapons. He gave him an hour and then went to inspect the haul.

"Really Travis, is this the best you could come up with?" Against the wall of one of the outer buildings of the abbey Travis had piled a motley collection of farm implements and a few tools from the blacksmiths. There were scythes, flails, hammers, wicked looking bill-hooks and several pairs of long-nosed pliers.

"The abbot won't let us use any of the abbey's proper weapons Sir Roger. He told me he doesn't want to know anything about what you have planned."

Sir Roger grunted at this. He poked the pile with his foot then stooped to pick up a pair of pliers. "And what exactly are they going to do with these? Pull a few teeth?"

Travis looked crestfallen. "I'm sorry Sir Roger."

Sir Roger held up his hand. "Don't whine Travis we don't have the time. I suppose it will have to do. Some coin to each of the lay brothers should boost their enthusiasm. I hope you've done better finding us some suitable raiders. Did you bring the cider?"

Travis nodded. He disappeared around the corner of the building and returned with a large stoppered jug. He said, "It's very potent my lord."

"Give it here, let me try it." Travis handed over the heavy jug and Sir Roger un-stoppered it and took a long swig. "God's teeth," he spluttered, "if that doesn't get them fired up I don't know what will. Right lets go find them. Bring the cider." He tossed the heavy jug back to Travis, who was nearly floored by the flying object.

~

Sir Roger had given Travis a simple list of criteria. This was to find him the largest, meanest, greediest and possibly stupidest of the abbey's lay brothers. On this occasion, Travis's efforts met with approval. The group of individuals who had gathered in one of the outer courtyards wouldn't have disgraced the troop of mercenaries Sir Roger had once commanded. Dressed in the rough brown woolen cloaks with hoods that all the lay brothers of the abbey wore, they collectively scowled at him as he approached. As rabbles went, this one was excellent. Sir Roger rubbed his hands together. He said, "Travis we'll need two of those cloaks ourselves to blend in."

"Do you really need me to come with you my lord? I'll only get in the way."

Sir Roger's hand shot out and grabbed Travis by the throat. He lifted him off the ground and brought his face close to Travis's. "You little worm. Of course you're coming. Surely you don't want to miss all the fun, do you?"

"No, no, it was just a thought my lord."

"You can leave the thinking to me Travis." Mudstone released his grip, and a chastised Travis fell to the ground. He stepped over him and grinned at the twenty or so cloaked figures before him. He rubbed his hands together again and said, "Good evening brothers. My name is Sir Roger Mudstone. Tonight I'm going to give you an evening of entertainment you'll never forget. Let's start with a drink. Travis the cider..."

Half an hour later and Sir Roger felt the rabble was suitably inebriated. For good measure he'd given them four pennies each. He and Travis led them out along the road towards Sodham. Once they were out of sight of the main abbey, he had Travis light each of their torches with some smouldering charcoal he'd brought from the abbey's cookhouse in a pot. Sir Roger looked on approvingly. "Excellent, excellent, you'll put the fear of God into anyone we run across. Remember spare nobody, these peasants are like vermin, they need exterminating. Right lads, let's be off."

∽

The crowd in the Man and Scythe were just settling in for the evening. It had been a long day of work for many and the ale was flowing freely. Bernard and Osbert had just eaten in the chamber above and went to join the throng downstairs. Taverner, in between supervising the tap boys, had joined them now and again to ask their opinion on various details of the St Traed's bones work. His enthusiasm had surprised them all, and he was a born organiser. Of all those in the village, he seemed to understand best of all that this was a last chance for Sodham. The church had already been white washed and tomorrow they were going to start on the thatch. They expected Will back in a day or two with the apprentice masons and they could start getting the temporary bridge in place. Much of the fallen stonework from the centre of the river had already been moved and piled on the far bank. For the first time in years there was a feeling of purpose in Sodham.

Bernard was stood at the door of the tavern with a drink in his hand when he first saw the lights high up on the hillside, a line of bobbing bright spots in the gloom. They were an eerie sight and induced a shiver down his spine. He couldn't understand what they could be. After a minute or two, the lights slowly started to descend in a strung out line following the course of the road. There was something vaguely familiar about the scene. He tried hard to remember. It had been a long time ago, and he'd been not much more than a boy. Then it came to him and it was as though a cold hand had seized his heart. He'd been on campaign with Gifford and his father. A night time raid on the enemy's camp. They'd all carried flaming torches and it had been brutal. He dived back into the inn grabbed a startled Taverner by the arm and dragged him to the doorway. He pointed up the valley at the lights. Taverner's mouth gaped open at the bizarre sight. He stood transfixed.

Bernard grabbed hold of Taverner's face between his huge hands and yanked it around so that he was staring directly at him. "Snap out of it man. Now listen to me, there isn't much time. Something very bad is about to happen. That's a band of men coming down the road and they're carrying torches. At the very least, they probably mean to do us injury, more than likely they'll try to kill us if they can. You need to do exactly as I ask. Do you understand me?"

Taverner slowly nodded his head.

"Go into the inn and bar the doors, close the shutters.

Lock the place down as though your life depends on it because it does. Don't stop to explain, by the time you do, it will be too late. Whatever happens don't let anyone out and especially don't let anyone in unless it's me. Whoever's inside will be relatively safe, anyone else will have to take their chances. I'm going to do what I can out here. Now go." He shoved Taverner back through the doorway and pushed the heavy wooden door closed from the outside. Seconds later he heard the heavy bars being put in place behind the door.

Bernard rushed up the stone steps behind the inn that led to the upper rooms. He grabbed his crossbow and bolts from his pack in the backroom and dashed back to the open doorway. He struggled up onto the inn's roof, then crawled to the ridgeline and looked down on the unfolding mayhem.

∽

The mob, their torches held high, hardly paused in their stride as they crossed the river beside the ruined bridge. As they had descended the hillside, Sir Roger had let the more headstrong of them take the lead. He hadn't lived this long by charging head first into the unknown. He preferred to lead from the rear. The head of the mob came to a stop in front of the church and hurled his burning torch into the thatch of the roof. Several of his companions followed his example. Sir Roger looked on approvingly. He lived for times like this, the crackle of the burning thatch and the acrid smoke brought a wicked smile to his lips. From down the street a figure came running towards them, shouting something about fire, uncomprehending of the danger. One of the lay brothers shouted an incoherent challenge and charged towards him, swinging the scythe he carried. The figure was neatly cut off at the ankles and the bloodletting had begun.

Sir Roger shouted, "Burn everything and kill everyone." And the cry was taken up by the braying mob as they started to run amok through Sodham. Sir Roger grabbed hold of a couple of the brothers before they could join the mob and bellowed, "Wait with me!"

Soon there were roofs burning all around and the sounds of screams and shouting filled the air. By now the church roof was well alight and Sir Roger turned his attention to the inn that lay across the street. The door was shut and the shutters covered the windows. He gestured to the two waiting brothers and started towards the building. That was when the first crossbow bolt struck with a sound like a butcher's cleaver cutting a prime joint. The man next to Sir Roger sank to his knees and toppled over onto his side a bolt stuck firmly through his forehead and out the back of his bald head. The remaining brother scuttled away. Sir Roger dived to the ground and rapidly crawled into cover. Travis was still on his feet. Sir Roger grabbed him by the ankle and yanked him to the ground. "Get down fool. There's a man with a crossbow."

"I saw no one master."

"Of course you didn't, you're a blind fool. Now shut up and get over here."

Travis crawled after his master who was now firmly lodged behind a stack of firewood. Sir Roger stuck his head above the wood pile momentarily and tried to spy their attacker. A bolt thudded into the log just inches away from his head sending splinters of wood flying into his face. "Gods teeth!" he hissed. This was not going as smoothly as he'd planned.

Judging by the direction of flight, the bolt had come

from somewhere above. Sir Roger realised that they were now dangerously illuminated by the burning church behind them. Further down the street came a gurgling cry as another one of the lay brothers took a bolt straight through the throat. The injured man came staggering up the street directly towards them, his hands clasping at the shaft of wood embedded into his throat. He gazed at them with a puzzled look then fell face down into the mud and expired with a gurgle.

From his position on the rooftop of the inn, Bernard had a clear view down the long track that composed the main street of Sodham. Most of the thatched buildings were now well ablaze. Only the light from the burning thatch and his years of soldiering with the bishop had enabled him to get off the few bolts he'd fired. Two of the attackers lay dead in the mud, he'd probably injured another and he had some others pinned down directly across the street. But there was only so much one man could do. He could now feel the intense heat from the burning church on his face. He hoped to God it was burning the backsides of the men hiding across the road. The whole of Sodham appeared to be going up in flames and all their plans with it. His only thoughts now were to keep them away from the inn. If he could at least do that something might be salvaged of the whole enterprise.

Above the background din he could hear a man's voice shouting angrily, "Touch me devil's spawn and I swear you'll be excommunicated!" He recognised the voice of Father Mathew and sure enough the familiar figure came pounding down the street towards the burning church. He was scattering the dark hooded figures before him. One made to reach for him but he shoved the figure back violently with a hand to the chest.

"You'd dare attack a priest?" he bellowed. "You'll burn in hell!"

Bernard felt sure they'd hack him down but amazingly the attackers in the street shrank back before his rage. The priest came to a momentary halt in front of his church then plunged through the flame lit doorway.

Bernard clinging to the roof tiles watched open-mouthed as the priest disappeared into the burning building. He couldn't understand what had possessed the man, any fool could see that the building was finished. It would be a miracle if he made it out alive. A light breeze only served to fan the blazing church. Flames started to shoot out of the open doorway. The heat was becoming intense. The priest was surely dead.

Suddenly a blackened and smouldering figure staggered from the building, a leather bag cradled in its arms. It fell to its knees with a soft moan. It was the priest, barely alive. By now most of the lay brothers had wandered back to the church and stood transfixed looking at the hideously burned man before them. Some brothers started to cross themselves. The smell of burnt flesh wafted on the wind.

"It's a miracle, how can a man come out of there alive," one whispered.

"It's a sign from God," said another. "What is it that you have there priest?" he asked.

The blackened figure looked up at him. "Bones," croaked the man, "Saint Traed's bones."

"A saint's bones? Forgive me father for what I have done here."

Another lay brother fell to his knees in front of the priest. "Forgive me father."

∼

Sir Roger, watching from the woodpile, grudgingly admired the priest's stamina. He was burnt to a crisp and couldn't have long to live. But the effect of his miraculous survival on the lay brothers couldn't be allowed to continue. Things had turned out badly enough without turning the bloody man into a martyr as well. Sir Roger darted out impulsively from behind the firewood a short dagger in his hand and headed directly for the priest. The bolt took him by surprise, embedding itself in the soft flesh of his right buttock. The pain made him gasp for air. It felt like someone had thrust a red hot poker into his backside. All thoughts of killing the priest were overridden by the searing pain. He sank to his knees. "Travis," he croaked over his shoulder, "Get over here. Give me your arm."

"What is it master?"

"Can't you see fool, I've been hit in the bloody arse!"

Travis looked at his master rear and could see the bolt stuck through Sir Roger's cloak.

"It's time to leave Travis. Get me back to the abbey." Travis grabbed his master under his armpits and with some effort begin to drag him back into the shadows.

∼

Bernard made his way down from the roof and pushed his way through the lay brothers, cross bow slung in one hand. He crouched down beside the priest, took the leather bag from his burnt hands, and gently lay him down onto the ground. He looked up at the brother's horrified faces. "Who ordered this? Tell me? Was it the abbot?"

He stood up clamped his hands around a lay brother's head and began to squeeze. The terrified man gasped in pain and struggled, his fists pounding against Bernard's chest and sides to no effect. It was one of the other hooded figures who blurted out the answer. "It was that man Mudstone. Plied us with drink and led us down here to sin." Bernard released his grip and the man slumped to his knees with a groan of relief.

With barely controlled rage Bernard hissed at the others, "Go. Go back to your abbey and pray for your miserable souls. Tell your abbot that the Bishop of Draychester will hear of this nights work, the King too. As God is my witness, there will be a terrible reckoning for all of you. Now be gone!"

Two of them hauled the kneeling man upright and backed away from Bernard. He picked the leather bag of bones up from where it lay next to the priest. He held it high with outstretched arms and advanced on them. They scattered before him like leaves in the wind.

29

SPREADING THE WORD

Hik had been trying out his new routine for the past couple of hours. He'd decided to enlist the help of two of his afflicted associates to add some authenticity to the scheme. Close to the minster he would suddenly jump out of his wheelbarrow in front of a group of pilgrims and run up to them. His companions would drop to their knees and start crying with joy and shouting in amazement. He'd weep and shout that St Traed had cured him. The locals paid him scant attention, they knew him all too well, but the pilgrims were more impressionable. The questions came thick and fast, the first was generally, "What did you say the name of this saint was?" And then inevitably, "Where did you say I can see these bones?"

After the first dozen or so miraculous cures his little band had the routine down to a finely honed performance. He'd even managed to squeeze in an additional fund raising sequence that the sergeant might not have approved of. He claimed he was collecting funds to help build a shrine to St Traed in Sodham. He had no intention of handing over anything he collected and also had no intention of ever setting foot outside the city walls if he could help it. The fact that he was also getting paid by the forces of law and order was the final bonus.

By the end of the day Saint Traed's name was starting to circulate amongst the pilgrims as was the name of the place one could see these miraculous bones. One or two had even decided to make the trip out to Sodham themselves and seek the saint's blessing. The fact that Sodham was two days hard walk over the dangerous moors didn't seem to be a deterrent. The self-sacrifice seemed more rewarding for the particularly pious amongst them. An element of risk and the unknown always attracted the thrill seekers, they wore it like a badge of honour. More would follow once the pilgrimage became established.

∼

Padget, the sheriff's sergeant, watched from the entry to a dark alleyway across the street. He soon decided that picking Hik for the job had been the right choice. Their paths had crossed many time over the years. Hik was a rogue and a charlatan to be sure, but Padget had a grudging respect for him. He was never violent or malicious like some he knew. He used the few gifts God had given him to survive the best way he could. Above all, he was a convincing performer and Padget judged the Bishop of Draychester's money well spent. The coins Hik was secretly hiding away would find their way back to Sodham whether Hik liked it or not, Padget would relieve him of them later in the day. He knew all the taverns favoured by Hik when he wasn't plying his trade. As he made his way through the city streets he heard the name of Saint Traed on many a passing pilgrim's lips which brought a wry smile to his own.

There was still one more thing to take care of for the bishop's men, and he made his way to Coppergate where he knew just the man for the job.

Richard Bradshaw was a metalworker who kept a modest shop at the end of the street. When Padget's family had first come to York they'd rented a small place from Richard's father. Padget had come to know the son well and felt he could trust him. There was a lad he didn't know, presumably one of Richards's apprentices, in the shop as he entered. "Is your master in lad?"

"He is sir, who shall I say asks?"

"Tell him it's David Padget, he knows me well."

A few moments later a small pot-bellied man with a big smile on his face emerged from a door at the rear of the shop. "David this is a surprise and a pleasure I might add. How long has it been?"

"Too long my friend, far too long, the sheriff keeps me busy!"

"Well you know you're always welcome, my Meg would be happy to see you, she'd have you matched and married off in no time mind you."

Padget laughed. "Ah, it's not your wife's match making abilities, ferocious though they are that I'm after today my friend. Tell me, do you know somebody that can make me some pilgrim badges?"

Bradshaw looked at him in surprise. "I feel there's a good tale behind that request. Well you've come to the right man, I've supplied my fair share over the years. I've cast them here in the workshop in the past although I've bought them in as well. But what on earth do you want with pilgrim badges?"

"It's a long story," said Padget.

"Then come into the back and tell it to me over some wine my friend."

∼

An hour later after telling his tale and outlining what he required he left the shop with the promise of two hundred pewter Saint Traed's feet. Bradshaw had said ten days and Padget promised to come back and collect them himself. He'd get them out to Sodham somehow. When he arrived back at the castle the sheriff's clerk was waiting for him at the gatehouse. His face was grim. "The sheriff wants to see you in his quarters now."

"What is it man? You look like you've been struck in the face with a skillet."

"He's in a fearsome rage Sergeant. He's not drunk a drop since the messenger arrived which is a bad sign."

"Well spit it out man what's the cause?"

"Sodham in a word. It appears all hells broke loose, village and church burned, men injured or dead..."

"God's teeth! Where's this messenger?"

"The lads up there now, the sheriff is questioning him."

Padget sprinted across the inner courtyard and up the stairs to the sheriff's quarters. The clerk hurried behind him. From behind the door he could hear the sheriff's angry ranting. He pulled up at the door to the chamber, brushed his hands through his hair, took a deep breath, knocked once and entered.

The sheriff said, "Where the bloody hell have you been Padget? You need to hear this sorry tale first hand."

A bedraggled youth sat slumped on the bench opposite the sheriff. He was mud splattered and sweat stained. Padget recognized him as one of Taverner's stable boys from the inn at Sodham. He looked half terrorised, no doubt the sheriff had been his usual calm self. "I'm sorry my lord, my duties took me to the other side of the city."

"You will be bloody sorry Padget. Gifford's men have apparently stirred up a wasp's nest out in Sodham. You were only there two days ago, I thought the situation was under control?"

"It was quiet when I left my lord, I don't understand what's happened."

The sheriff stabbed his finger at the boy. "Tell him boy. Tell him what a bucket full of shite you have brought to my door."

The boy turned his white face to the sergeant, his eyes wide. "It were the lay brothers from the abbey Sergeant. They came at dusk, two days ago, carrying torches."

Padget crouched down in front of the boy. "Its Michael isn't it?" The boy nodded. "It's all right Michael, tell me slowly, what did these men do?"

"Burnt everything sir, the church, most of the village, Father Mathew is near death and many others with him."

The sheriff slumped back against the wall. "Hear that Padget, even attacked the bloody priest. I know Jocelyn Gifford, once he learns of this we'll have no end of trouble. As if we didn't have a difficult enough job already. It's a bloody disaster!"

Padget ignored the sheriff's rant. "The inn Michael, they burnt that as well?"

The boy shook his head. "No, the inns still stands. Taverner sent me to bring word. I rode all last night and today."

"And the bishop's men they're harmed?"

The boy shook his head again. "The big man, he killed

some of the lay brothers with his crossbow. He climbed up on the roof. The clerk was with us, barricaded in the inn."

Padget smiled in grim satisfaction. "That would be Bernard with the crossbow. He told me himself that he campaigned with Gifford in his younger days. A hard man to come up against in a fight."

The sheriff looked at Padget in despair. "You make it sound like that's a good thing. We've got Gifford's men killing the bloody monks from Ribsdale Abbey. Have you any idea the mess this is? It's even worse than I thought."

Padget snapped, "I'm not a fool my lord. I understand the situation. If the king thinks we can't keep order he'll have us replaced."

"Replaced? He'll have me strung up for God's sake. As for you Padget, if you're lucky you'll be spending the rest of your days cleaning out the cess pits at some castle on the Welsh border. Do you understand me?"

"Perfectly my lord. Let me take some of the men from the garrison and ride out there."

The sheriff got to his feet, his face looked like thunder. "You'll take twenty men and horses and get out there at once. I keep order in this shire, I want to know what the hell is going on. Do you understand me? I won't have it Padget, do you hear me, there will be order!"

"Yes my lord."

30

THE MESSAGE

One of Padget's men found Will as he was leaving the cathedral archives. They were soon hurrying back to the castle. Will's newly gained knowledge of the priest's past only added to the alarm he felt. He didn't doubt Father Mathew had killed William of Wallcot. The question was what else he would do to conceal his crime. Although concerned for the companions he'd left behind in Sodham he also worried for his own future. God alone knew what the bishop's reaction would be if this turned into a disaster. He needed to get back to Sodham as fast as possible.

Padget and a host of armed men were already gathered in the castle yard when he arrived. He saw his own horse amongst them. "You've heard what's happened?" shouted Padget over the swirling mass of men and horses.

Will shouted back, "Yes, and I've made some troubling discoveries of my own. I need to get back there."

"Your horse is already saddled, grab your pack and we'll be on our way. The sheriff is furious, he wants to know what harm has come to your companions."

"What about Sodham, is he not worried about the villagers as well?" asked Will sarcastically.

Padget gave him a sour look and said, "The sheriff fears the bishop and the king's retribution, he cares little for Sodham itself Will. He looks to save his own neck, remember, the higher one rises the harder one falls."

Will nodded wearily in acknowledgment. "We'd better be on our way then. I've enough worry for everyone."

31

A REAL MARTYR

It was two days after the raid that Will and the sheriff's men returned to Sodham. They had ridden as hard as they could, continuing well into the dusk on the first day. Finally they had called a halt and camped at the roadside high on the moors. It had been an uncomfortable night, and they had set off again at first light with hardly a pause to eat. As they rode down into the village, Will was grim faced as he saw the damage. The inn was virtually untouched, but as for the rest, it made him boil with anger.

Will brought his horse to a halt in front of the burnt out church. Bernard had watched the riders come down the road into the valley and he wearily walked over to join them, Osbert despondently trailing after him. Bernard looked up at Will and said, "A bad business lad, but it could have been worse and they didn't get away without cost."

Will shook his head and contemplated the smouldering remains of the village. "Taverner's boy said it was some of the lay brothers from the abbey?"

Bernard nodded. "It was, they were led by that bastard Roger Mudstone, I'd know him anywhere. I'm sure I hit him with a bolt from my crossbow. From what I could see he might have trouble sitting down for a while. We'd have had him but some lackey hauled him off in the confusion. I suspect he's up at the abbey's infirmary getting his sore arse sorted."

Padget said, "Well I'm going to take a ride up the valley to the abbey with my men. Strictly speaking it's out of our jurisdiction, but I'm sure the sheriff wouldn't object to us putting on a show of force in the circumstances. Twenty armed men sat in his courtyard should focus the abbot's mind on whether to shelter this Mudstone character. We might swing down to that manor of his as well."

Bernard said, "You'd better hurry then. I know his type, he'll go to ground to lick his wounds. Better be careful sergeant."

Padget nodded. "We'll be back by night fall. Hopefully with Mudstone." He called to his men, and they were soon on the move again up the valley.

∼

Will climbed down from his horse with some difficulty, his limbs were stiff and sore from the hard riding. "What of Father Mathew, is he still alive?" he asked Bernard.

"Barely, I'd be surprised if he lasts the morning."

"But is he conscious?"

"Only for a few minutes at a time, why?"

"I need to ask him about what I found in York."

"The poor bugger is finished lad, we should leave him in peace."

"I believe he killed Walcott and I think I know why."

Bernard swore under his breath. "I knew he wasn't telling us everything, but murder! You have proof?"

Will nodded. "I went to the church archives at the minister. He'd definitely met William Walcott before, back in his youth in York. There was a murdered girl involved. The priest was sent here to get him out of the way and to do penance. Our man Walcott turning up here I'm sure was probably chance, but the priest recognised him, of that I'm sure. Where is he?"

Bernard pointed over towards the ruined church. "We lay him on his bed in his shack behind the church, its undamaged. Not much else we could do for him. Taverner's daughter is tending him. I'm not sure what sense you'll get out of him. Once you see the state he's in you'll realise it'll be a death bed confession."

As they walked around to the small shack behind the burnt out wreck of the church, Will told Bernard what he'd discovered back in the city. The shack had been spared the flames and looked virtually untouched. When they entered the smell in the confined space almost made Will gag. He'd remember that smell for the rest of his life, sickeningly sweet, like burnt pork. Taverner's daughter was on her knees with a damp cloth held to the priest's face. She squeezed some drops onto his parched lips.

"Is he conscious?" asked Will

The burnt man's eyes flickered open at his voice.

"I hear you bishop's man," he rasped.

Will said, "I've been to York Father Mathew, I know your story."

A thin cough that could have been a laugh came from the injured man's throat. "You know some of it. I suspect you want to know all of it. Better come closer boy, my voice is going." Bernard gestured for the girl to leave them. They knelt either side of the straw bed so they could catch his words. "I was sent here from York to do penance, that much you probably know. As for the girl in York, Helene was her name, I loved her. If that's a sin then I was guilty, but I swear I didn't kill her. She was the love of my life. They butchered her with no more regard than if she'd been a sow." His eyes were a watery washed out blue. With some effort, he raised his head up and looked at each of them in turn. "I've no reason to lie to you now."

Will nodded his acknowledgment. "I believe you Father, I do. But what of William Walcott, you recognised him of course?"

"I knew him again as soon as I laid eyes on him. How could I ever forget that face?"

"What happened?" said Bernard.

"He didn't know me at first, or at least he wasn't sure. I'm not much to look at these days. Twenty years on the moors in all weathers does that to a man. Still, I knew what must be done."

"And what was that Father?" asked Will.

The priest said slowly as if to a child, "Why, he had to be destroyed of course. The man was the spawn of the devil my son. He wasn't fit to walk on God's earth."

Bernard said, "Are you saying God told you to murder him?"

The priest looked confused. "In a way I suppose he did. It wasn't hard. He was drunk, laying in his bed in the chamber above the inn. There was a knife on the table. I picked it up and I laid his neck open like he had done to my poor sweet Helene all those years ago. He didn't even wake, it was an easier death than he deserved."

Bernard and Will exchanged a startled look. Will said, "As for Wallcot, I can understand your reasons Father, but why did you go back into the burning church? The bones, you of all people know that they don't belong to a real saint."

Father Mathew managed one last smile and whispered, "People need things to believe in. Call it my penance for the sins I've committed. You'll come to understand my actions my son. Remember only God can say what is real and what isn't." He lay back on the bed and closed his eyes and said no more.

They left him in peace under the watch once again of Taverner's daughter. He died around noon, never regaining consciousness. The girl came to tell them as they were surveying the damage to the rest of the village. Bernard, Will and Osbert trudged back to the shelter.

"Bloody fool," Bernard said, gazing at the dead man sadly. "Still, I dare say Sodham can lay claim to a real martyr now."

Osbert looked at him scandalised, "He was a brave man to risk his life for the relics."

"Relics my arse and I didn't say he wasn't brave lad. That doesn't mean to say he wasn't a bloody fool to go into the flames for a few old bones, although I think I understand his reasons."

Osbert said, "It was God's will surely."

"Maybe so lad, maybe so."

Osbert stared glumly at the dead man, "What are we to do now?"

Will put a hand on Osbert's shoulder and said, "Sodham still needs a reason to exist. In his own way Father Mathew has just made its future a lot more secure. I suppose that's some sort of legacy at least."

Osbert looked puzzled. "I'm not sure I understand you?"

Bernard smiled. "Well of course you don't, you're really a rather simple soul Osbert. Anyway now that the sheriff has sent us half the York city watch I doubt we need fear for our security, but we could certainly do with their labour for a week or so."

Later that afternoon some women from the village washed as best they could Father Mathew's battered and burnt body and sewed him into a shroud. On Bernard's instruction, they left him on his bed in the shelter behind the burnt out church. His funeral would have to wait awhile longer.

~

The bishop's men now accompanied by Taverner continued with their inspection of the village. Apart from the church, which was a burnt out wreck, about a third of the houses had some damage. The thatched roofs had burned readily and the wattle and daub walls had been easily tumbled. There were half a dozen villagers dead, the same number injured. The abbey's men had taken their own dead and injured with them. If they had been left behind the villagers would no doubt have taken their own vengeance. Bernard wished he could have done more, but it would have been suicidal to tackle the mob head on. Taverner said as much to him, "You couldn't have done anything else. If you hadn't gotten us to barricade the inn, we'd most likely all be dead and Sodham finished."

Bernard shook his head sadly. "On days like this I feel like I'm getting too old for the bishop's service. One thing I do know Taverner, there'll be a reckoning for this, our bishop is not a man to cross."

Tavener poked his foot at a pile of ash and said, "That's as maybe, but what are we to do in the meantime?"

Will, with as determined a look as any of them had ever

seen on his face, said, "We follow the plan we had, nothing's changed in that respect. The bridge still needs rebuilding and the church needs a new roof now. We need to get people to want to come here again. I know the man's barely cold, but once word spreads about Father Mathew we could build a shrine to a real martyr now."

32

TROUBLE AT THE ABBEY

The abbot of Ribsdale was in a cold rage. The news of the disastrous raid had reached him as he'd been indulging in one of his many vices, namely food. The truth was, he was at an age where he was starting to prefer a good meat pie more than a romp with one of the kitchen girls. The prior had burst in as he was about to start a sumptuous private banquet for one. "Prior Robert, you better have a good excuse for interrupting me yet again. It's becoming tiresome in the extreme. These pies are ruined if you don't eat them while they're hot."

The prior's face was grey and drawn, "My lord..."

"Yes what is it man? Spit it out."

"It's Mudstone, I'm afraid he made a terrible mess of things."

The abbot sighed and put down his pie. "It's becoming harder and harder to find the right sort of help, do you know that Robert? At my time of life I should be slowing down and enjoying the fruit of my labours."

"Yes my lord."

Prior Robert led the abbot to the abbey's infirmary. They

found Sir Roger lying face down naked on a straw mattress, presenting his hairy arse to the world. Brother John, the abbey's infirmerer, had just removed the crossbow bolt from his backside. It had proved an extremely painful exercise. Sir Roger had forsaken the infirmerer's offer of a pain-relieving draft and had instead drunk a whole keg of the abbey's finest cider. He was roaring drunk. The abbot said, "Prior Robert tells me four of our lay brothers are dead Mudstone. I believe you've allowed things to get out of hand. Your little escapade has turned into a fiasco."

"Well, well, I wondered when you'd show your face. If it isn't our fat master in person," Sir Roger said turning over to face the abbot. He painfully hauled himself onto his feet. Taking a swig from the keg of cider he hobbled over towards the abbot who backed away somewhat alarmed.

Prior Robert stepped between them outraged. "How dare you speak to my lord abbot in such a way and for God's sake man cover yourself up!"

"Cover myself up!" roared Sir Roger, "You cowardly little turd. I know your type, let others do the dirty work but turn tail when the going gets tough."

The abbot turned red with rage and indignation, he fought to gain his breath but could only splutter an outraged, "You..."

Prior Robert said, "Let us leave my lord, the man's clearly drunk."

"Drunk. You're right I'm drunk and I'm in the mood to throttle the life out of both of you." He lunged forward at them and managed to tear the front of Prior Robert's cowl. The now petrified prior turned and pushed the abbot back through the doorway of the infirmary, swiftly followed by Sir Roger. The two monks hurried up the corridor pursued by the naked man waving the cider keg menacingly.

"That's it, run for your life you fat little turds," he roared, "I'm going to rip your hearts out if I catch you."

It was Travis, fearful for both of them who finally brought Sir Roger to a halt by clinging to his legs. "My lord, we must leave."

Sir Roger's rage subsided enough to realise that charging naked through the abbey might not be the best of ideas. He kicked Travis hard a few times to vent his anger but the man wouldn't let go. "Please my lord, I already have our belongings packed, and the horses saddled. The cook tells me she spotted a party of soldiers on the road only this morning. They're surely heading to Sodham and then here."

"Soldiers eh, I'll take them all on. Bring them on, do you hear me Travis you little worm, I'll take them all on."

"At least let me get you some clothes master."

Travis released his grip and Sir Roger looked down at him. He said, "I'm surrounded by incompetents Travis, do you know that?"

"Yes my lord."

Sir Roger sighed heavily. "Find me some clothes Travis. We'd better ride, the abbot will have to wait."

∼

A short time later, and they were on the road leading away from the abbey to the west. It rose high out of the valley and headed out across the moors. Sir Roger quickly sobered up in the cool air. Red Eyes, his war horse, was a ferocious beast in a fight but he wasn't built for prolonged speed and they made slow progress out of the valley. "Do you think someone will follow master?" said Travis. He looked anxiously back down towards the abbey.

"Not the good brothers. Have no fear there, they have no

spine for a fight, but look past the abbey Travis. What do you see?"

Travis squinted hard trying to make out anything in the haze of the valley bottom. Then he saw what the eagle-eyed Sir Roger had already seen. Tiny figures on horseback, perhaps fifteen or more, it was difficult to be certain. They were moving fast along the road towards the abbey. "Men on horses. Soldiers?"

"Let's not find out. If you have any regard for that scrawny backside of yours then make haste Travis." Sir Roger dug his spurred heels into the horse's flank and the beast snorted angrily but picked up speed. Travis dug his boots and knees into his own horse but soon found himself trailing Sir Roger.

∼

Padget had no expectation of a warm welcome at Ribsdale Abbey. The sheriff's and by extension his own authority did not extend to the abbot's domain. Still the man needed to be reminded that there were always limits. If they had any chance of snaring Mudstone, he needed to give the abbot no time to think.

They rode fast and hard and covered the few miles between Sodham and the abbey in a little less than half an hour. As luck would have it, the main gates were open, a heavy cart lumbering out of the gateway. Padget, without dismounting urged his horse down the side of the cart and through the gateway followed by his men. There was a startled shout from the gatekeeper as they thundered past into the inner courtyard. He ran after them shouting angrily. "You can't just ride in here without warning. Who are you and what do you want?"

Padget gestured to one of his men who rode over to the gatekeeper and caught the back of his hood. He dragged the startled man across the cobbles of the courtyard and dumped him in front of Padget's horse. Padget pointed a finger at him and said, "If I were you I'd shut your mouth and listen very carefully. Don't speak again unless it's answering my questions, do you understand?"

The man nodded open mouthed.

"Sir Roger Mudstone, where is he?"

Before the man could answer him, from a doorway on the far side of the courtyard emerged the fat abbot, the prior and several of the other brothers. The abbot came storming over to them. "What is the meaning of this outrage? Who the devil are you to burst in here like this?"

"I've no doubt you have a good idea who we are my lord and why we're here. My names Padget, sergeant in the sheriff's service. We've just come from Sodham, it's not a pretty sight, I believe you have some involvement in the deed?"

"I don't know what you're talking about man. You have no authority here, sheriff's man or not. I demand you and your men leave at once. This is outrageous."

Padget stared the abbot directly in the eyes and said, "I'll tell you what's outrageous my lord, that a man such as you would let loose a thug like Mudstone to do your dirty work. Now tell me quickly where Sir Roger Mudstone is or, God is my witness, I'll tear this abbey apart in the search."

"You dare to threaten me Padget?"

Padget bent down closer to the abbot and whispered, "It's not a threat my lord abbot, it's a promise..."

They glared at each other for a minute neither willing to bow to the others will. Padget gestured to his men who started to dismount and the abbot suddenly buckled under the pressure. "He's gone, less than a half hour ago," he spluttered.

"Where?" hissed Padget.

"I know not. He's not a men to reveal his intentions. He took the road to the west."

"How many of them?"

"Just him and his man, they took their horses and packs and were gone. Good riddance to them."

Padget looked at him for a moment, decided he'd pushed it as far as he'd dare and made the slightest of bows with his head. "My lord." He turned to his men, "Come on, we may catch him yet."

And they were gone as swiftly as they had arrived, leaving a fuming but humbled abbot in their wake. They followed the road west. The track and the surrounding landscape seem deserted apart from the abbey's flocks grazing. They pressed on and were soon rewarded with the sight of two figures on horseback in the far distance. They crested a ridge and vanished from sight again. Padget grinned and said, "It's them. They're no more than a quarter mile ahead and they can't keep that pace up."

Excited with the chase, they thundered down the road after Sir Roger. Padget knew this way, he'd been up here often enough as a lad. Ahead over the ridge of the hill, the track branched left back down into the next valley and to Coxington. The main route continued west over the moors.

∽

Once out of sight of the pursuing soldiers Sir Roger made a split second decision and brought his mount to an abrupt halt, causing Travis's own horse to run into the back of them. Sir Roger jumped down, reached back up, and pulled his bewildered retainer from his own horse. He threw Travis headfirst into a water-filled ditch that was set back from the road and shielded from it by a long line of bilberry bushes. Quickly tying the reins of Travis's horse to the saddle of his own he pointed the head of the great beast towards the track into the valley. He took a short dagger hidden in his boot and plunged it into the rump of the warhorse. The enraged beast shot forward dragging the other horse along behind. They plunged down into the valley and were soon lost from sight.

~

Padget was first to the ridge. He could see for miles across the moors yet the way ahead was empty. His quarry could only have gone down the track to the left and was now hidden in the trees that lined the route down into the valley. He urged his horse to the left and down, swiftly followed by his men.

Sir Roger and Travis watched from the ditch, hidden from sight, as Padget and his men took the road into the valley. Sir Roger said, "Pity about Red Eyes. That beast was worth three of you Travis. Still, needs must." He hauled Travis to his feet. The man was soaked to the skin and shivering violently in the cold breeze coming off the moors. "Well don't just stand there man. We need to put a few miles between us and them before nightfall. We'll need to avoid the road of course, too obvious by far." He pointed out into the bleak, featureless moorland that lay to the right of the road. "That way. Get moving."

~

Padget continued into the valley bottom to Coxington. On their way down they had heard horses ahead. They were always just out of sight as the road twisted and turned down the hillside. At the bottom they found Mudstone's remaining manor deserted. From what they could see no one had been there for days if not weeks. A great warhorse stood in the centre of the deserted street, its sides heaving. A dagger was buried up to the hilt in its rump and blood ran freely down its sides. Another horse stood behind it head down munching grass from the verge.

Padget was in a rage. "Damn the man, I fear he's given us the slip back there on the moor. It must have been at the turning. He's set these two loose to confuse us."

One of his men looked up at the sky and said, "It's getting late sarge, they'll be out across the moor by now. We won't catch them before dark."

Padget nodded. "I know it. We're going to have to get some dogs from Sodham, track them from first light. They won't get far up there on foot."

33

THE REBUILD

Padget and the bishop's men were taking breakfast in the room over the inn in Sodham. After two days of fruitless searching, Padget had admitted defeat and conceded that Mudstone had somehow given them the slip. "I don't know where the bastard has gone but I've no doubt the sheriff will do all in his power to have him declared an outlaw. Maybe Bishop Gifford will even stump up a price on his head?"

Bernard grunted his agreement and said, "I'm sure he will. That turd will surface somewhere you can be sure of it and when he does, we'll hear. My lord bishop has eyes and ears across the kingdom."

Will said, "Can you not stay for a few days at least Sergeant? We could do with the manpower to get things underway."

"I can give you a few days young Will, if only to postpone having to give my report to the sheriff. He'll not be happy that Mudstone has managed to get away. What will you have us do?"

"Help with the thatch on the church for a start. Then there's the bridge."

"I see the mason's lads arrived last night."

"They're down by the river now looking at what's left of our bridge. I know the master mason at York has given them some ideas on what can be salvaged. I did my best to give him a description of the ruins. If we can at least get people across the river without getting their feet wet, it'll be a start. Getting carts across can come later."

The four of them finished their bread and cheese and then walked down to the river. The two apprentice masons were knee deep in the river by the old bridge examining the remains of the piers. "What's the verdict lads?" Bernard shouted.

The smaller of the two waded across to the river bank and clambered out beside them. "Well the piers aren't as bad as we feared. They're sound for a year or two. They'll need replacing if you ever want a proper bridge again, but for now we can patch them up. We can get a wooden walkway across for you."

Bernard grunted his approval. "That'll do for a start. Will we able to get pack horses across?"

The lad nodded. "I think so, with care."

"How long will it take do you think?" said Will anxiously.

"To patch the piers up, a week, more likely two, depends if the weather holds. We'll need some labour to shift the stone."

"Then you'd better make the best use of me and my men. I can give you a few days," said Padget.

"Don't worry there's plenty to do," said the lad with a grin. He turned to Will. "We're going to need your carpenter.

I'll talk with him about the walkway. That's going to take another week at least."

Will nodded. "Whatever help you need, whoever you need, you just have to ask, the faster we do this the better. I'm hoping to see our first pilgrims anytime soon."

"About Agnes," said Will. "If she's to become our bridge hermit then she'll need some permanent shelter."

Osbert said, "If you're serious, I'd suggest it's on the far side of the bridge, if only for the sanity of the rest of the village."

Bernard laughed. "What else are we to do with her? She will need something simple but warm and dry, we could have pilgrims coming at all hours of the day wanting to cross the bridge."

Osbert said, "I must say your optimism is amazing."

"Have faith Osbert, they'll come…"

They left the mason's lads to their work and walked back up to the church. They stood in the graveyard and looked at the burnt-out shell of the building.

Will said, "I believe the carpenter has already built us a simple reliquary for the bones. Fortunately he'd not taken it into the church before the attack. Which brings me back to poor Father Mathew. Shouldn't we bury him? I can't think he would have wanted to be anywhere else but this church yard?"

Bernard said, "I think you're right lad and the village needs to move on. They must still have a grave digger about the place?"

"Unless he's amongst the dead of course," Osbert said.

"Cheerful sod as always aren't you. If he is then you'll be doing the grave digging, I'll supervise," said Bernard.

Osbert look suitably outraged. "Scribes don't dig, we record events!"

Before the argument could development any further Will said, "We'd best start on the church. The walls look sound, but we need timber for the roof beams and thatch. Oh and whitewash, we need lots of whitewash."

∼

They buried Father Mathew and his dead parishioners in the churchyard the following day. It was a brief affair, people paid their respects but Will felt a desperation in their need not to linger over the dead. The living recognised this was Sodham's last chance. The choice was now to rebuild or to move on. If the village survived, they would need a new priest. He'd leave that problem to the Bishop of Draychester. He was sure he'd hear of it in Osbert's next dispatch.

∼

A week and a half passed and the piers were repaired as best as they were going to be. The carpenter, his apprentice and various other folk roped into the business had started to erect a scaffold that fanned out from the piers and supported a slender wooden walkway two planks wide. It would only last a season or two at best, Will was under no illusion otherwise, but the sight made his heart soar. On the far riverbank at the entrance to the walkway, they had built a small hut made of wattle and daub for Agnes.

The blacked walls of the church had been painted a brilliant white both inside and out. The roof was still open to the sky, but the roof timbers were neatly stacked outside alongside the new straw thatch ready to be put in place. Will had been spending the money the bishop had given them freely. He hoped the bishop would agree it had been spent wisely, Osbert was keeping a full account of it, he was sure. A few days more and the church was finished. The wooden reliquary was put in place. It was a square wooden box of polished oak, with Saint Traed's bones visible through a sliding door on the side. It was placed in the centre of a flat stone slab they had dragged up from the riverside, once part of the bridge. One of the mason's lads had spent a day smoothing the rough surface down. There was just enough room for the reliquary to sit in the middle and for candles to surround it. For all its simplicity, in the darkened interior of the church, the effect was impressive.

34

FIRST PILGRIM

It was Taverner's boy Michael who brought them the news first. He ran down the road from the high moorland into the valley, past Agnes's new hut, across the temporary bridge and came to a breathless stop in front of the inn. Bernard had sent him up there every morning for the last week to watch the road.

"They're coming," he gasped. "A party of them, must be at least twenty."

"Who boy? Soldiers, monks?" asked Bernard anxiously.

"No, pilgrims on foot, they even have staffs and hats."

Will said, "Are you absolutely sure?"

Michael was jigging about from one foot to the other with excitement. "Recognised some of them I did. From when I was in York. They were at the great church there."

"The minister you mean," said Osbert.

"That's what I said, the big church."

They stood there half in shock. Will was the first to recover. He grinned and said, "I can hardly believe it, it's worked!"

Osbert said sourly, "Yes a miracle indeed."

"We need to get to work before they arrive. Bernard, where's Agnes? She's needs to be in position to collect a bridge toll," said Will.

"She will be asleep in her hut over there. Can't get her out of the place since we finished it."

"Can someone go and wake her up then."

"I'll walk down there myself and wake the old crone up, although God alone knows what the pilgrims will make of her."

Will punched Osbert playfully on the arm. "Osbert you and I are going to light the candles in the church around our ancient reliquary and be available to tell the tale of Saint Traed if anyone asks."

Osbert grimaced. "I think the story of Father Mathew rescuing the bones from the blaze would be more truthful."

"Frankly I don't care as long as you tell it well," said Will.

"I'm sure our visitors will be hungry and thirsty and hopefully want a bed for the night," Taverner said rubbing his hands together in anticipation.

Bernard quickly roused Agnes from her slumbers in the hut. She was soon stood by the entrance to the bridge softly chortling to herself. Bernard positioned himself on the bridge and leaned against one of the new wooden railings. He wouldn't have missed this for the world. What they would make of Agnes he didn't know, but it was sure to be entertaining.

∽

The pilgrims who emerged on the road from the top of the valley were what Bernard could fairly describe as the hard core kind. Not for them the simple novelty of the journey or a single day out at the nearest shrine. No, he knew this type well, they could be found at all the major shrines and on the roads in between. In Bernard's experience, those who went on pilgrimage as a matter of pure faith were few and far between. From what he could see these were travelling as penance for some sin or in hopes of a cure for illness. Dressed in black and brown cloaks they wore broad-brimmed hats and walked with a wooden staff. Secured by a shoulder strap, they each carried a large leather satchel. Even at a distance he could see the multiple pilgrims' badges pinned to their cloaks.

The lead figure was a formidable-looking woman of indeterminate age, stout build and ferocious expression. She carried a metal-tipped staff which she smashed into the ground with each relentless stride forward. Her cloak was adorned with the largest collection of pilgrims badges Bernard had ever seen. There was no doubt who was in charge and the others followed along in her wake. There were four or five women, one not much more than a girl. The rest of the party consisted of two old men who hobbled along supporting each other, a thin grey faced man and what could only be his son as they looked so much alike, three well-dressed fellows and two others who were dressed like beggars. As they approached the bridge, Agnes shuffled into their path and gave her best ear shrieking cackle.

Even the lead pilgrim looked suitably taken aback by the performance. Bernard couldn't help but stifle a chuckle. He'd no doubt they'd been to a lot of shrines before, but he was pretty sure they'd never encountered anyone quite like Agnes. She looked Agnes up and down and said, "God's teeth, what ails you Woman, are you of feeble mind?"

Agnes stuck out her hand and cackled. The woman moved to step around her. Agnes shuffled with surprising speed to block her way.

"Can't you see Matilda, the Woman is a bridge hermit. We need to pay for our passage." It was the thin man who had spoken. The rest of the party came to a stop behind him.

"Well she should say so, we haven't got all day," the woman snapped back. She undid the leather script she wore, dug around and retrieved a penny which she dropped in Agnes's hand and then swiftly stepped around the old crone and made her way onto the bridge. The others followed suit and Agnes and Sodham was soon twenty pennies the richer. The woman, Matilda, paused to speak to Bernard at the halfway point across the bridge. "We've journeyed from York. I take it this is Sodham?"

"Oh yes, this is Sodham all right," beamed Bernard.

"The shrine of Saint Traed, is it far?"

"Err the shrine. Well let me see, no it's not far good woman. See, the church is just there." He pointed to the far side of the bridge.

"That's it? It's very small."

"True, it's a small shrine, but then Saint Tread was a humble man."

"You knew him?" she asked.

"Not personally, but he was well known around these parts."

"Hmmph. Well I've heard in York of some miraculous cures taking place here. It's been a long journey, I hope we won't be disappointed."

"What sort of miracle are you looking for?" asked Bernard curiously

"It's not for me you understand, " the woman said, seemingly evading the question. "Some of my companions are afflicted."

"Ah, you seek cures then?"

"For them, yes of course." Seemingly not willing to part with any more information she moved on across the narrow plank walkway, her companions trailing after. Bernard gave them a minute and then followed. Behind him he could hear the faint cackling of Agnes. At least someone was happy.

~

An hour later and Taverner was also a happy man. He had twenty guests to accommodate. The inn hadn't been as busy in years. The pilgrims had opted to seek accommodation and a meal before the more spiritual matters across at the church. Will and Osbert loitered nervously at the church door. Osbert said, "You'd think having come all this way they'd at least have the decency to come in here first."

"I think we may have underestimated the draw of Taverner's hot stew and a pot of ale," said Will sarcastically.

"Well I'm going to blow some candles out, we have little enough funds for anymore."

"If you must. Just be ready to light them again if they decide to come over. I wouldn't want to ruin the effect." In the end Will walked across to the inn. The pilgrims were having a meal. There was a great deal of noise and laughter. He looked meaningfully at Taverner who was hovering around the table waiting on his customers. He just grinned and shrugged. They didn't look in any hurry to see Saint Traed's bones.

Bernard, who had been sitting with the party, got up and walked over. He whispered, "Don't be so impatient lad, they're here aren't they. They'll take a look across at the church soon enough. Let them enjoy the meal and the inn, it's all part of the experience. The more content they are, the better this will work."

"I suppose you're right but I can't help but think we should have spent more time on the church."

"We did all we could with what we had lad. It a bloody miracle the place even has a roof on it. Look, let's give them some time to finish their meal and down a few more ales and I'll bring them over myself. In the mean time I'll spin the tale of our late priest rescuing the bones from the fire, you can't deny it's a dramatic story."

Will went back over to the church to keep Osbert company. When he had judged a half hour had passed, they lit most of the candles again around the wooden reliquary of Saint Traed's feet. Not long after Bernard led the group of pilgrims into the interior and they stood in a hushed group in front of the candles.

~

In the flickering candlelight the little group began to shuffle slowly around the reliquary led by Bernard. The pilgrims mouthing a prayer as they circled the relic three times. Will reflected that the effect would be better led by a priest but in the circumstances he thought Bernard had done the right thing. Some of the pilgrims then knelt down and began to pray in front of the relic.

Bernard backed away from the group and stood beside Will. He whispered in his ear, "Give them a moment or two and offer to open the reliquary door so they can touch the saint's feet."

"Are you absolutely sure, it's not even real is it?" Will whispered back, somewhat taken aback at the effect the so-called relics were having.

"You heard what Father Mathew said, it's all about belief Will. Just look at them" Bernard grinned. A couple of the pilgrims had now crawled forward on their knees and were kissing the flat stone surface in front of the reliquary. "Let's make sure they make a suitable offering on the way out. Pity the pilgrim badges haven't arrived yet."

"And I thought I was bad," muttered Will shaking his head.

Even so he walked slowly forward and whispered softly behind the group of pilgrims. "For those of you afflicted with various ailments I will open the reliquary. Feel free to briefly touch Saint Traed's feet. I hope he brings you the healing you desire."

"Amen," said the stout woman named Matilda.

Will went around the side of the group and gently leaned over the wooden reliquary and slid back the side door. There were some audible gasps from the pilgrims behind. The sight was undeniably striking. Saint Tread's worn leather boots complete with two shin bones popping out over the tops stood just within the wooden box. He gently eased back and allowed the pilgrims to approach.

"The boots are Saint Traed's?" whispered Matilda.

"The very same," said Will straight faced.

The pilgrims had formed themselves into a queue and were slowly shuffling forward and each reverently touched the tip of one of Saint Traed's boots. Will was beginning to feel decidedly guilty. He felt Osbert's eyes on the back of his head. Sure enough, when he turned around Osbert was glaring at him. He shrugged in the dim light of the church. Osbert could be as disapproving as he liked, but needs must.

The woman Matilda came back to stand next to him. They both stood looking at the pilgrims in front of the shrine. Eventually the woman murmured, "This is an interesting place. Have Saint Traed's bones been here long?"

"Not long, the bones were rediscovered only recently."

The woman sniffed. "I see. That's why the church is simple and unadorned and the reliquary plain?"

Will didn't know where the conversation was going. "The village has suffered some recent misfortune as you may have heard. We try our best."

"I think I may be able to help."

Will was taken aback. "Well that's very kind of you. Perhaps your party could help us. We still have some whitewashing to do and…"

She cut him off with a brisk, "That's not what I had in mind."

"Ah well…" Will was at a loss.

"Don't let my dress as a pilgrim fool you young man. I'm a very wealthy woman. Tell me, what exactly is your position here?"

Will was starting to feel quite uncomfortable. "I'm an official of the Bishop of Draychester. William Blackburne at your service."

The woman's eyes widened with surprise, "You're Jocelyn Gifford's man? He's the lord of this manor?"

Will pulled his seal from under his shirt and lay it in the palm of his hand to show her. "I am and he is."

"Well, well, that is interesting. Come, walk me back to the tavern William."

Will thought there was something about this woman that was vaguely familiar, perhaps they had met before, but that couldn't be, he would definitely have remembered her.

"Have you served Jocelyn long?"

"I've been in the bishop's service for only a few weeks."

"And before that?" she asked. Will hesitated which made

the woman smile and say, "Never mind, no need to answer that, let's just say I know how Jocelyn works. If you're in his service he must see something in you."

Will looked at her curiously. She smiled again and said, "I know your bishop well, or at least I did."

"Ah I see," said Will not knowing quite how to take this piece of information.

She continued, "It's been many years since we've seen each other. I've been on pilgrimage, first to Santiago and on to the Holy Land and then back. I've visited most of the holy shrines in England and I sense there's more to this one than meets the eye young William, am I right?"

Will decided he could trust her with at least some of the facts. They entered the inn and he led her to one of the tables near the fire. He called Bernard over and hurriedly whispered in his ear that the woman seemed to know their master well. Over cups of the inn's finest ale she slowly coaxed the recent weeks' events out of them. When they had finished she said, "I mentioned to William earlier that I think I may be able to help you and do some good for my own soul as well. Do you think fifteen pounds would be enough to repair the bridge properly and embellish the shrine and church?"

Will and Bernard just looked at her in amazement.

"Well don't just sit there with your mouths open."

Will recovered his wits first. "That would be very generous. Perhaps in the form of a gift to the Four and Twenty of Sodham?" He swiftly explained the Four and Twenty's role in the manor.

Matilda said, "Of course you'll need to make provision for prayers for my immortal soul to be said in perpetuity before the shrine of Saint Traed."

Will nodded his agreement. "Of course, of course. They

can begin at once, although thinking about it I'm sorry to say we no longer have a priest."

"I'm sure the bishop will appoint someone suitable when he hears what has gone on here. Which brings to mind that perhaps it's also time I wrote to him. It's been far too long. I feel my days as a pilgrim are coming to an end. I grow old."

Bernard tutted into his beer. "Surely not my lady. Your stride seemed strong when I saw you on the road earlier today."

She smiled at him indulgently. "Then perhaps it's that I grow weary of the road itself. My husband died many years ago and my children lead their own lives. If my pilgrimage is to end, then I find myself at a loose end. I can see I can be of some help here and I'm sure your bishop wouldn't mind a little interference in his plans for this place?"

At that Bernard choked on his ale. Will clapped him helpfully on the back before he could say anything. If the woman wanted to give them a small fortune towards the successful outcome of the task who was Will to deny her? He was sure Osbert would be reporting this back to the bishop long before the lady's own letter reached him. Will nodded over to where the other pilgrims were sat, "Your companions lady, they travelled with you to the Holy Land?"

"The old man and his son were in the original party. The rest, well I seem to have a habit of acquiring waifs and strays. As I've made my way around the shrines of the kingdom my little party has grown." She stifled a yawn. "I grow tired. Can you have your clerk draw up some papers so we can formalise the gift?"

"Of course my lady, Osbert, our clerk, can draw up the necessary documents tomorrow."

35

THE BISHOP ON THE MOVE

Jocelyn Gifford, Bishop of Draychester was on the move. The cathedral owned properties that were scattered across the length and breadth of the kingdom. He spent a good portion of the year on the road. He could have left it all to his officials of course but, truth be told, he enjoyed the travelling. In his youth he'd been a soldier, and he'd never really given up his nomadic lifestyle. He liked well enough the comforts of the bishop's palace at Draychester but as he grew older he had no wish to become soft like some of his fellow clergymen. The bishop and his retinue on the road were a splendid sight to behold projecting both power and wealth. It was a calculated display in these trouble times. They were some ten miles south of the city of York. Ostensibly they were on their way to visit Archbishop Waldby, but they intended to press on to Sodham as soon as they could. Near the very head of the column on a beautiful grey mare rode Gifford himself; alongside him was Scrivener, his chief clerk and adviser of many years. Immediately around Gifford and Scrivener were the bishop's men at arms, twenty-five heavily armed mounted guards. Strung out along the road behind them rode the bishop's senior officials, aides and messengers. Further back, and in some cases trudging on foot, came a collection of the lesser members of the bishop's household; junior scribes down to the cooks and scullion boys. At the very back were stragglers who had attached themselves to the column over the course of their journey. They sought safe travel within its numbers as only the suicidal would dare to attack a retinue such as Gifford's. All told the column stretched a good half a mile.

∼

"Let's not tarry too long with the Archbishop in York Scrivener. I'm eager to see Sodham myself."

"A day or two at the most should satisfy convention my lord. He'll be offended with anything less."

"Archbishop Waldby is a pious old bore Scrivener, we both know that. I don't think he's had an original thought in his entire life. Two days in his company is about all I can stand. God alone knows what the King sees in him."

"A safe pair of hands I would say my lord. He's predictable which means he's rarely a threat."

"That's as maybe but it's not you who has to accompany him to endless prayer sessions. So two days at most Scrivener, do you hear me? Whether we offend or not."

"Yes my lord."

"And our first business in York will be to send for the sheriff's man, what's his name again?"

"David Padget, a sergeant in the sheriff's employ. According to the dispatches from my nephew Osbert, he's been most useful to us in Sodham and also in this issue with the Abbot of Ribsdale."

"Ah yes, the Abbot of Ribsdale. I think we are going to pay that bloody man an unannounced visit Scrivener. He needs reminding of just who I am and who owns Sodham."

"As you wish my lord."

~

In the late afternoon they reached Micklegate Bar the main gate into the city from the south.

As soon as they were within the walls, Gifford said, "Scrivener, ride to the castle and see if you can locate this man Padget. Bring him back with you if possible. I suppose I will have to pay my respects to Archbishop Waldby, God help me."

Scrivener was back within the hour with David Padget in tow. Giffard was sitting with Waldby in the archbishop's private dining chamber. He said, "Ah Scrivener, back at last. And you must be Padget?"

"My lords," Padget said somewhat nervously nodding his head in deference to the two bishops.

Gifford said, "I feel I owe you my thanks Sergeant. It seems you have been of great service in Sodham."

"Thank you my lord, the sheriff asked me to assist and I have followed his orders."

"No need to be modest Sergeant. I know the sheriff, he's not an easy man to work for I imagine?"

Padget just smiled and said nothing. Who knew what part of this conversation might get back to the sheriff. He took the view of always being on the side of caution when dealing with the nobles. They didn't obey the same rules as everyone else.

"Come sit with us Padget, we'd appreciate your account of recent events."

Padget spent the next hour relating all that he knew. He was glad to finally take his leave, he felt slightly uncomfortable in Gifford's presence. The man had the unnerving ability to extract every bit of detail without appearing to ask anything much at all.

~

"A bad business Jocelyn," said Archbishop Waldby sipping his wine slowly.

Gifford felt he had to take the opportunity to press his case against Ribsdale Abbey. If he had to suffer the archbishop's company for the next two days, then he could at least use his time wisely. "Yes, it would appear so. I am most surprised by the Abbott of Ribsdale's behaviour."

"Disgraceful and undignified for a man of God. Perhaps you should pay him a visit Jocelyn. I take it you are going out to Sodham? I believe the abbey is only a short distance away?"

"Indeed, indeed. I hadn't thought to, but at your suggestion I think I shall of course visit him." He added mischievously, "Perhaps you could offer some advice as to my course of action?"

"He should do penance for his undoubted sins!"

"Yes penance indeed. I shall pass on your advice to him of course."

"Prayer is the answer Jocelyn. Perhaps you would join me tomorrow in the minster and we can pray for guidance in this matter together.

Gifford gave Scrivener a hard stare and then turned back

to the archbishop. "But of course Archbishop, I'd be delighted to."

That evening Gifford had Scrivener send a messenger to Sodham with a letter. They would spend one more day in York before making their way over the moors to see the place for themselves.

36

SIR ROGERS FLIGHT

"Travis if you don't get a bloody move on, I swear I am going to take my very sharp sword and stick it up your arse. You remember my sword don't you?"

Travis was up to his waist in a peat bog carrying Sir Roger on his shoulders. He momentarily considered the threat but concluded that Sir Roger was unlikely to want to get his feet wet. In any case an increase in speed whist wading through the foul smelling water and rotting vegetation was physically impossible.

After a few more minutes Sir Roger said, "Tell me Travis, how far do you think we've come since we abandoned the horses?"

"Ten or more miles I think master, it's hard to tell. There're no landmarks to speak of."

"Well at least we don't seem to have any pursuers. Which is probably because no one in their right mind would attempt to cross this on foot, especially not at night." He suddenly pulled himself higher on Travis's swaying shoulders and peered ahead. He dropped back down and grabbed

Travis's head by the ears, he twisted it to the right. "Over there Travis, some rocks, do you see them?"

Travis wiped the mud from his eyes with a grubby hand and peered into the gloom. On the far horizon there seemed to be a series of dark bumps raising slightly above the surface of the bog. He grunted an acknowledgment and started to plod towards them. Sir Roger dug his still booted and spurred feet into Travis's sides to give him some encouragement.

Ten minutes later a weary Travis hauled himself and Sir Roger onto a ridge of rocks that marked the transition of bog back into rough moorland grass. Sir Roger climbed down and cuffed Travis over the head with an evil grin. It was about as close to a sign of affection as he ever showed his faithful servant. Travis painfully removed the large pack he had also been carrying and lay it down on the rocks.

"See Travis, if you put your back into it, anything's possible. I think this is as far as we go tonight. I feel fatigued, find some wood and make a fire." Sir Roger lay down on the flat surface of the rock, propped his head against the pack, and promptly started snoring.

Travis peered around in the fading light. There probably wasn't a stick, let alone a tree, in ten miles. He wondered whether Sir Roger had been joking, he found it increasingly hard to tell these days. He briefly toyed with the thought of wandering off on his own and leaving Sir Roger for good, his master was sound asleep and no one would stop him. He dismissed the idea. If Sir Roger caught up with him, he'd die in some hideous way he couldn't even imagine. His fate was bound up with the man and there seemed to be no escape this side of death.

In the morning they came across a well-worn path heading down off the moors. They followed it for a mile or so. It crossed a narrow but fast flowing moorland stream via a little stone bridge that was just wide enough for a man leading a horse.

"We're on a pack horse route Travis. I think the time for walking is over."

"I don't understand master."

"Of course you don't. If I let you do the thinking we'd still be stuck up to our necks in that bog. Anyway, I'm sick of walking. We're going to wait here by the bridge, there'll be someone along today, this path is well used."

"We've nothing to buy horses with."

"Travis have I told you how incredibly stupid you are?"

"Frequently master."

"Shut up and get down here under the bridge."

"Yes master."

They hadn't long to wait. From higher up the hillside they could hear the jingling of harnesses and the tinkle of bells. Soon a line of five sturdy pack horses started to descend the rough track towards the bridge. The lead animal had a collar of bells and each horse carried a large bulging pack laid over the flanks and tied underneath. There was a chubby little man sat on the first horse, as he rode he whistled a tuneless ditty. On the last horse sat a young girl who appeared to be sound asleep on her mount. Sir Roger and Travis kept out of sight crouched down under the small arch of the bridge. Travis was up to his waist in the stream as there wasn't room for both on the narrow bank. Sir Roger naturally didn't want to get his feet wet.

"Just stay out of sight Travis until I've clubbed the peasant at the front. You can grab the girl then, just make sure she doesn't run off. We don't want any witnesses." Sir

Roger pulled a long dagger from his belt then slipped up the bank and crouched down behind the low wall at the entrance to the bridge. He waited until the man leading the first pack horse was almost on top of him. He jumped up and grabbed the startled man by his tunic and pulled him off the horse in the process deliberately bashing his head against the wall of the bridge. The man slumped to the ground unconscious. Sir Roger thumped the man's head on the ground just to make sure. The line of horses came to a halt half way across the bridge.

Travis emerged from under the bridge and approached the girl on the rear horse who still appeared to be asleep. Just as he was about to grab her she suddenly started screaming at the top of her lungs, "Thieves! We're being robbed. Murderers, thieves!"

"Shut her up for God's sake!" called Sir Roger. "She'll wake up half the bloody shire."

The girl slid off the horse and dodged around the outstretched arms of Travis. She jumped up onto the wall of the bridge and skilfully ran out to the centre. She balanced there, unsure of what to do next. Sir Roger beckoned to her and said, "You'd better come here girl or I'll make sure you regret it. We've little time and I've even less patience."

The girl gave him a shrewd look and said, "Think I'm stupid mister. You've done for chubby John, what'd you do to me? We've run into thieves before."

Sir Roger said, "I'm no common thief child. I'm a knight. We're on important business, I need your horses."

"Don't look like any kind of knight to me mister. Where's your own horse and armour? Only kind of business you're up to is thieving."

Sir Roger hated children. To be fair he hated everyone else as well, but the young made him feel awkward. They had the unnerving knack of saying to him what most adults would never dare. He hauled the unconscious man into an upright position and held the knife to his throat. "If you don't come here, I'm going to slit his throat. Do you understand me?"

The girl shrugged her shoulders. "Makes no difference to me mister. Chubby has been poking my mum since dad died, he drinks something fearful and beats us both. You'd be doing me a favour."

"Travis get across the stream to the other side of the bridge."

Travis dutifully splashed through the water and with some difficulty hauled himself up the steep bank and blocked the other side of the bridge. The girl looked from one to the other. "I can help you. You can't just ride down the valley with the horses. Everyone knows us and these beasts. Twice a month we're through here. There'll be questions."

Sir Roger tutted and wagged a finger at her. "My, my for one so young you have a lot to say my girl. Maybe we'll just throw you in the water here and take our chances. What say you Travis?"

"She's just a girl master."

"I'll be useful. I know all the tracks and the stops between here and Bolton Priory."

"Is that where you were heading girl?"

"Yes, to the monks at the priory."

"What's your name?"

"Anny."

Sir Roger took his dagger from the man's throat and cut through the rope holding one of the packs. It fell to the ground, and he pulled back the rough cloth and found a block of salt. He was beginning to see how this could work. "Tell me Anny. How much do the monks pay you for this?"

"Not ours, we're just shifting it. Comes from the Durham coast, not sure where that is but it's what Chubby says. He gets paid for moving it that's all. The monks have already paid for the salt. He gets his money when we deliver it."

"What do you carry on the return journey?"

"Wool usually."

Sir Roger contemplated the block of salt for a minute and then came to a decision. "Get down off that wall child. I'm not going to do you any harm. I believe I do need your help. Your friend Chubby ends his journey here though. He won't be needing his clothes either but we will. Travis I think I have a plan to revive our fortunes."

Travis inwardly groaned. He was sure whatever Sir Roger had in mind would result in some sort of suffering for Travis. It was the way of the world. "Yes master."

∽

The girl indeed seemed to know every track and pathway in a hundred miles. From what they gleamed from her incessant chatter she had been virtually brought up on the back of one of the packhorses. They skirted around Bolton Priory. Sir Roger wasn't interested in delivering the goods to their rightful owners. They came to a halt near another bridge that crossed a small stream. So far they'd passed few other travellers. Sir Roger, dressed in the unremarkable but oversized clothes of Chubby looked like any other pack horse master going about his business. He said, "I want to head for the coast. Think carefully child, have you ever been farther to the west, all the way to the sea perhaps?"

"Been to a place on a river, saw ships there, that's way to

the west of here. Lancaster, I think. Delivered salt to the priory there once with Chubby."

"Do you think you can remember the way and the places to stop overnight?"

"Maybe."

"Think harder."

"Yes, I'm sure."

"Good. Now first we need to turn this salt into coin. I'm sure there's plenty of unscrupulous rogues in this business?"

"What's unscrupulous?"

"Thieves he means child," said Travis.

Sir Roger nodded. "Yes indeed Travis. Thieves who'll buy this salt from us with few questions asked. You know somewhere we'll find them child?"

"Oh, that's easy, we need to stop at the Moorcock. That's an inn down the bottom of this valley. Chubby says it's a den of thieves, although it's never stopped him drinking the night away in there."

"Excellent, it sounds the ideal place."

∽

A skinny, runny-nosed lad with red hair and not much older than Anny was stood in the yard of the inn as they arrived. He grinned at the girl. "All right Anny. Where's Chubby then?"

"All right Ginger. With me Uncle Roger this time," she jabbed a finger in Sir Roger's direction and continued, "Chubby isn't with us"

"No loss there then, miserable bugger is Chubby."

The girl smiled nervously. "Is Hamo the Hand here?"

Ginger looked at her curiously. "Hamo, no, he's not here

yet, but he will be later. What do you want with that one? He's as mean as they come?"

She nodded at Sir Roger and Travis. "Uncle Roger and his man want to do some business."

Ginger looked at Sir Roger with a cynical eye, sniffed and said, "Business is it. Well I'll be sure to let him know."

Sir Roger came and stood beside the girl. "You do that lad. Penny in it for you if you point him in my direction. Why is he called Hamo the Hand?"

"On account he only has one. Hand that is."

"What a very appropriate name he has then, Hamo the Hand. How'd he lose it?" Sir Roger's sarcasm seemed to go over Ginger's head.

"Chopped off it was. My dad says it's because he put it in too many places he shouldn't have."

"Ginger's dad is the inn keeper," added Anny helpfully.

"I'm sure your father is a very perceptive man Ginger. Now lad, take me to some drink and hot food. Travis, see to the horses and keep an eye on the goods and the girl."

∽

Sir Roger was slumped at one of the low trestle tables in the dim and smoky interior of the Moorcock when Hamo the Hand made his entrance. Hamo did indeed have a missing appendage which he more than made up for in flesh with his double and triple chins. He had the figure of a squat barrel on legs. He waddled over to Sir Roger and sat down heavily on the end of the bench. It groaned ominously under the strain. "Young Ginger out there tells me you want to do some business. So what you got that I need?"

"Ah, Master Hand, good of you to join me and straight to the point, how refreshing."

Hamo rested the stump of his arm on the table and scratched it somewhat irritably with the grubby fingernails of his remaining hand. "I don't believe in beating about the bush, although I wouldn't mind a drink before we start negotiating."

"Feel free," Sir Roger said gesturing towards the flagon on the table. "The ale's like ditch water but I suppose you're used to it up here on the moors."

Hamo poured himself a generous measure took a long swig and smacked his lips. "Can't say I've noticed, anyway it always tastes better when somebody else is buying."

"You do a lot of business do you?"

"Now and again. You know how it is, the odd misplaced thing crosses my path and I help it on its way."

"Is salt one of those misplaced things?"

"Salt?"

"I thought you said you didn't beat about the bush. I'm sure you already know what I have, what I'm asking is do you want it?"

"Depends who might come looking for it after you're gone. Chubby and some monks for instance?"

"Oh I wouldn't worry about Chubby."

"Had an accident has he?"

"Run into some thieves I believe. An occupational hazard no doubt."

"An occu what?"

"Never mind, let's just say Chubby will not be bothering you."

"And the girl?"

"Don't worry about the girl, she was useful for a while but I doubt that'll last. Let's talk price."

"Be hard to move that lot, how many pack horses you got out there, four, five?"

"Five and I'm sure you can stash it somewhere. Keep tagging one onto the end of another train. A few days and it'll all be elsewhere."

"The monks will come looking before long."

"And by then it'll all be on its way elsewhere and I'm sure you'll deny ever having seen it. Go find Chubby's corpse, you can say he and the girl were robbed and killed. I'm sure you'll have no difficulty making something up. So make me an offer."

"What's stopping me just taking it from you? You're two men and a young girl. I can call on ten men, you wouldn't make it a half mile from here."

"Do I look like a man you can easily take things from?"

Hamo took in the grim determination on the other man's face. "No. No you don't. What you look like is a born killer."

Sir Roger nodded. "Good, so, you're not as stupid as you look then. Why take the chance, I guarantee some of you will die and I'll make it a point to single you out. Why make life hard my friend, just make me an offer."

"I'll give you a pound."

"Don't insult me, there's five times that amount in salt."

"Take it or leave it. I don't see any other buyers in here do you?"

"Three and I'll throw in the girl."

"Two and the girl.'"

"Done."

Hamo spat into the palm of his one good hand and held it out to shake and seal the deal. Sir Roger looked at Hamo's grubby hand in disgust. He pulled a leather glove from inside his pocket, donned it and reluctantly shook Hamo's hand. Afterwards he took the glove off and tossed it on the table. "You can keep that as a souvenir, how fortunate that you only need the one." Hamo grinned toothlessly, he couldn't quite work out if he'd been insulted or not but he handed over the money regardless.

∼

Sir Roger found Travis and the girl in the stable. They were sat in the straw sharing a lump of cheese and some bread. Travis stood up as his master entered. Sir Roger flicked a coin between his fingers. "The deal is done. Two pounds and I threw the girl in as well. Seems Hamo has shown a liking for her. It's not as much as I'd like but it'll do for now."

The girl looked thunderstruck. "You need me. I know the way and the best places to stop at."

Sir Roger looked at the child who looked back at him with pleading eyes. "Don't whine child. I'm sure we'll survive without you. The deal's been done and you stay."

Travis laid a hand on the child's head protectively. He swallowed hard and said, "Master you can't give her to Hamo, she's just a child."

Sir Rogers's eyes narrowed. His hand shot out and grabbed Travis around the throat and began to slowly throttle him. "Never, ever, tell me what I can or can't do Travis."

Travis clawed at the hand around his windpipe as Sir Roger pressed harder. Finally he was released to fall in a retching heap. Sir Roger gave him a painful boot in the ribs to emphasise the point. "Sentiment makes you weak Travis." He bent down and hauled the wheezing man to his feet. "Now pick out the two best pack horses. The salt, the girl and the rest we leave for Hamo. I want to be away from here within the hour."

After Sir Roger had left the stable Travis sank back to his

knees. The girl said, "He'll kill you someday Travis. Why do you stay with him?"

Travis shrugged his shoulders. "It's too late for me child, I know no other life. Listen to me. You need to get away from this place. Do you think you can find your way to Whalley Abbey?"

"Of course, me and Chubby have been there dozens of times."

"When Sir Roger and I leave, sneak away out the back. Make your way to the abbey, don't stop until you get there and avoid others on the roads if you can. The monks will look after you." He quickly put together a small pack for her from the supplies he'd bought from the inn. He handed it over and said, "Here girl, hide this under the straw for now. At least you won't starve on the journey. Now stay out of sight in here until we leave. That's when Hamo will be most distracted."

"I'd rather stay with you Travis, won't you come with me?"

Travis gave a bitter sounding laugh. "We wouldn't get a mile girl before Sir Roger's blade was stuck in our backs. You need to be brave child, I'll pray God guides your path, it's the best I can do for you."

"Thank you Travis."

He smiled at her, no one had thanked him for anything in a long time, it felt good.

37

A BISHOP IN SODHAM

It was Tavener's lad, Michael who spotted the rider first. The boy came hurrying to the upper room over the inn. "There's a rider coming down the road. Fancy looking he is, dressed all in green."

"He's all in green you say, you're sure?"

"Head to toe master. Lovely horse he has too, beauty it is," replied Michael.

Bernard, Osbert and Will rushed to the outer door and stood at the top of the steps and peered across the valley. "That's the bishop's livery, I'd know it anywhere. A messenger I'd say," said Bernard. The rider was just approaching the bridge. He came to an abrupt halt as the figure of Agnes suddenly sprang in front of his horse. They could hear the cackling even from here. Will winced. Agnes could take things a little too far. They heard an outraged voice raised in protest and a moment later the rider continued across the bridge.

Two minutes later and the messenger came to a halt outside the inn and expertly dismounted. Bernard recognised the man instantly. "Ralph, it's been a long time."

The man smiled broadly. "Morning Bernard, too long indeed, the bishop keeps me busy my friend. Your bridge hermit took me by surprise, a nice touch though."

"We think so too. Come far?"

"From York, left two days ago."

Osbert scowled at the man. "Please tell me we're ordered back to Draychester Ralph?"

"Ah, Osbert, good to see you too, and as cheerful as ever." He turned back to his horse, reached up and took down a pack from behind his saddle and retrieved a sealed letter from within. "I have a letter here for the Bishop's Official of Sodham, which must be you young sir. I don't think I've had the pleasure as yet. Ralph Little is my name, bishop's messenger."

"William Blackburne," mumbled Will as he snatched the letter from Ralph's hand. He broke the red wax seal and quickly read the single sheet. His jaw dropped.

"Bad news?" said Osbert in a tone that was more a statement of fact than a question.

Will looked up. "The bishop is coming here. He's in York now, he's leaving Wednesday. What day is today?"

"Thursday," said Ralph cheerfully.

"Which means what, he could be here tomorrow?"

Ralph shrugged. "More likely Saturday morning, it's a hard ride across the moors."

Matilda and some of the other pilgrims had come out of the inn and stood listening.

"Jocelyn Gifford is coming here?" she asked.

"Indeed he," replied Ralph.

"Well, well. God works in mysterious ways indeed." They all looked at her curiously but she said no more and disappeared back inside the inn.

Bernard clapped Ralph on the back. "So my friend, how is my lord bishop? Curiosity got the better of him I take it? That's why he's coming on this little inspection?"

Ralph laughed. "I don't suppose to know the intentions of our master Bernard. I think Osbert's uncle, Scrivener, is the only one who knows his mind. What I do know is that he won't lodge here. He intends to spend some time with the good monks down the road at Ribbsdale Abbey. From what I hear it won't be entirely a social visit."

This time it was Will's turn to laugh. "I take it the abbot has no idea he's about to get a visitor?"

"I think not. The whole of the bishop's household is on the move. It will no doubt be horrendously expensive to put them all up."

Bernard once again clapped Ralph on the back and said, "Well I for one hope the bishop stays a month and drains that weasels' coffers down to the last penny."

"Vengeance is mine said the lord."

"Oh shut up Osbert!" they all said in chorus.

∼

Will suddenly looked in horror towards the far side of the bridge, "God's teeth, I forgot about Agnes. Will she try to collect from them?"

Bernard shrugged. "I would certainly hope so. I'm sure the bishop would expect nothing less from our bridge hermit."

"Well I'm glad you're so calm about it. I think we need to get over there."

"Relax my young friend. I know Gifford. Let Agnes be."

As the bishop's party approached the makeshift bridge,

Agnes emerged from her shack. The bishop himself took the lead and stopped before the disheveled figure. "So Agnes. Escaped from the nunnery again? Perhaps you've found an occupation more to your liking?" She gave a nervous cackle. The bishop hadn't really expected an answer. "I suppose you'll be wanting a toll eh? Strictly speaking it is my bridge you know?"

Another nervous cackle greeted the bishop's good humoured question. He reached beneath his cloak and dropped a heavy leather pouch of coins into Agnes's hands. "I think that's about fair for a party this size." Agnes bowed low and with a final cackle shuffled back into her shack. The bishop urged his horse onwards and the rest of the household streamed across behind him.

~

Gifford looked down from his horse at the little group assembled outside the inn. He smiled broadly and said, "Well then, here you all are. Hale and hearty I hope?" Before anyone could answer, he jumped down from his horse and put an arm around Bernard's shoulder. "Bernard my old friend, good to see you."

"And you my lord."

He moved on to Will, grabbing his hand and shaking it vigorously. "William, you have been using your talents to good effect I hear?"

"Welcome my lord. I hope you'll approve."

The bishop smiled and moved on to ruffle Osbert's hair much to his embarrassment. "And young Osbert, your dispatches have been most enlightening. Even your Uncle Scrivener says so, isn't that right Scrivener."

"Quite my lord."

"Thank you, I've tried to do my best," said Osbert blushing a deep red.

The bishop turned to the rest of the group and suddenly stopped dead, his mouth hanging open, "Good God! Mathilda!"

"Well I must say, is that any greeting for your sister?"

The rest of the welcoming party turned around almost as one. Will could see the likeness at once. He thought she'd looked familiar, it was obvious now he studied her face. The bishop pushed past them and embraced his sister warmly. "Forgive me sister, it's just such a surprise to see you, a most welcome one I might add. You were at Canterbury the last time you wrote. What on earth are you doing here?"

She grinned and said, "Well I've come to see the shrine of Saint Traed of course. At York there was much talk about its miraculous healing powers." She gestured to the church and continued, "Your men seem to have done a most thorough job although it could have done with a women's touch here and there."

"I have no idea what you're talking about," he said with a twinkle in his eyes. He took her arm and said, "I don't know about the rest of you but I could use a drink and some food. Shall we?" With that he pulled his chuckling sister towards the inn.

∽

Later that night, in the guesthouse at Ribsdale Abbey, Bishop Gifford sat opposite Scrivener, a shared flagon of ale on the tabletop between them.

The bishop put down his cup and sighed. "This man Mudstone, I fear we may have underestimated him. Perhaps we should have just taken care of him back in Draychester but that's the benefit of hindsight my friend eh?"

Scrivener reflected that he had in fact advocated this course of action months ago, but he thought better than voicing his thoughts. Some things were better left unsaid. "Yes indeed my lord. He seems to have disappeared over the moors towards the west of here. My guess is he's making for the coast."

"Well if he's any sense he'll leave the realm. He's declared outlaw of course with a hefty price on his head. I've made sure the abbot of this place will be a most generous contributor as well. Mudstone will hang and worse if he's caught. You have no news of him at all? He's not sought sanctuary anywhere?"

"Not a word of him my lord, a man like him can't go far without leaving a trail of death and destruction behind. It's only a matter of time before we hear something."

"I hope you're right Scrivener. To other matters. Young William, he did well you think?"

"He shows promise my lord I must confess. The church and the bones were a touch of genius, almost worthy of one of your own schemes. What would you have me do with him now?"

"I think the lad needs to be kept busy Scrivener. We wouldn't want his talents to lead him astray. I may have another task suited to him."

"I thought you might my lord. May I ask what?"

"You may Scrivener. Something has occurred in Wales."

"Wales? Is that strictly safe my lord? I hear there's trouble brewing again."

"Safe no, trouble yes."

"And he's expendable of course?"

"Scrivener, I do believe you are getting ever more cynical as the years pass. It'll be good experience for the lad."

"He'll need his wits about him in Wales. May I suggest my lord that you send along my nephew again? Perhaps you'll allow Bernard to accompany them at least for some of the journey, to keep an eye on them both?"

"Agreed."

AFTERWORD

FROM THE AUTHOR

Dear Reader,

Thank you for reading one of my books. I've always been an avid reader of historical fiction but also harboured the thought, like so many of us do, that I'd try and write something myself. What you have been reading was the first book I published. It took me a long time to finish the first one and have the confidence to put it out into the world. I worked in the IT and Telecoms industry here in the UK for many years, ended up running my own company, and inevitably life and job got in the way. I'd do some research, make some progress on the book, then leave it again.

In early 2018 a close family member became seriously ill. Writing offered me an escape from some of the stress and worry involved and gave me the motivation to get the first book over the finishing line.

After I'd completed that first book, I wrote the next two in the series in a just over a year. I learned a lot writing them. What I got over that period was validation from readers they enjoyed my work, which in turn encouraged me to keep on writing and improving.

The writing process can be both uplifting and disheartening in equal measure. I really appreciate every review you guys give my books. Every time you leave some feedback, good or bad, it helps validate that at least someone is out there reading them. I look at each review posted and take your comments to heart and hope to become a better writer because of them.

On Amazon, I've found it makes a huge difference for independent authors like me when prospective readers can learn more about a book from others who post a review. So, if you can spare a minute and share your impressions of the book that would be amazing.

Did you enjoy the book? What did you like about it? Who were your favourite characters? Should the series continue? Give me your thoughts via a review or rating on Amazon.

Be the first to receive the news of upcoming books in the series, exclusive offers and free downloads. Join my newsletter and...

Get your free copy of
Death Of The Messenger
The Prequel to the
Draychester Chronicles

You can sign up at this link:-
www.westerbone.com/newsletter

For lots more information visit my author website,

www.westerbone.com

You can also connect with me on Facebook,

www.facebook.com/mjwesterbone

and on twitter,

www.twitter.com/westerbone

@westerbone

Available Now
Book 2 of the Draychester Chronicles

Death Of The Vintner

Available Now
Book 3 of the Draychester Chronicles

Death Of The Anchorite

Hope to see you soon,
M J Westerbone,
Hindley Green, England, U.K

COPYRIGHT

Copyright © 2021 by M J Westerbone.
All rights reserved. Published by Irene Storvik Ltd, Hindley Green, Lancashire, UK. This is a work of fiction. Any resemblance to actual persons living or dead is purely coincidental. Reproduction in whole or part of this publication without express written consent is strictly prohibited.

Printed in Great Britain
by Amazon